CAGED

CAGED

Terry Brykczynski

CROWN PUBLISHERS, INC. · NEW YORK

All the characters and events in this novel are fictional. Any reference to publications, products, or locations is purely coincidental.

Inquiries should be addressed to Crown Publishers, Inc., One Park Avenue, New York, New York 10016

Published simultaneously in Canada by General Publishing Company Limited

Printed in the United States of America

Library of Congress Cataloging in Publication Data

Brykczynski, Terry.
    Caged.
EM
    I. Title.
PZ4.B91577Cag 1980   [PS3552.R98]   813'.5'4

ISBN: 0-517-539950   79-21786

Book Design by Deborah B. Kerner

10 9 8 7 6 5 4 3 2 1

First edition

For Amanda

CAGED

She was an antelope, an American pronghorn, and she rested on the ground with her spindly forelegs tucked under. It was a typical pose of mock awkwardness that the fleet animals often adopt. The white patch on her chest contrasted sharply with the reddish earth packed hard and flat by the herd's countless pawings. Her neck stretched out but for some reason her nose didn't seek the cool shade of a nearby manzanita shrub. She smelled the odors of familiar grasses and plants by rubbing her cheeks slowly, haltingly, across the ground. The dipping sun warmed her chilled flanks; perhaps soon the flies would cease to be a problem. They had bothered her ever since the wetness had started to seep from her neck. She wanted to move away from the flies and she didn't understand why her legs were so tired.

For the second time she smelled the human odor. This time her nose detected the two men before she saw them. They were hidden by a row of scrubby bushes and the sound of their shoes was muffled by years of constant practice.

She snorted in terror and jerked up on her forelegs. Her ears, her ears that had failed her, sprang tight and locked in place. Her nose sprayed flecks of foam.

When the two men passed the manzanita, one froze. The other pointed.

"It's the doe all right," one of them said. *"Jesus."*

"I came as soon as I could," said the other.

She lifted herself up then, an almost impossible task. She bleated once, twice, and fell. With her forelegs crumpled underneath, her belly contracted violently and shuddered in a spasm.

"Jesus," repeated the first man, with a choke that came from a frozen throat.

The antelope heaved and collapsed in a quivering, shaking mass of rippling muscles. She kicked her forelegs in an ineffectual attempt at escape but it was useless.

"When do you think it . . ." the first man asked, his voice trailing off. He really didn't want to think about it.

"I checked on the pack this morning. Everything was fine, so I went on to the paddock. About ten minutes ago I came back for the afternoon count and came up one short. But I figured she was still sleeping here in the brush. Then—then the fence started shaking."

The two men looked at the doe's hindquarters. Both the back legs had somehow kicked through the fence. The chain links had driven into the tendons and pinned her like a steel snare. As the two men stared, a fresh pool of red liquid spurted from the hindquarters to cover the old, clotted black blood. The doe had evacuated her bowels and smeared a layer of dung over her back.

The taller of the two men stirred uncomfortably and began to move his hands around because he didn't know where to put them. "What do you want me to do, Doc? Are you going to put a cast on her?"

"A cast?" the other man asked incredulously. "Do you see those legs? There's nothing left. She's smashed her bones into splinters. Both legs are useless."

"But what are we going to *do?*" wailed the shorter man.

Instead of answering, the veterinarian ran his eyes along the length of the downed animal. His practiced examination was quick and sure; what he saw made him sick. He began to stare intently at the antelope's neck. Scratching his chin nervously, he moved closer and stopped.

"Bob?" the vet questioned.

"Yes?"

"Who else knows about this?"

"What?"

"Who else was around?" the vet demanded.

The keeper looked behind him. Through the thick stand of brush he could barely make out the exhibition meadow and the visitors' fence. It was nearly closing time and the paths were deserted.

"I found her ten minutes ago," the keeper said. "Nobody was around. I don't think people can see this far back with the bushes and all."

"But you're certain there was nobody around when you found her? You're certain?"

"Yes. If somebody was around they could have done something, helped. An accident like this—" The keeper looked at the vet's face but the vet was staring at the animal's neck. A thin red line crossed half her throat. Neither of them had noticed this injury before.

The keeper bent down and saw the stained patch of blood-soaked ground under the antelope's neck. He reached out a hand but the animal bleated in renewed terror.

"What is that, Dr. Lewis?" he asked. His voice was unsteady, and it trembled as he tried to control it.

"The neck wound?" Dr. Lewis said. "I think a substantial amount of blood loss. Very close to the jugular vein. In fact, it couldn't have missed it less."

"No, Doc," the keeper said, violently shaking his head. "What *did* it?"

The vet pursed his lips. When he spoke, his voice tried to sound confident. "Well, you're right, Bob. If someone *had* been around, they could have stopped this. Pulled her leg out of the fence. Calmed her down. But nobody was here. The neck wound? I'm not sure."

"What do you mean?"

"Could be a number of things. Another antelope could have done it easily with a hoof. Or she could have caught her neck on a twisted part of the fence. Even a broken branch, if it was very sharp and—"

"No, Doc," the keeper said. His voice began to rise. "No branch did that. She couldn't have twisted around at the fence. No hoof did that . . . Doc, that's not an accident."

"There was nobody around," the vet firmly stated. "You said that yourself."

"A knife did that!" the keeper blurted hysterically.

"Nonsense. Who could have done it? There aren't any footprints."

"Don't you see? Can't you see?" The keeper stared at the vet. "What are we going to do?"

In answer, Dr. Lewis laid his satchel on the ground and kneeled to open it. With two swift clicks, the bag sprang open. He unzipped a pouch, removed a box, and examined a tiny vial. Reaching into a tray, he took out a syringe and plunged it into the rubber-capped vial, where twenty milliliters of a colorless fluid was withdrawn. Turning to the keeper, Dr. Lewis snapped his order.

"Put your coat over her eyes. Hold her steady."

The keeper stared at the glistening needle. He shook his head. "We have to get help. We have to move her to the stall. She's dying. We need help."

"There's nothing left to do," the vet said coldly. "Calm down."

"You're going to kill her, aren't you?"

The antelope snorted. A trickle of blood started to run from both her nostrils.

"Bob, hold her head steady."

The keeper shook his head. "You can't kill her without the director's orders. You know that."

"We don't have a director," the vet exploded. "Nobody told you? Gordon had a heart attack this morning. Will you just let me do what I have to?"

"Heart attack?"

"Yes, damn it. Didn't you hear the ambulance?"

"But—"

"There's no time. Are you going to cover her eyes?"

The keeper was stunned. An even greater shock spread over his bloodless face. "Call somebody. You have to call somebody."

"I'm not calling anyone. There's nobody to call." The syringe in his hand began to shake. "Will you do what I say? I'm taking responsibility. This antelope is dying; she can't be saved. She's suffering. Look at her. Goddammit, *look!*"

The keeper stared numbly at the quivering body. The antelope's ears were trembling and her left foreleg pawed aimlessly at the ground. The flies buzzed hungrily.

Without another word, the keeper took off his coat. He held it stiffly before him, advancing slowly toward the animal.

"Cover her eyes," the vet ordered.

The antelope grew calm. The darkness felt good. Her flank became still and smooth. Dr. Lewis knelt beside her on the ground and raised the needle. The darkness felt better.

The last tram of the day rolled to a stop on the crest of the little hill. On one side was dense shrubbery, while the other looked out onto a magnificent vista of manicured meadows, pine-shrouded dells, and seemingly limitless grassland.

"We're leaving the antelopes now," the pretty guide explained through her microphone. "What I'd like to show you next is our African plains landscaping with the Central Asia exhibit in the distance."

The half-full tramload craned their necks to gaze with mechanical interest at the picturesque view. Cameras began snapping and binoculars focused with almost military precision. While the people gaped at the perfectly planted expanse, a man stepped casually out of the bushes and climbed aboard. Taking a vacant seat, he also began to view with interest the details of the African plains. The electric tram gave a soft whir and crawled down the hill toward the main plaza.

"I think you're sitting on my gloves," an elderly lady said

somewhat stiffly. She was bundled up in an old cotton cloak, and the wind had spilled grey hair from two ancient amber barrettes.

"Oh?" the man said in a concerned voice. "I'm terribly sorry." He half rose while the lady retrieved her frayed and rather tacky gloves. "I didn't see them. I hope you'll excuse me."

"I put them down," the lady patiently explained, "because nobody was sitting there."

"I changed my seat because of the view," the man said, smiling sweetly. "I hope you don't mind my company. Do you come to the zoo often?"

"I'm a Society member." She pointed to a badge pinned on her shoulder. "When you join the Society you get in free."

"Ah, yes. I've been meaning to look into that."

"Also," she continued pointedly, "you don't have to buy a ticket for the tram ride like everyone else."

The man nodded politely and turned to stare at a water buffalo. He turned rather quickly, for an energetic tic had erupted from the corner of his mouth. The twitch had begun under the old woman's stare and now it jerked like a metronome to her insistent eye blinks.

"Do you have a cigarette?" the lady asked, leaning closer.

"Yes, of course." The man fumbled in his coat and brought out a pack. He offered it to the lady but as he did so, he stared at his hand. Jerking it back before she picked a cigarette, he seemed somewhat flustered. He awkwardly rearranged his fingers around the pack and offered it again. But the lady still stared at his hand.

"I think you've cut yourself," she said. "There's blood on your hand."

"Yes," the man said quickly.

"You probably didn't see it because you're wearing sunglasses. Blood looks black through sunglasses. It's an optical principle."

Under her critical gaze, he wiped his hands with a linen handkerchief. The cigarette pack slipped from his fingers and dropped out of the tram, where it was crushed by the rubber wheels.

"Do you want a bandage?" she asked with motherly concern.

"No. No, thank you." His hand awkwardly scratched a cheek, where the twitch threatened to overcome his jaw.

"I always carry them with me. You never know what will happen."

"I suppose not."

"First aid. First aid is very important. Sometimes you don't get a chance for second aid."

"Do you come to the zoo often?" he interrupted, trying to change the subject.

"I told you once before. Don't you remember? I am a member. This pin."

"Maybe you could tell me where the gibbons are. They never stop chattering, do they?"

The woman brightened. "I'd be happy to. They're my favorites. But then, I love all animals, don't you?"

"Animals?" the man repeated, considering the question in genuine earnest. His hand dropped limply to his lap as the tic suddenly vanished. "Why, I guess they're just about the most important things in my life."

■ ■ ■

The lecture hall was pitch-black. In the cavernous darkness beyond his lectern, Steven could hear the rustling of notebooks and the clicking of pens. He grinned to himself. It was the click-click of those pens that separated the Berkeley zoology student from nearly every other in the country. He thought back to his own undergraduate days just ten years ago when he was sitting in cramped seats himself and scrawling notes in pencil, languidly erasing and smudging scrap sheets. Could those days have really existed—the furious riots, the soul-searching angst of "relevancy," the doubts that anything learned in the classroom could ever compare with the real world outside? These days he had trouble recognizing the rigid bodies as students. There was a cold-blooded intensity to their eyes. They brought yellow legal notepads and thick pens charged with indelible ink. Did they ever make mistakes? Their fingers worked like furious automatons, copying his utterances with the thoroughness of court reporters. It wasn't eagerness, he would have welcomed eagerness, but rather it was efficiency and grim determination, as if they had taken personally to their hearts his introductory remarks on Darwin's competition and the survival of the fittest. They were, in a word, hard-assed.

The projector whirred. A burst of light exploded on the screen. Steven heard the inadvertent gasps as the students gaped at the first slide.

A full-length mountain gorilla reared majestically on his haunches. The brilliant Kodachrome slide caught his magnificent ebony hair, his ivory fangs, and even the scarlet capillaries that crisscrossed his limpid, haunting eyes. The green fronds of banana palms shimmered like emeralds; the blue haze of the African crater range wavered with postcard lushness. The gorilla loomed so close that with a step it could have lurched off the screen and taken a seat in the first row.

"This is Boss-Man," Steven said through his microphone. "I gave him that name for obvious reasons."

"Did you take that shot with a telephoto lens?" A mechanical voice posed the question like an interrogation.

"No," Steven said. "It was a moderate wide-angle lens, twenty-eight-millimeter focal length, if I recall. It's not really that difficult to get near gorillas in the wild. All you have to do is follow the tribe for eight months, sit in the rain, and sleep in the shade when the sun boils at a hundred and twenty degrees. After another year or so they'll let you come within a hundred yards before they turn and run. After that you take one step closer every week, and if you're lucky, like I was, the tribe will suffer you at twenty feet but no closer."

"How *did* the tribe accept you?" A different voice spoke up.

"Good point," Steven said, reacting positively to the intelligence of the question. "If I can lapse for a moment into anthropomorphic terms, I suspect Boss-Man and his group considered me a poor outcast, driven from my proper tribe because

of my obvious bare-skinned ugliness and puny physical dis-
abilities. Can you call it pity? Was some compassionate altruism
operating toward an obvious ineptly palefaced country bumpkin?
Remember, I didn't know the first thing about constructing a
banana-leaf nest or how to attract the amorous attentions of even
the most receptive female. In short, they accepted me as some
dim-witted relative who meant no harm and gave up his seat
when asked."

"The way you talk about Boss-Man—he seems like a *person.*"

Steven paused. In his mind he traveled back to his years in
Africa on the postgraduate fellowship that resulted in the univer-
sity offering him the youngest full-professorship in departmental
history. He had learned more from Boss-Man than from his entire academic treadmill.

"Boss-Man *was* a person," Steven said slowly. "He had feel-
ings. He had urges. And he had *reason.* That brings me to the
point of today's lecture. I want you to realize the impossibility of
discovering the thoughts and individuality of animals unless you
study them in the wild, in their natural surroundings. Only then
will their true nature be revealed. Only then will their character
traits make sense, as intelligent adaptations to an intricate en-
vironment. You could *never* know Boss-Man from staring at him
exhibited in a circus or caged in a zoo. Locked up in cement
boxes in what pass for 'natural' homes, an animal can never be
understood, no matter what species. To be caged is to be incar-
cerated; it is to destroy individuality, pride, their very *being.*"

Steven stopped suddenly. His hands tightened around the microphone and he was glad the darkness hid the hint of sweat
appearing like a thin film over his temple. "Excuse me," he apolo-
gized. "I didn't mean to launch into what seems to be my favorite
harangue against zoos. Sometimes I catch myself talking like a
liberal, and we all know what happens to those in Berkeley."

He waited expectantly for the laughter that never came. A few
desultory coughs broke the silence-shrouded lecture hall. Steven
shrugged. If the hard-assed grinds couldn't afford a laugh, they
could rot and petrify in the library for all he cared. The joke had
been *funny,* damn it. Funny enough to hurt.

"Next slide, please."

The rest of Boss-Man's troupe appeared on the screen. Like a series of family portraits, the candid photographs froze the gorillas in their most unguarded moments—examining feces from a sick infant, peering with monumentally bored eyes at one another in a thick downpour, copulating enthusiastically. Steven's voice accompanied the slides like the words of a diary suddenly springing to life and re-creating the emotions, the discoveries, and the wonder. He knew the slides by heart but, as each one leaped on the screen, he still could smell the overripe fruits; he could feel the buzzing heat and the cramps in his neck and the hellish welts of beetles crawling over his thighs that he dared not remove for fear of stampeding Boss-Man's family.

Midway through the lecture, one of his teaching assistants slipped him a note.

"They said it was urgent," the graduate student whispered.

"Who did?" Steven asked softly.

"The department secretary. She said to give it to you right away, even if you were lecturing."

Steven paused, letting the slide of Boss-Man's fight with a rival dominate the screen. Some of the projector light fell on the slip of paper and his hands trembled as he read the short message.

Dr. Cooper,
A Mrs. Harriet Adams called the department and said you must be contacted. Your father has just suffered a heart attack and has been taken to the hospital. You are to please get in touch *immediately* with your uncle.

He didn't remember mumbling at his assistant to finish the lecture, nor did he remember stumbling out of the dark hall to the brightly lit corridor where he leaned his body into a corner and covered his face. He did remember his body shaking, his neck breaking out in an icy sweat, and the fight to keep the tears inside. And even as his body shook he remembered clamping his jaws tightly, so tightly, to lock the cries inside. He was so *observant,* so trained to record the slightest detail, and now in the corner he realized the signs his father had given that went completely unnoticed. The handwritten letters with the slight shakiness that Steven ignored. The arguments on the phone punctuated by breathing pauses that Steven had mistaken as irascibility. He had visited his father only a few times since returning from Africa and the meetings had always ended with the same red-faced stammering arguments. Gordon loosened his collar and gulped like a fish. As always, Steven stalked away in the middle of the act. *But why was he still calling it an act?*

The tears blinded his eyes; he knew students were walking quickly by and avoiding his face. Why was he holding back his tears? Was he still trying to win those stupid arguments? His mind, his mind that he had trained in countless lessons not to interfere, not to disturb, was now dissolving as it had done only once before. There was a slide he kept in his drawer, one that he would never show to any class. It was of Boss-Man, his hair grey at the tips, his eyes blinking in confusion as he lay underneath the panting body of a younger, stronger male. Boss-Man's spine had been snapped, his body paralyzed except for the rolling of his eyes. Boss-Man had died, and Steven had taken pictures.

He pushed himself away from the corner and stumbled down the corridor to a bank of phones, hearing every stray noise and sound as if a switch had suddenly been released in his head. He slid open the booth door and it roared on its hinges. The coins exploded in the slot. The crackling dial pierced his ears. The call never completed its first ring.

"Yes?" the voice immediately answered.

"It's me, Harriet."

"Steven, I—"

"Is he all right? Where did they take him?"

"The ambulance left." The voice wavered, lost in a bad connection. "Steven, I can't explain . . . I don't know. He was in his office with Charlie and—"

"Just tell me, where is he now?"

"I don't *know*. Charlie's supposed to call me."

"Damn it, didn't Charlie tell you the hospital?"

"Did you get the message? Charlie has to see you."

"Why?"

"He's at City Hall. The Council Chambers. He said you *have* to get down there now."

"The only place I have to go is the hospital."

"Steven, you have to see Charlie. There's a letter. I can't explain, I don't know. You have to see him right away."

— — —

The noon hour traffic was jammed as Steven's battered Volkswagen crept along the backed-up approach to the Bay bridge. Steaming fumes and acrid smog from the Emeryville industrial parks clogged his sinus cavities and he swore. Across the Bay, a dismal haze shrouded San Francisco and Steven wondered how many tourists would mistake it for fog. He threw his money at the toll taker, flinging it at him as if to a beggar. The bridge was bumper to bumper and only at the freeway on the other side could he accelerate to a decent speed. He roared off the City Hall exit and in a few minutes reached the golden-domed monument.

Charlie stood in the rotunda. Steven's shoes clicked loudly on the polished marble floor and when the two met, they exchanged suspicious stares.

"Where is Gordon?" Steven demanded.

Charlie's face was haggard. Steven was tall, but Charlie's bulk towered far above. His uncle's thick grey hair, usually neatly combed, drooped in tired clumps. His huge hands were stuffed in the side pockets of a tailored Abercrombie & Fitch suede coat that he had worn for so long the outline of his massive shoulders bulged without a crease. Years of sun had bronzed his face; the scars of sandstorms and heat exposure had long since molded his skin to a toughness that approached the inflexibility of a hide. His checkered L. L. Bean shirt was soaked at the collar with sweat.

Charlie didn't say a word. He removed his pawlike hands, dark and wrinkled as his face, and tugged at a ridiculous string tie that looped around his veined neck. Set on the tie was a huge lump of raw Australian opal that he had bought in the outback on his first trip around the world and carried ever since. Charlie coughed, a rumbling phlegm-choked smoker's cough, and he stared down at his hand-tooled boots.

In the years since Charlie had retired, Steven could never remember his uncle wearing anything different. He had always seemed dressed as if emerging from the hold of a tramp steamer swearing at stevedores. If it wasn't a freighter, it would have been the running board of a four-wheel-drive Land-Rover screaming to a dust-swirling halt in front of a makeshift airstrip where a chartered Vickers Vernon squatted, waiting for Charlie's orders. Steven stared at the patch on Charlie's shoulder, the strip of hard leather where the rifle butt fitted snugly to absorb the recoil. The stitching around the strip was designed to be temporary; Charlie had worn through many patches.

"Steven," Charlie said slowly. "Gordon's okay. There's nothing more we can do for him at the hospital."

"There's nothing we can do here. Where is he?"

"UC Med Center."

Steven turned to leave. Charlie's eyes rose from his boots and he barked, "Where the hell do you think you're going?"

"I'm going where I should be. Where both of us should be."

"Stay," Charlie barked again.

"I'm in a hurry."

"So am I," Charlie growled. "Don't go."

Steven whirled around. "I have to see Gordon."

"You can't see him. Nobody can. They put him under the tent. He's plugged in. He's under goddamn intensive care. They won't let you see him."

"There's got to be something I can do."

"Stay here."

Steven almost exploded. "What in hell are you talking about?"

Charlie hadn't moved a muscle since Steven arrived. Even his voice was slightly slurred, as if his throat were constricted. "Somebody," he said, "has to take care of the zoo."

"Worry about that later. Don't you think Gordon's more important?"

"There's no time."

· 13 ·

"Why are you so worried about the zoo all of a sudden?"

"I always have been."

"So what are you doing here? Trying to get yourself appointed director?" Steven asked sarcastically.

"That's exactly what I'm trying to do," Charlie snapped.

Steven's jaw dropped. "You've got to be kidding."

"I've got to get appointed before the Mayor comes back from Washington tomorrow."

"What's the Mayor got to do with it? I don't understand."

"There's a lot you don't understand, Steven. Gordon tried to explain a million things but you, you were always arguing."

"What's the Mayor got to do with it?"

"Wise up. He's been trying to screw the zoo for years, just waiting for Gordon to make a mistake. They've always been on each other's back. The Council usually supports Gordon. But if he can't take care of himself, the Mayor will cram some damn accountant into acting director."

"So what?"

"I need help," Charlie said without emotion. His hands were back inside his coat and he stared at his nephew with vacant eyes.

Steven shook his head. "Charlie, I don't know where you got this crazy idea. Stay here if you want, I don't care. You can reach me at the hospital. I'm leaving."

"Harriet just gave me this," said Charlie. His hand came out of the pocket holding an envelope. He shoved it at his nephew.

Steven opened it warily, reading to himself the typewritten note.

Charlie, I haven't been feeling well and if you're reading this you probably know a lot more than I do now. I'm going to ask Harriet to give you this just in case something happens. I have to ask you to do something. I never asked anything of you before. Keep it for me, Charlie. Keep the zoo. Do what you have to, but make sure it stays. We've talked about this a hundred times, I don't have to repeat the problems with money, the Mayor, or anything else. Do your best, Charlie. I don't know how long I'll be gone. If it's a long time, make sure you find someone to take over who *knows.* He's got to be an animal man, Charlie, you know what I mean. I've tried to talk to Steven but between you and me, he'd rather see the place burned down. I can't argue with him anymore, I just can't anymore. Whatever you do, don't listen to his poison. Keep the zoo, Charlie. Keep it for me.

Steven stared at the typewritten letter. His fingers seemed to burn, as if the paper were licking flames across his skin. Charlie slowly snaked out his arm and retrieved the letter. He folded it carefully and put it back in his pocket.

"I don't think Gordon wanted you to read that," Charlie said finally.

"Why did you let me?"

"Because we can talk. You and I always could talk."

"No, Charlie. I always listened. I was always listening to you."

"I need help, Steven. The zoo . . ."

Steven clamped his eyes shut. *Poison.* The word seared him. Was that what his father thought? It wasn't true. All Gordon had to do was listen; Steven could have explained. Now it was too late. But was he always going to be too late?

Charlie stirred. "The animals," he muttered. "Gordon wants them looked after."

"So do I," Steven said. "But you know what I think."

His uncle shrugged. "I'm older than Gordon, too old to argue with you. I just need your help, that's all. You can go back to your school in a few minutes and leave the zoo to me."

"What do you want from me? Charlie, you don't really think you can get appointed director, do you? Are you going to show them your scrapbook? Are you going to show them the safaris and the rows of heads, the dead elephants and the rhinos? Are you going to show them the *Life* article?"

"I was an animal collector before that, Steven. I'm not apologizing for anything. I know animals."

"I'm not arguing there. You can keep the zoo, Charlie. You can do it a thousand times better than I could. But don't you think it's a little ludicrous? The Great White Hunter who's slaughtered more animals than ten zoos could fill?"

"I don't do that anymore," Charlie repeated firmly. "Are you going to help me?"

"I'll help the animals. I'll always do that."

"I don't want the damn job but someone has to do it. I know what you're saying. I know what they're going to think in there. That's why I need you."

"What do you expect me to do?"

"I'm sixty-four. I never finished high school. I learned what I know where it counts. You, you're a hotshot professor. A goddamn degree."

"Three of them," Steven said, suddenly grinning. "I've got three of them."

"And you can wipe your ass with all three of them. But I need someone to tell them I know animals."

Steven didn't hesitate. "You got that. I'll go in there with you and here's what I'll do, period. If they want a recommendation, I'll say that in my professional opinion, there isn't another man in the state who knows more about animals than Mr. Charles Cooper. The gentleman has gained an astounding repertoire of practical experience; his field studies, though crude by academic standards, have nevertheless been performed impeccably, and if he doesn't appear to have lengthy rigorous credentials, I can assure them that Charles Cooper has worked with more animals in his career than ten zoologists would in a lifetime. I'll swear to that, on a stack of Bibles. What I'd like to say is that the ten zoologists couldn't work with the animals because it was you and people like you that wiped them off the face of the earth."

"Steven—"

"I'd *like* to say that. I won't."

Charlie's throat growled. His neck rumbled and he patted his pockets for his cigars. "That's all I need."

"That's all you're going to get."

"Sit on the bench over there and write it out, will you?"

"I'll go in there with you."

"No. I don't want you to."

"Why not?"

Charlie lit his cigar. A huge cloud of blue smoke drifted up the skylit dome. "Look at you. A goddamn professor and you're wearing blue jeans. Look at that shirt. That's a ditch digger's shirt. Sandals. No socks. For Christ's sake, you're thirty years old and you're wearing sandals. You need a haircut. No, no thank you. Just sit down and write something. Big words, lots of important big words. And write down all your degrees. All three of them. But don't, don't let them see you."

Steven threw up his hands and muttered, "I give up. You got it, Charlie. Whatever you say."

Steven walked to a bench and carefully composed a glowing account of his uncle's practical experience. It was easier to do than he thought. No matter what Charlie had done twenty years ago, he knew animals. Before he organized safaris he had collected for nearly every major zoo in the world. He had trapped in every jungle, desert, island, and swamp on six continents. He had been the best. And if trapping animals was hard, keeping them alive in broken-down freighters for the exhausting transport across oceans was infinitely harder. But Charlie had done it; he needed the money.

Steven silently handed the note to his uncle, who read it while stubbing his cigar out in a sand-filled urn. Charlie nodded, mumbled something unintelligible, and disappeared into the Council Chambers.

As soon as he was gone, Steven called the hospital. But just as Charlie said, no visitors were allowed to Gordon's room. His condition was "stable," he was under intensive care, and everything possible was being done.

Steven returned to the rotunda. The minutes passed; he watched the sunlight crawl across the marble floor. He wanted to wait for Charlie, to tell him how he felt about Gordon. How he was wrong in arguing and how he would never bother him again about poison. He just wouldn't talk about it. Charlie would do a good job as director; he'd yell at the keepers and he'd check on the feed deliveries. What else is needed for a zoo? All you have to do is just baby-sit it. The San Francisco Zoo was a snap, quieter than a nursery. Can't hear a sound through the concrete and iron. The Council would be happy, the visitors would be happy. No complaints, no trouble. As for himself, things would go back to how they were before. He'd visit the zoo when Gordon recovered and he'd praise the "progress." He'd agree that things were bad but they were always getting better, weren't they? He just wasn't going to argue anymore. And the animals? At least they wouldn't be worse off. Sure, things were bad, but they're always getting better, right?

An hour and a half later, the door opened and Charlie ambled out. Steven looked at his face and for the first time he realized just how old his uncle was. His cheeks sagged. The jowls under his chin wobbled and although his back was straight, his heels never quite lifted as far as they should. His lips trembled and his hands hung limply at his side. Steven knew it then, and the jittery feeling in his own stomach was fear. He didn't have to ask to know that they had rejected this old fighter; they didn't want to take a chance on this faded, cursing, pigheaded, once vital mountain of a man.

Charlie stopped. His wagged his head at the floor, too exhausted to raise his eyes. "They don't want me, Steven. The bastards are scared to stick their necks out before the Mayor comes."

"You tried, Charlie. Let's get to the hospital, okay?"

"No, you don't understand."

"You did your best. I understand that."

"No." Charlie raised his head and stared at his nephew's eyes. "They don't want me, Steven. They want *you.*"

Steven saw then. He saw the eyes. "Out," he muttered, "I'm getting out of here." Steven made his move quickly. He twisted around the ashtray and quickened his pace toward the doors. He darted across the marble but he should have known better.

Charlie melted in front of him. He had come from a dozen steps behind and overtaken Steven in a second, cutting him off like a sheep dog working a flock. Steven was blocked. How had the old man moved so fast? Charlie's suddenly alive body rested perfectly, the weight evenly distributed on the balls of his feet. His eyes read every muscle in Steven's legs; he knew his moves even before Steven thought them.

"No," Steven growled. He shook his head violently. "Get out of my way. I'm not going to do it."

"You don't understand."

"I understand, damn it. I'm not going to do it."

Steven knew he should keep his gaze down, sideways, anywhere but at Charlie's eyes. He knew what he would see. Charlie's eyes had broken bosun's mates; they had stared down sunken-faced Masai chieftains and thin-lipped Chinese traders. The eyes . . .

"Calm down, Steven. What's the matter? All I want to do is talk with you. We could always talk. Right?"

At two fifty-seven, three minutes before adjournment, the minutes recorded the emergency appointment by a vote of six to four of Steven Cooper, B.S., M.S., Ph.D., to the position of acting director of the San Francisco Zoological Park. The term was to last until either the elder Cooper returned or until subsequent votes elected a new permanent director.

■ ■ ■

Steven worked into the night arranging his departure from the zoology department. He filed the papers requesting emergency leave of absence and above the blank line for explanation he scrawled "personal reasons." Steven himself didn't know the reasons, but they were certainly personal. He didn't take over the zoo totally because of Charlie. But even of that he couldn't be sure. He wondered why Charlie had "neglected" to tell Harriet the hospital. Why had he been lured to City Hall? The more he thought about it, the more the whole situation smelled like a craftily constructed snare. Hard evidence was scant but the scent of a master woodsman hung like fresh spoor over the trail.

Steven packed his books and research notes, emptying his office of current projects. His teaching duties could be taken over by assistants since a detailed course outline existed. He was leaving a score of half-written journal articles but he could work on them at the zoo. He wondered how much real time it would take to baby-sit the animals, certainly not much. He would mother them just as long as it took for Gordon to recover.

It was really for his father that he was doing it, Steven decided. He gritted his teeth. The line that separated family from friends was the only point that ultimately forced you to do something you didn't want to do. But he would do the job; he'd be a good caretaker. And the minute Gordon stepped through the gate he'd hand the nursery over and wash his hands of it.

The zoo had just opened its gates at ten o'clock when Steven lugged his hastily packed suitcase toward the ticket line. The guard peered at him strangely, then smiled in recognition. He tipped his cap and swung open the employees' gate.

Steven paused. An unexplainable feeling passed through him and instead of being waved through, he joined the line of visitors waiting to buy tickets.

"How many?" the bored voice drawled.

"One," Steven said.

"Seventy-five cents to go in."

"How much to leave?" Steven joked. His second attempt in as many days thudded flat.

After clicking through the turnstile, Steven stuffed the ticket stub deep in his pants pocket as if he were afraid of losing it. He felt crazy doing it, superstitious and totally unreasonable. But he hoped the stub would be a charm, a token of his impermanence. Maybe that was why he smiled as he patted his pocket. Superstition was wickedly antiscientific, but Steven liked to cover all bets.

Walking across the main plaza, he breathed the tangy smell of eucalyptus and pine. A faint hint of fresh elephant dung tickled his nose. The old familiar cat smells, the camel heaps, the bear dens—it still smelled the same.

When he was going to college he had lived at the zoo every summer—in the old director's cottage tucked away in a thick pine grove. He hardly ever left the grounds then, being exhausted every evening from cleaning cages, hauling feed, and nursing sick animals back to health in his bathroom that more often than not held enough beasts to qualify as a menagerie. But after he left for graduate school in the East his summer visits shortened to weeks, then to days. It was then that the change in him started, the vague uneasiness toward zoos that grew from a nagging self-doubt into a more virulent disgust. After his four years in the craters of Africa, the transformation had been completed. And as much as Steven shifted his loyalties, the deeper the gulf yawned between him and his father. Poison? The word might be correct, but he wasn't sure that he was the only one oozing venom.

There were few morning visitors in the plaza, mainly older regulars and a few uncertain tourists studying maps of the grounds. Steven trudged up the gravel path to the office. His hand paused as it gripped the handle of the screen door. Something seemed wrong.

It took several seconds to identify the uneasiness. Then it came. The handle—the handle was too low. He remembered having to lift his arm before. He smiled when he realized that the door hadn't changed as much as he had. Steven shrugged and quickly entered.

"Well," he said, grinning widely. "It's good to see you, Harriet."

The plump lady at the desk rose from the ancient clacking Remington and brushed her glasses into grey hair arranged like a crane's nest above her head. She laughed, waddling from the desk and flashing neat pearl teeth.

Her hair hadn't changed a bit. Steven always remembered objects disappearing into it; eyeglasses, pencils, paper clips, and a quill pen Gordon had given her as a gift for staying with him fifteen years. The quill pen had long since disintegrated with age but Harriet's hair always remained the same.

"You haven't changed a bit," Steven greeted her.

"Neither have you," Harriet said, cocking her head and beaming. "Except you're about ten feet taller."

Steven looked around the outer office and absorbed the memories, the bits and stuff of what had been another life of his. He couldn't help thinking about the door handle and how low it had seemed. For over an hour he talked with Harriet, taking in the changes in the zoo since he had last visited. As he suspected, nothing had changed.

"Harriet, I want to go over Gordon's records. The plans, budgets, animal charts—everything you can lay your hands on. I'd like you to take care of the normal calls and whatever until I can get prepared."

Harriet bobbed her head. "No problem."

For the next two days Steven buried himself in the scraps and jotted notes that Gordon called his records. Journals were scattered helter-skelter in the office, hidden among the filing cabinets like pieces of a giant puzzle. It was Steven's approach to throw himself into a job headfirst, figuring the more work he did in the beginning the fewer his problems would become. He worked far into the night and was at his desk in the morning even before Harriet arrived. The shape of the puzzle finally became clear and it was frightening.

Gordon had been juggling. For how long, Steven wasn't certain, but he winced as he saw the building inspector's survey. The cat house was leaking, extensive interior cracking; recommendation—demolition and new construction. Stapled to the report was his father's appropriation request to the Mayor's Department of Parks and Recreation. They allocated one-third what he asked, only enough for minimal repatching. The story was similar all down the line. Old exhibits long overdue for renovation had been woefully underfunded. Sometimes even that money had been diverted toward feed bills and medical supplies.

But it wasn't simply a problem of insufficient planning. There was a huge stack of designs drawn up by the most prestigious architectural firms in San Francisco. They were all alike, containing beautiful drawings and conceptions, projecting wildly inflated bids, and extending profuse honors to the Mayor for the instigation of yet another important civic program. Naturally their survey work and estimate fees were "severely" reduced with the public welfare in mind.

And Gordon juggled. As Steven plotted the attendance figures, they showed an alarming fall—not sharp, but a steady, sickening decline. He wasn't surprised. There was no question that some of the exhibits were frighteningly ugly. It made me stay away, Steven thought. He grimly concluded that it was only a question of time before the animals began to suffer. Steven had to admit that his father had kept them healthy so far. Gordon's mortality rate had always been among the lowest of the country's top zoo directors. But as Steven had argued with him countless times, there was no space in any medical report for animal psychiatry.

When Steven finished, he was more firmly convinced than ever of the relics that zoos had become. They might have served a purpose once but there was no need for them now. They kidnapped animals from their natural homes and, forgoing a trial, jailed them like political prisoners. The question had never been raised, but Steven was certain the case would be instantly thrown out in a *real* kangaroo court. Zoos were dungeons, medieval chambers, with the torture simply a matter of degree. Unlike any other oppressed minority, however, animals had no advocates, no public defenders.

Poison! The word hovered in the office like a ghostly echo. Steven shook his head. He was not going to get involved. He had a job to do and he'd do it to the best of his abilities—until the minute Gordon returned.

Finally he caught up with the survey of the zoo's condition and Steven began assuming more routine work. He began one morning with the backed-up mail. Most of the letters were normal—meat bills, animal dealer lists, upcoming conventions. Channel Five asked to film a *Birth at the Zoo* story or, if that couldn't be "arranged," at least a *Summertime Blues* angle with wilted penguins and disgruntled polar bears. The rest of the letters were from the general public. Steven wrote replies to the first few and then stopped when he had an idea. He sorted the letters and put them in a box for his father, thinking they would be good for Gordon to tackle when his condition improved. It wouldn't be strenuous and might be cheerful therapy.

They were letters from teachers, thank-you notes together

with class projects, or simple questions on the length of a hamster's gestation period. People's canaries were going bald and would the director have the time to prescribe treatment? Steven smiled; these were the letters Gordon liked best. But the smile turned to a frown when he scanned one sheet of coarse school paper with the kind of wide ruling used for learning handwriting. The message was scrawled in a curious red ink.

Direktor,
Don't you think you've got just a bit too much power for your own good? I'm talking about the animals, direktor. A lot of people like me don't like to see them the way they are. Maybe you'd better think about this.

Sieg Heil, Commandant

PS The antelope was unfortunate, what else is next?

Steven grimaced as he crumpled up the paper and threw it in the trash can. The zoo always got its share of crank letters and many times he remembered his father being awakened in the middle of the night by some slurring drunk who "just wanted to settle a little bet."

He promptly forgot the irritating note and spent the rest of the morning going over keepers' reports. Buried near the end was the weekly veterinarian file. By this time his eyes were drooping, but at the third page they sprang open. He reread a paragraph, then snapped the intercom switch.

"Harriet?"

"Yes?"

"Get me Dr. Lewis on the phone, will you?" A second later he snapped, "Forget that. I'll go over and see him. If anything comes up, I'll be at the vet's compound."

As Steven put on his coat, he glanced worriedly at the report once more and then went out his private door. It took only a few minutes to cross the gardens around the flamingo pool, where the vet had his laboratory.

He found Dr. Lewis stocking drugs in his cabinets. He was a

gnome of a man, standing on a chair to reach the higher shelves. Steven had never seen him without a huge briar pipe clenched between his tiny lips—usually an uprooted tree stump with gnarled projections and charred cavities. The bowl was continually crammed overfull with tobacco; the flakes spilled onto his lab frock, which over the years had absorbed the brown juices like fine meerschaum. Charlie always chortled over the sheen of Dr. Lewis's lab coat, chuckling that it was "as brown as the breast of a West Indies Negress."

When the vet carefully eased his fragile frame off the chair, Steven was surprised to see the pipe dangle limply from his lips. The pipe looked heavier than Steven remembered; the bowl weighted the old man's head down. Dr. Lewis absentmindedly waved Steven into a chair while he used a hand to support his smoke-spewing briar. His shoulders slumped in a permanent slouch and his eyes were slightly tearing from the strain and heat of the pipe.

As they chatted for a few minutes, Steven noticed that the vet's voice had grown softer, weaker, and he tended to ramble a bit more. And Steven gradually became aware of a curious similarity between his father, Charlie, and Dr. Lewis. The parallels were so strong. The three men were all old but, more important, they shared a quality. An old guard quality perhaps, like self-imposed exiles isolated from the contemporary world. They were a class to themselves—the old zoo men—the men who had been children at the period in America when cities west of New York had felt both the pangs of inferiority and the heady swelling of boosterism. Zoos sprang up faster than weeds on undeveloped outskirts, and as the cities grew they absorbed the parks amoeba-like within their centers and marched outward again. The cities had changed; the zoos and the men who tended them hadn't.

At a pause in the conversation, Steven brought up the matter he had come to discuss. "I read your report a few minutes ago. I'm sorry I wasn't able to get to it sooner."

Dr. Lewis nodded. "Quite understandable under the circumstances."

"There was something in it that I'd like to clear up."

"Oh?"

"You mentioned that you had to destroy a pronghorn. I believe you administered an overdose of pentobarbital."

"Ah, yes," the vet nodded, wagging his chin sadly. "A doe. Very unfortunate. Such a fine creature."

"You wrote the keeper reported it injured, an accident with the fence."

"You know pronghorns, Steven. The most jittery exhibit we have. It could have been anything, a car backfire, a loud noise. Anything will set them off. She kicked through the fence and caught her back legs."

"There was nothing you could have done?"

Dr. Lewis shook his head. "Nothing. Their bones are like glass; hers were shattered, impossible to mend. She lost too much blood."

"You were quite sure of that?"

"Positive," the vet said sadly. He sucked on his pipe and the briar gurgled its agreement.

"It's hard for me to say this, Dr. Lewis, because I've known you for so long. You taught me quite a bit when I was working summers here."

"You learned fast. I couldn't teach you anymore."

"I'm just going to be here until Gordon gets out of the hospital. But until then, I have to run it as he would."

"Of course. I understand perfectly."

"Good . . . but that means that I'll be the one to make the decisions. Just like Gordon does. And that applies to everything. But especially any decision on animal destructions. Is that clear?"

Dr. Lewis's face reddened and he stirred uncomfortably. Looking away, he cleared his throat noisily. When he finally spoke, his voice quavered. "Now, Steven, I hope you don't— What I mean is that I was forced to do what I did. Gordon wasn't there. Nobody—"

Steven interrupted gently. "I understand. From what you've told me, there's no doubt in my mind that either Gordon or I would have agreed with you. The circumstances were extraordinary and you were correct. I just want you and me to have an understanding for the future—that the final authority rests with me and me alone."

The vet sucked on his pipe. The blush eased from his face and he vigorously bobbed his head. "You're perfectly right. The rules must be followed. Perhaps I exceeded my authority, but I was acting in the name of mercy. The poor antelope was suffering. I hope you don't think I was acting irresponsibly, like some crazy concentration camp commandant."

Steven froze. It was only then, with that particular turn of phrase, that he stopped. He had heard that word before. The letter he threw in the trash can. When he read the vet's report, the only misgiving he had concerning the antelope was to make sure Dr. Lewis would consult him in the future. He never connected the two events. But the letter had something about commandants in it, something about antelopes.

Steven frowned. "Was there anything unusual about the pronghorn's death? Apart from the accident, I mean."

"The accident itself was unusual, a freak occurrence."

"Yes. But nothing was strange about the injury?"

"You read my report, Steven. Multiple fractures in both hind legs, severed nerves and muscle tissue damage, massive hemorrhaging. The animal had bolted toward the fence, struggled, and entangled herself. The fence had been mended at that point and the crimps weren't snipped smooth. The jagged edges cut through her flesh at several points—hindquarters, neck—"

"Her neck?"

"Yes, her upper throat. There were tufts of hair stuck in the fence. She must have contorted her body quite severely. Unusual? Steven, you know as well as I do the mortality rate in zoos. But we're quite proud of Gordon's record. It's far better than most."

"*Any* death is a bad record," Steven blurted before he could stop himself.

Dr. Lewis removed his pipe from his lips and nervously licked them. "I'm sorry, Steven."

Steven abruptly rose, but before starting for the door, he remembered something else.

"By the way," he said, flipping through a small notebook, "the hooved-stock keeper mentioned that one of the imported okapis seemed under the weather."

"Yes," Dr. Lewis confirmed. "The new male we got from New York quarantine."

"Oh?" Steven said. "You checked for blood parasites?"

Dr. Lewis shook his head. "Blood parasites don't live in okapi habitats."

"But they can be transferred by flies. There was an article in last year's—" Steven quickly checked himself. He continued in a friendly tone. "I've got a pile of journals I've finished with, taking up a hell of a lot of room. Would you like me to drop some off? There's quite a lot of new stuff. I'm sure you'd find them interesting."

Dr. Lewis stared back. He returned his pipe to his mouth and puffed silently. Then he pointed with the stem to a corner of the laboratory. "Do you see those, Steven? Those are *my* journals. They're very neat. They're straight and unbent. They're that way because I haven't had a chance in four years to read them. I'm lucky if I have time to stack them away in the corner. All day I give inoculations, set bones, and take pregnancy tests. At night I'm running stool samples to the labs or filling out quarantine forms."

"Do you need more help?"

"I *have* help," Dr. Lewis snapped. "I hire help every six months. College degrees. I tell them I can't pay them much. Then I ask them why they're here and everyone says the same thing. *Experience,* they say, *it's good experience.* Then they get their experience and go running off to start a dog and cat private practice in the suburbs and drive Cadillacs. Help like that I don't need. Steven, what is it with these college people? The zoo should be a place they come *after* they get the experience. They should come to the zoo because they can't be anywhere else. Steven, what is it with the college—"

Dr. Lewis stopped in midsentence. The words he formed froze in his lips. "I don't mean you, Steven. You haven't changed. You're still the same."

"If there's anything you need, you'll tell me, won't you?"

"Yes. Of course," Dr. Lewis muttered. The clouds began pouring again from his pipe and he blinked his eyes through the blue fumes.

And as Steven left the compound and crossed the plaza, he noted that Dr. Lewis had been the second one to tell him that he hadn't changed. Harriet had said the same thing. It was no use explaining to them they were wrong. But it was more than that; Steven didn't want to impose on them, to disturb their faith. It wasn't faith in him; rather it was an affirmation of their own life and he respected it. Only Charlie had never said it. Perhaps he of all the rest had the least faith to sustain.

■ ■ ■

It was on a Saturday morning, three minutes before the zoo opened, when Steven found himself standing alone on a high, grassy knoll. The vantage point afforded a spectacular view of the main entrance, the introductory gardens, and the first quarter of the grounds. It was quiet, too quiet, and suddenly he realized why. Around him were none of the free-roaming animals, the semi-tamed birds and rodents that were allowed the run of the zoo. While most people thought the dozens of peacocks, guinea fowl, cranes, and squirrels were a decorative touch thoughtfully provided for the benefit of their cameras, actually they were let loose to eat bugs. Without them, the pathways and benches would be crawling with insects feeding on wads of gum, hot dogs, and spilled popcorn strewn helter-skelter over the zoo by confirmed garbage droppers.

But the peacocks were quiet now, hidden in brush along with the bantams. This was their defense against insanity, their period of contemplation. They rested in preparation for the coming army of careless shoes, clutching fingers, and rolling baby carriage wheels.

The noise started then. The jarring recording erupted from

the loudspeakers near the entrance and Steven gritted his teeth. Unconsciously his fists tightened as he stared with disgust at the speakers. They were grouped in a semicircle not on zoo grounds proper, but just at the perimeter. They belonged to the carnival that was more or less permanently camped at the side entrance. The carnival had long been a source of irritation both to Steven and to his father but the concession right was impossible to tear loose from the hands of the Mayor, who extracted an annual rakeoff for the city's budget by pointing out that, after all, it wasn't on zoo property.

The lights on the ferris wheel sprang on; the merry-go-round lumbered into motion and churned out its insistent pipe, piping. Muffled sputters of the go-cart rides cracked in the air and a cloud of white steam rose above a popcorn stand. Steven stared at the carousel, feeling his stomach burn. He hated the carnival. They were fine somewhere else, Steven thought, but not next to the zoo. It was another sign of the degradation of zoos. It hurt him to hear the blaring music; it sickened him to see the people stumbling from the carnival into the zoo with their sense of equilibrium destroyed by machines. They lurched with a characteristic whirl, their eyes wide and locking mechanically on moving objects, colors, shapes. I'm crazy, thought Steven, shaking his head. I'm thinking they're mindless zombies.

The zoo gates opened. The huge iron grating swung to the side and the rush was on. Steven had to burst out laughing. The first ten kids, part of a school group, threw their tickets at the taker and shot inside. Their teacher ran after them, then stopped in confusion as the guard demanded her ticket. She wavered, yelling at the scampering children, and then glared at the guard. The rest of the class stood deathly silent behind the gate, staring in horror at their teacher's loss of authority.

Meanwhile, a half-dozen old women in sun hats and floral prints took advantage of the momentary confusion to squeeze past the children. Then the entire crowd deserted their lines and charged forward in a surging, pressing riot.

As order was restored and the flow checked, Steven shook his head in amazement. He hadn't seen the opening ritual for years and the view of the mob from his hilltop location made it seem funny. It made him feel good. In all his life he had never rushed the gates because since childhood he had always been inside.

He felt good walking down from the hill. At last he had time to leave the office and reacquaint himself with the old keepers and introduce himself to the new ones. As he headed across the plaza, he smiled at the visitors milling in the open square. Some were studying maps or buying film while others hurried down familiar paths toward favorite exhibits. He walked past the electric tram ride when he suddenly felt a whim. It was a giddy feeling and it must have been due to the tingling smell of eucalyptus. If he wanted the feeling of coming to a zoo for the first time, the tram tour was a perfect opportunity.

The tram was almost full but Steven broke into a run and landed on the last seat in the back. The ticket seller was about to come over and curse him out until he recognized Steven's face. Steven smiled and shrugged his shoulders awkwardly as if to say I don't know what the hell I'm doing here either. The tram started to roll.

On board, the guide reached out a hand to steady herself and switched on her hand mike. Steven didn't know her; she must have come to the zoo in the last couple of years. She was properly bright and cheerful, looking pert in her blue-and-gold windbreaker uniform.

"Good morning, ladies and gentlemen," she began. Her voice assumed the usual singsong melody of guides everywhere. "My name is Amanda. First of all, I'd like to welcome you to the San Francisco Zoological Park or, if you prefer, just 'the zoo.' This is *your* zoo if you live here in California, but if you're from out of state, I'd like to extend a warm welcome to you also. As our tram continues, I'd like to remind you that arms and legs should be kept inside; remember, these are animals here and they might misinterpret your actions."

Steven winced. Do *people* always interpret correctly?

"As we move along, I'd like to give you some statistics on the zoo, some facts and figures." Here she paused, and a mischievous smirk emerged from her lips. "I said I'd *like* to. But do you really want to hear a lot of numbers on acres or what year the zoo was built or how many animals we have?"

She looked at the people intently and for an instant they stared mutely back. Then all at once pandemonium broke loose. The kids in the front violently shook their heads and yelled, "No, no, *no.*" The young parents smiled shyly while the camera-toting tourists sighed in obvious relief.

"Well, neither do I," agreed the girl, flashing a conspiratorial smile. She had won them, they were hers. After a space of twenty seconds they were butter in her hands. "I'll make a deal with you, okay? If you don't tell my boss I skipped the lecture, I'll tell the driver to go slower and we'll see more. You want to see the animals, right?" A slight frown crossed her brow. "What kind of a group are we? I asked you a question and all you do is stare back at me. Is that how we're going to be? No? Then all right, I'll try again. If you're too shy to say anything, raise your hands. *We want to see the animals, don't we?*" There were sixty seats on the tram. Immediately fifty-nine hands crowded the air.

Steven was dumbstruck. He had written the script for the lecture years ago for his father. It was meant to be informative, an alternative to the guidebooks and signs. What insubordination possessed her to skip the lecture?

"Unanimous," the girl cheered. "Or as near as you can get," she added, passing the faintest frown toward Steven's folded hands. "I'm glad," she continued, "that I have such a good group. We're going to see the bears first, but before we get there I want you all to ask me questions—any questions—about the zoo. Remember, my best groups always have the most questions."

Immediately a boy shot up his hand and plaintively cried, "Where are the snakes?"

"There!" the girl shouted, pointing at the space directly beneath his seat. The boy's mouth dropped and he froze. The people roared their approval and as the gales of laughter pealed from the tram, the boy's face relaxed and he smiled.

Steven groaned audibly and almost buried his face in his hands. What was she doing? "Snakes," the girl said, "are there. They're everywhere. And you did the right thing when I told you a snake was next to you. Did everyone see that? What's your name?"

"Arthur."

"Arthur remained calm and didn't get excited, which is the worst thing you can do around snakes. You're pretty smart, Arthur. If you want to see a lot of snakes, I'll show you the Reptile House, where you can go after the tram ride. Next question?"

A well-dressed man in a tailored suit raised his arm quite delicately. An extravagant ruby set in gold flashed from his hand but the people behind him ignored that and rather openly stared at the tightly bound turban wrapped around his head.

"Yes?" the guide asked.

"Please tell me," the man said in a heavily cultured tone. "I have heard much of this curious animal of yours. The great bald bird. The one pictured on your country's coins?"

"The bald eagle?"

The man brightened. "Yes. The eagle. But he's not really hairless, is he?"

"No." The girl smiled. "That's a common misconception, lots of people make that mistake. It's just that the whiteness of his feathers makes him look bald."

"I'm afraid I don't understand. A white-feathered bird in my country would never be thought of as hairless. A brown-colored one perhaps, I could understand that. But a white one? It's rather confusing."

The girl's face assumed the faintest trace of a frown which she was frantically trying to dispel. Finally she thought of an escape and she bobbed her head in agreement. "That's a *very* good question. Did everybody hear that? Who would like to tell the gentleman from India why the bald eagle isn't bald?"

"He ain't bald," spoke up a confident man in the front. "He's just *called* bald."

"Ah," the man from India said, nodding his head happily. "You stated the problem exactly." He politely waited for the man to continue his explanation but as the silence grew longer, his face grew even more puzzled.

"Excuse me?" Another man raised his hand and directed his

attention toward the Hindu. "Can I ask *you* a question?"

"Certainly," the Hindu replied, quietly relieved that the embarrassing silence was broken.

The man cleared his throat. "You come from India?"

"Yes. I do."

The questioner's voice hardened. "Why do you worship cows? Why do you let them run loose in the streets? Why don't you eat them if all of you are starving?"

All eyes turned to the man from India. People twisted in their seats to get a better view and all became quiet. The intense silence indicated a profound interest in the answer to this question.

Steven groaned and buried his face in his hands. He alone felt the horror, the dread, the ignorance and undercurrents of confrontation. He began to pray that somebody would *do* something, move the tram faster, anything. Instead, the Hindu smiled.

"Why don't we eat cows?" he asked. Smiling, he turned in his seat to look at everyone. His voice assumed the tone of an elder explaining the obvious to a slightly dull child. "I come from India. We have our cows. Here in America," he said, lifting a hand in a graceful gesture, "you have your dogs."

If the air before had been tense, then the stunned vacuum that greeted his response was cataclysmic. People dropped their jaws. Their eyes widened. Steven slowly raised his head and groaned.

"Bears!" shouted the guide. She almost screamed the word into the microphone and waved her arms furiously. The tram had crawled to a stop in front of the brown bear grotto and the girl seized upon the event. "I want you all to meet Yogi the bear. Yogi is our star performer here at the zoo and is really our unofficial greeter. You'll see what I mean. What we're going to try to do now is see how glad Yogi is to meet us. Right, Yogi?"

On his haunches, the bear stared blankly at the tram. He had heard his name called. His tiny eyes were buried under a carpet of hair as his nose twitched suspiciously.

"Here you are, Yogi," the girl continued quickly. She reached in a pail and withdrew a large biscuit. Waving it, she exhibited the morsel with a series of friendly urgings. "Show us how glad you are to see us, Yogi."

As the bear remained motionless, again there was the flicker of indecision on the girl's face. Turning to the people on the tram, she explained the situation. "Yogi needs a little encouragement. Let's show him first how happy we are to see *him,* okay? Let's wave at Yogi. Like this. . . . Does everybody know how to wave?"

Again fifty-nine hands began a furious assault on the bear's attention. Fifty-nine hands waved in friendly insistence.

"That's right," the girl beamed, exhorting them on. "Let's show Yogi how much we like him."

The bear made a slight movement with his paw. The tramload increased their fervor in anticipation but they wilted when the bear checked his movement. He froze. The girl bit her lips and hurled the biscuit at his chest. It landed ten feet from his paws, clattered, and broke in half. The bear ignored it. He had caught a scent in the air and he sniffed harder. He smelled Steven.

Steven watched Yogi with increasing nervousness as the bear stood and moved toward him. He was in the last bench of the tram and as the bear waddled closer, Steven began to slink down in his seat. By now the crowd was growing weary and the frantic sea of arms had diminished to a dribble of hopeful jerks.

The bear rose on his haunches to bellow at Steven. Yogi's weak eyes couldn't see far but the old scent was unmistakable. The restless tramload began to look elsewhere. They wanted to leave. But the guide had noticed Yogi's movement and now she frowned.

Steven's eyes locked on the bear. Damn it, he cursed silently, why don't you wave and get it over with? But as Yogi bellowed another friendly greeting, Steven realized that the bear would perform only if he did something. Trying hard not to let anyone see him, Steven tentatively stuck out his hand away from the tram and waved it quickly in a familiar shake.

Yogi roared his approval. The bear's massive arm shot out and his paw began to flap furiously. He rested on his legs and jerked his arm at Steven as if his life depended on it. Steven slowly drew in his arm and slunk back into his seat while the crowd went wild. He thought he had been unobserved but he didn't notice the eyes of the guide examining him minutely.

She faced the crowd and flashed her winning smile. "Now *there's* the Yogi we know. He was just being a little shy. Everybody wave now." She waved herself to show them she meant it and threw another biscuit at Yogi, who this time snatched it greedily. The crowd cheered, the guide exhaled silently in relief, and the tram moved on.

It rolled down the pathways, stopping at interesting animals or at points on the grounds where the vista opened suddenly to expose meadows of grazing antelope and sleeping lions. Murmurs of excitement oozed from lips, cameras worked into position, and everywhere people craned their necks.

"This is More-More," the guide said brightly, introducing the stopped tramload to a monstrous hulking orange orangutan. The beast was lying on his back with his hairy legs weaving slowly in the air. He looked at the tram with a slight touch of contempt, flapping his massive jowls. Then he inserted a fat finger in his nose. "Orangs are very proud creatures," the guide continued. "They're very rare now in the wild; their natural habitat is being destroyed. They tell me that More-More here is among the handsomest of his kind in any zoo in the country. Believe it or not." She paused for the automatic laughter. It came loudly and quickly.

They laughed, Steven noted with an irritated frown. They laugh at *her* stupid jokes.

Picking a peanut from her treat bag, she tossed it at More-More. It was a perfect throw, the peanut landing less than a foot from the orang's hands.

More-More turned his head slowly and stared at the peanut for what seemed an eternity. Slowly and deliberately, he reached toward it. His fingers were like fat cigars but they were incredibly nimble. With an almost dainty touch, he plucked the peanut up and preciously examined it in what seemed to be timeless contemplation. His mouth quivered slightly. He snorted and flung the peanut back at the guide.

It was at Monkey Island when the incident with the garbage can started. It wasn't really an incident, thought Steven later, but what was it?

The tram stopped near the pool of water surrounding Monkey Island and, as usual, the troupe teased the people by disappearing to the other side. They would gather in one corner, lure the tram closer, and then scamper off to repeat the process. It was their favorite game. The guide was obviously frustrated and she began to hurl dark looks at the monkeys.

But when the troupe's leader spied Steven in the back seat, he chirruped a greeting and furiously waved his hand. So caught up in his excitement the monkey began vigorously masturbating, using both hands instead of his usual one. He sat on his rear end, his legs spread grandly apart, and jabbered away in spurts of contentment. The rest of the troupe gathered around, secure in the knowledge that while he was thus occupied he would forgo the usual bites, snarls, and pounding that go along with the top job.

The guide's face turned scarlet. She started to mumble something in the microphone but instead bit her lips. It was then that she followed the head monkey's gaze back, across the moat, across the rear of the tram to Steven. She frowned. Bending down, she whispered a few words in the driver's ear. The tram moved a few yards and stopped.

As Steven sat, he began to be aware of a faint buzzing. Slightly annoying at first, it became more pronounced when he found the source. The tram had stopped with Steven's seat immediately next to a garbage can. About two dozen wasps were hovering over the prize feeding hole, dive-bombing the brightly colored boxes and paper bags. As they tired of the boxes, a few scouts began to investigate the buttons in Steven's shirt. He tried to brush them away but the movement only attracted the rest of the swarm. He swatted one that landed on his cuff and started to crawl inside. The nasty hum that emanated from the insect made him instantly regret his decision.

Slowly, incredibly slowly, he put his hands in his pockets and he concentrated. He knew what he was going to do, exactly. He remained motionless, letting the wasps fly around him until they got bored. They zoomed past his nose and hovered around his ears but Steven had only one thing on his mind. He stared at the girl. He knew she had made the driver park the tram in the spot. There wasn't much doubt about that. But why?

She never looked at him. Steven stared from the back of the tram, his arms rigid and his eyes unblinking. She was looking everywhere, everywhere else.

The tram finally pulled away from Monkey Island. The head monkey tired of Steven's rejection so he began pounding the head of the nearest male, who immediately fled across the rocks. The rest of the pack followed in hot pursuit.

"That . . ." the guide explained grimly, "is Monkey Island."

The tram ride was almost over. Nearing the area for disembarkation, the rain of questions became a flood as the people tried to stall the end. "Why aren't the flamingos pink? Where are the turtles? Can a lion kill a tiger? What is a bongo? Where are the rest rooms? When are the lions fed?"

"Please," the guide said through her mike. "I want to remind you. Will you all do me a favor while you're here at the zoo? Please take care of the animals. Don't tease them. A few days ago I saw a visitor climbing over the fence of the pronghorn antelopes and that's strictly against the rules. He should have known better. Please respect the animals."

Steven sat up. He had only been half listening to the guide's patter when she mentioned the antelopes. His mind began to churn. Someone—a visitor—had climbed over the fence? This time the coincidence was too great. Something was going on.

Steven rose from his seat but was pushed off the tram by the surging crowd. He kept his eyes on the guide but the stream of people shoved him farther away. When he finally fought his way through, she was gone. What was her name, he thought feverishly. Sandy? Sandra?

He remembered the employees' file at the office; it would have her name. He took a half-dozen steps when he felt someone tugging his sleeve.

"Hey!" she demanded. "What do you mean lousing up my ride like that?"

Steven turned in astonishment, confused by her sudden appearance. "What?"

"So you wanted to hear the lecture, huh? I figured it. When

everybody in the load raises their hands except *one,* yeah, I know he's trouble. I saw you bother the bear. The monkeys, too. Are you a pervert? What's the matter with you?"

A rush of anger flooded Steven's face. He forgot about the antelope as his hackles rose. "I happen to *like* lectures. Can you understand that?"

"Good. Then I'll give you one. I saw you sneak on the tram. I know you didn't buy a ticket. I don't care about the other stuff and how you fouled it up but I *am* mad about the ticket. What's the matter, are you cheap? That money goes to the zoo, not me. You think you pulled one over, don't you? I have half a mind to turn you in to the guard but I can't prove anything. The zoo needs that money."

"Do you know who I am?"

"Yeah," she said, "a cheap jerk."

Steven's mouth dropped. "Do they—" he waved a hand toward his office—"know you're going around insulting visitors? I have half a mind—"

"That's right, half a mind. Look, I don't need this job, get that? I don't care what they think. I don't care who you complain to. I, *I* could be a tour guide at Universal."

"Why don't you," Steven suggested dryly.

"Because I'm—" she hesitated for a split second—"between pictures. I'm just hanging around here because I like animals. And because I like them, I don't like to see them get short-changed, got that? Now what you're going to do right now is go over to that booth and buy a guidebook for two lousy dollars."

"I don't need a guidebook."

"That's just why you're going to do it."

"And if I don't?"

The objection didn't faze her for a moment. She rigidly braced her chin and curled her lips. Her eyes assumed the most haughty combination of pity, contempt, and maliciousness. "Because," she hissed in a low, powerful whisper, "because I've got friends here who handle snakes. Very poisonous and very dangerous snakes. Mambas. Black mambas and puff udders. I don't have to tell you what can happen."

"Oh, yeah?"

· 39 ·

"Yeah."

The ridiculous threat hung melodramatically in the air as Steven shrugged his shoulders. He thought of telling her who he was but then he reconsidered. In her present condition, whatever it was, she wouldn't believe him. It would be much more effective if she found out herself, later. He stared coolly into her eyes and ordered calmly, "Who did you see climbing the antelope fence?"

"And why do you want to know?"

"I think I might have seen the guy," Steven lied. "Maybe we can find him and take him to your friend with the snakes. What did he look like?"

Her eyes narrowed as she looked at him with suspicion. She crossed her arms but didn't answer.

"Well?" Steven prodded. "What did he look like?"

"It was *you*, wasn't it," she accused in a low voice. "It was almost closing time and I was working the last tram. I didn't get a good look at you but I guess I saw enough. What do you want? Why are you doing this?"

The girl began to back away. There was genuine bewilderment in her face but it was mixed with a growing terror. She crept several more steps back.

"It wasn't me," Steven said, advancing toward her. "Was it someone who looked like me? Was he my height? What was he wearing?"

"Go away," the girl said.

"All I want to know is what he looked like."

"Quit bothering me," she shouted.

"Tell me, damn it!" Steven lost control. His hand clamped on her shoulder. "I'm the director. Answer me. I have to know."

"Do you want me to call the cops?"

The girl twisted free and broke into a run. Steven followed, but as he pushed through a group of people he tripped on a carriage wheel. Sprawling onto the asphalt, he slammed his kneecap hard. Wincing with pain, he struggled to his feet but the girl had vanished.

"*Adders*," he spat viciously. The girl's stupid error upset him far more than his scraped knee. He swore again. "Puff *adders!*"

■ ■ ■

Each employee's photograph was in the corner of his or her personnel record. At the N's he found her. Amanda Newman, age twenty-seven. Her picture had a professional gloss to it, much different from the other snapshot Polaroids. Snipped from a commercial agency composite? Occupation—actress. *Working* actress, she had added in a neat script. The lighting did her justice—long auburn hair, wide grin, healthy teeth. The woman *breathed* healthiness. Then he read further and nodded—native Californian.

The record showed her being hired two years ago as a guidebook model. She worked several months as prop girl for the seal show and the next summer as tram guide and greeter. She turned down a full-time offer and was available only for seasonal work.

Steven gave Harriet the folder. "I need to talk with this woman. Can you call her in for me?"

"Amanda Newman," Harriet read. "That rings a bell."

"How so?"

Harriet repeated the name out loud and checked her appointment calendar. "Yes. She tried to meet with Gordon several times but I couldn't fit her in."

"Well, I have to see her now."

"She gets a noon break from the tram."

"You'd better pull her in right now. Get someone to cover for her."

"Right."

"What's on the agenda for today?"

"Not much," Harriet said, handing him the mail. "The Mayor's office returned your call and they're finally sending over the preliminary budget proposals. Some representative from Purina wants to see you about an endorsement. Nothing else."

Steven took the mail and walked into his office. He spilled the sack of letters onto his desk and started to sort them. One of the envelopes immediately caught his attention. It was short and square. With growing uneasiness, he opened it to find the same coarse paper.

Direktor . . . Why haven't you done anything? You still have all of my angels shackled. Didn't you listen to the poor antelope? I tried to help her but I was interrupted. I listen to the screams every day. I hear them. Isn't anybody going to do something?

—one who listens—

PS Horses scream when they cross rivers, don't they?

Steven's hands shook as he held the paper. It had only been a few days since he had thrown the other letter into the garbage can. His mind began to race. Who was writing these letters? What was he saying? The last phrase. *Horses scream when they cross rivers, don't they?* What did that mean? Was this a veiled threat against the zoo's horses? They only had four. But they were exceedingly valuable Przewalskis. A rarer strain could not be found. There were no streams in their corral, only a water trough. No bushes to hide anybody either; the horses were in plain sight along a major pathway.

Steven decided to take no chances and pressed the intercom button. "Harriet?"

"Yes?"

"Call up the Przewalski paddock. Tell the keeper I'm coming over in a few minutes to check on something."

"Right."

Steven leaned back in his chair. A faint trace of sweat crept across his brow. It was just too impossible to believe. Two letters in a row was no coincidence; the antelope had been too much of one. For the first time Steven became aware of a chilly breeze, a cloud that swirled from somewhere beyond his comprehension.

Something was happening that he didn't understand. And it was frightening.

The intercom squawked. "Miss Newman," Harriet announced.

"Please send her in," Steven replied. He stared at the letter again and didn't notice the door when it finally cracked open.

Amanda sighed nervously. At last, she thought, they're letting me see the director. She closed her eyes and muttered, think positive. This is just another audition. If I don't sweet-talk this old man, I'll never get the transfer off the tram and into the children's zoo. Think positive. Find something to compliment him on. But why should he care that the tram was boring work? Why should he care that she wanted to work with animals in the petting zoo? Think positive. The point is that if she was going to work here, it was going to be a job she *liked*. And what's the point of working in a zoo if it's not with animals? There, that's positive enough. Maybe he's hard of hearing and she could run through a scene for him. What should she play? Sorrowful maiden? Cool efficiency? A sexy temptress? Cooper, his name was. How had he gotten out of the hospital so soon? No, she thought, definitely better not try the sexy bit.

Amanda started to turn toward the director's desk and introduce herself but she couldn't. Her jaw dropped as she suddenly saw the animal heads on the wall. Her eyes widened in awe.

Steven looked up then. He followed her gaze toward the stuffed heads. They were extraordinary. After dying, the animals had truly met their maker, for the finest craftsmanship of the taxidermic art had been employed. It was, after all, a prestige location. The partial heads were superior—a fine Kodiak bear, a gemsbok, a rare buffalo. The whole animals were no less extraordinary—a magnificent jaguar, a Canadian lynx, a saltwater iguana. The rest were birds, a special attachment of Gordon's— from the gargantuan horned owls to the dainty shorebirds, the brilliant jungle fowl and the plain and rather dumpy meadow songsters. Relics, Steven considered them, artifacts of an age when stuffing a dried hide in a natural pose was the sincerest form of religious adoration practiced by the keepers of the temple.

He knew them all intimately, of course. As a child he had crawled over the hides scattered around the room, climbed over the skin-covered chairs, and rubbed grimy hands over bleached white and thoroughly frightening skulls. As a teenager, he had minutely examined the furs, like a rug dealer mentally computing the value of a scarce and fine collection. As a graduate student he had looked upon them as companions of his father, compatriots gathered at the club to sip brandy and not to be stared at for their sedentary habits. Later, when he had received his doctorate in zoology and wandered into the room for the obligatory congratulations, he had noticed for the first time that the teeth of the Kodiak bear were yellowing and a slight layer of dust clouded its mane.

The girl gaped at the fierce fangs of the bear. Her back was to Steven and she shivered involuntarily.

"Good morning, Miss Newman," Steven said.

She whirled around and stiffened. Her mouth opened even wider. Then her purse dropped from her fingers and spilled open across the floor. A lipstick tube tumbled ten feet before wedging between the toes of a stuffed blue heron. She scrambled down out of sight, grabbing at the rolling bottles and boxes and coins.

"Good morning," Steven tried again.

"Don't rub it in," a surly voice warned from beneath the desk. When she finally appeared a minute later, Amanda didn't look at him. Instead, she sank into a chair, exhausted and irritably pushing back loose strands of hair. "I knew it," she said, staring at the ceiling. "I've been trying for three weeks to get in here and when I do—"

Steven interrupted. "Why did you want to come before?"

"I wanted," she blurted, "to get transferred off the damn tram. It's driving me crazy. I can't stand these people. My feet are killing me. My voice—it's not doing my voice any good. That wouldn't be so bad but I'm beginning to laugh at my own jokes. I think I'm hearing them for the first time. The drivers can't seem to find any places on my body they haven't pinched black and blue already but that doesn't stop them. I came back here to ask for a transfer. I want to work at the children's zoo and keep sheep from chewing off kids' buttons. But fat chance of that, huh?" She groaned again. "The feeling I have already, and it's beginning to grow, is that all I'm going to get is a nice long lecture. Maybe not so nice. But I don't blame you. Will you give me a chance to resign before you fire me? I think I've been set up."

The rush of words escaped from her mouth like air out of a burst balloon. She groaned again. What good did it do to think positive? Look what positive gets you. She slumped in her chair and wearily shut her eyes.

"Suppose," Steven began after a long pause, "suppose I make a deal with you." He noticed one eye flicker open suspiciously. "You don't tell my father I skipped giving you a lecture and I'll see what I can do about the transfer."

Her eyes blinked open. "Your father?"

"He's still in the hospital, recovering from his heart attack. I'm running the zoo until he comes back."

"I swear I didn't know it was you on the tram."

"Well? What about my deal? You seem to like making deals, as I remember."

"Why are you doing this?" Amanda asked, not quite believing what she had heard. "You should be yelling at me, standing up and shouting 'You're fired!' and holding out your hand for my official windbreaker and ripping off my emblem patch for dishonorable conduct."

"What for?"

"What for? I yelled at you. I screwed up the tram lecture. I—"

"I don't have time to worry about things like that. I have enough trouble with the animals. Don't you think I know what you go through? I had your job when I was seventeen and I wore out three pairs of shoes."

"You were a guide?"

"When they didn't have trams. Look, I know what a pain in the ass the public is. If it were up to me, I'd lock the gates and not let *anybody* in. They're a damn nuisance. Sometimes . . . they're trouble."

"Why are you doing this?"

"I just told you."

"You told me why you didn't like visitors. You didn't say anything about me."

Steven paused. He had to choose his words carefully. "I need something from you."

"What?"

"Something you wouldn't tell me before. It's become . . . important."

"About this guy with the antelopes?"

"How did you know?" Steven asked sharply.

"I figured it might be. In the plaza your face turned white when I told you. You scared me. That's why I thought the guy might have been you."

"I need to know everything about what you saw."

"Why?"

"Because I'm seeing the police later on. On a general matter." Steven tried to steer away from the truth. "They're trying to cut down security patrols in the neighborhood. They don't know what's going on. Vandalism, climbing fences, that sort of thing. I need evidence to back me up. Do you understand?"

Amanda nodded. She frowned as she concentrated. "There's not much I didn't tell you. . . . I was on the last tour of the day. We were coming around the antelope exhibit. I was standing on the highest part of the tram and caught a glimpse of him through a space in the bushes. He dropped from the fence."

"What did he look like?"

"I can't remember. The sun was in my eyes. Just ordinary, I guess."

"Isn't there anything you remember? How tall was he?"

"He had a brown coat and sunglasses," the girl said promptly.

"How do you remember that now?"

"Because he got on the tram."

"What?" Steven's jaw dropped.

"Yeah, he got on the tram. It must have been him. We stopped at the other end of the antelope exhibit and I was showing the people the bison. It was shedding and looked like a sorry rug. Real bad. The tram was half full and I remember turning around and seeing somebody sit down in the back. Brown coat and sunglasses. I figured he snuck on, a lot of people do, you know. That's why I got mad at you. But the ride was almost over anyway, so I let him."

"That's all?"

"Wait. I think I remember two guys running down the path. One of them wore a uniform, must have been a keeper. I can't remember what the other one looked like. He was carrying a bag, like a doctor. I didn't think anything of it. I guess I should have."

"There was nothing you could have done."

"What did he do, the guy with the sunglasses? You're after him, aren't you?"

Steven nodded slowly.

"Well, what did he do?" she asked again.

"He was bothering the animals."

The girl nodded. "It happens all the time. I guess I shouldn't be saying that but it's true. I see it from my tram. But there aren't any keepers around so what can you do? They throw food when they're not supposed to, they tease them."

"I know," Steven said, cutting her off. He rose from his desk. "Thank you . . . thank you, Amanda. You've been a great help. If you can think of anything else later . . ."

"I can."

"Oh?" Steven said hurriedly.

"I'm thinking about that transfer to the children's zoo."

"Let me see what I can do, all right?"

She nodded and started for the door. As she held the doorknob, she paused. "What do they call you?"

"What do you mean?"

"Do they call you Mr. Director? Dr. Cooper? Coop?"

"I'm sure they call me a lot of things. You can call me Steven."

"Okay. . . . By the way, I'm just wondering. Did you—did you buy that guidebook when I asked you?"

"I *wrote* the damn guidebook," Steven almost snarled. His voice rose a few decibels.

Amanda paled. She shrank and fled from the office, slamming the door behind her.

Steven shook his head in amazement. His father had always had trouble with summer help and this woman seemed no exception. An actress, he mused, scanning again her file photograph. Amanda's smile leaped from the glossy eight-by-ten, still seeming to mock him. She was a little older than the usual fresh-faced college temporaries looking for a short and easy taste of exotic work. But there was no doubt she was good with people, her tramload rapport proved that. Still though, he doubted whether he could trust her with animals in the petting zoo. He had had his fill of beautiful women complaining of goat smells. He shrugged and guessed she would forget about the transfer once she learned about the stall-cleaning chores.

With a weary shake, he cleared his mind and returned his attention to the letter. The piece of paper suddenly seemed more ominous after what Amanda reported. She had seen someone climbing the fence about the time Dr. Lewis's report said the animal had been injured. The first letter! Steven cursed himself for throwing it away. If only he had saved the postmark. Was that first letter mailed before or after the antelope was injured? He checked the envelope in his hand. It was stamped at the main post office early afternoon yesterday. But more important, there was this horse business.

"Steven?" the intercom squawked.

"Yes?"

"Charlie is here to see you."

"Send him right in."

Steven stuffed the letter in his pocket. Charlie came in, but before speaking, he also acknowledged the stuffed heads around the room. But his gaze was different from Amanda's wide-eyed awe. Charlie gave a short, almost formal nod of recognition. From his expeditions he had sent each of the heads to Gordon instead of postcards.

"I'm glad you came," Steven said. "I have to talk about something."

"Fine, fine," Charlie muttered. Then he licked his lips. "But

I'd rather be outside; this room is a box. A little sunshine never hurts, right? Let's grab a beer. I can't talk without a beer."

"We can get one on the way to the Przewalski paddock. I want to show you something there."

They left through the side door and crossed the plaza, stopping at a refreshment stand. With one gulp, Charlie drained his Dixie cup. He smacked his lips with the beer foam still clinging to his walrus mustache.

"Lousy beer," Charlie said. "But it's cold. Let me tell you about the beer in—"

Steven's attention drifted; he had heard the lecture before. The beer in Australia was somedays better, somedays worse, than the beer in Germany which was itself variable in quality compared with the suds in South Africa. And no matter which country, gin everywhere was bad.

Steven wondered why his uncle had avoided the zoo. Ever since Steven had taken over, Charlie seemed uncomfortable being around. At first Steven expected Charlie to share the workload and he suggested to his uncle that he be the liaison to the keepers. Charlie agreed unenthusiastically. But as the days passed, Steven found that instead of listening to the keepers' problems, Charlie had been more interested in telling sea stories and reliving safari expeditions. The keepers were fascinated, they were spellbound by Charlie's adventures—to the detriment of their work, as Steven had discovered. When Steven confronted his uncle, Charlie had shrugged it off and simply began avoiding the zoo. Perhaps it was just as well, Steven thought.

"—well water, the foam was absolutely green with mossy crud—"

Nevertheless, when Steven led Charlie toward the paddock he was glad his uncle had come. He needed Charlie's advice about the letters.

"Wake up there, Steven. You look like a ghost. You need more sun. You stay in that office too long and you'll start smelling like a mushroom."

"Charlie," Steven began. "There's something I have to tell you. Something serious."

"Eh? Shoot. What's up?"

"Charlie, somebody is—"

He never finished the sentence. Both of them froze. There! The sound came again. Steven's ears tingled as his neck moved toward the noise. It came again.

From across the zoo grounds in the direction of the aquatic area came dim noises of a crowd's screams. To anyone who works with the public, the sounds of people in excitement are common; they fade away in meaning by their repetition every second, every hour. The individual laughs, giggles, and shouts cease to have any significance. But there are times when a crowd acts like a *person*. And the sounds it makes are like those made by any other person in pain.

Steven dropped his beer and ran. He dimly perceived Charlie putting on a burst of speed and following but the noise from the crowd blocked out any other thoughts. Steven ran harder. He passed the plaza, the candy and food stands; he flew down paths along the side where there were fewer people. They stared at him curiously; they had heard the screams but for them it was nothing. At Monkey Island Steven glanced at the rocks and saw the pack grouped together at the very top, craning their necks toward the screams. They heard.

Charlie followed twenty steps behind. He ran heavily, his coat flapping wildly. Beads of sweat filled the wrinkles in his face but he ran after Steven without question.

Steven tore around the corner of the bear pits and headed toward the African exhibits. The screams were louder now; he could hear babies crying. He burst through an open courtyard and there, at the end, he saw people streaming toward the hippopotamus exhibit. The shouts of the crowd were luring others, drawing them closer in an insane desire to *see*, to *see*.

Steven choked. It hit him then. Horses . . . river. *Horses scream when they cross rivers.* . . . Hippopotamus. Greek. River horse. Damn it, why didn't he think of it before? It was on the sign in front of the exhibit. How could he have been so stupid? It wasn't the Przewalskis. There could have been time. He could have done something.

Steven tore into the crowd and began shoving. At first there was no resistance but the closer he got to the front, the denser the bodies became. He shoved hard, reaching over heads and prying shoulders apart. He heard Charlie cursing and screaming at the people to get out of the way. Steven plowed through. It was useless to yell because everyone was yelling and only vicious punches in the back made people wake up from their trances. He reached the railing; it slammed into his belly and he leaned forward into the pit. Charlie came up behind and when they saw the hippo, they gasped.

Directly in front of the railing the dry moat plunged sharply twenty feet. Where the cement rose again in a steep incline, blunt iron spikes kept any animal from falling into the moat. Beyond the spikes was the pool the hippo soaked in and a mud space maybe ten feet wide for basking.

The hippo's back legs were still in the pool but the rest of his dozen-foot length and four thousand pounds stretched out in the mud. His tremendous head leaned over the spikes, his jaws working spastically. What the people were screaming about were the gallons of blood pouring from his throat and running like buckets of red paint down the moat. His huge mouth gaped and again the crowd screamed. The jaws revealed a mass of bloody froth and lacerated flesh. The carnage spread over rows of ivory teeth and spurted from his fat lips. He bellowed. A dark cloud of blood droplets sprayed from his nose.

Steven's face was blocked by the elbow of a man trying to take a picture. Steven slammed the camera into the man's face, pushing more people away. Then with a deep breath and a prayer, he vaulted over the railing. He flung himself over, holding on until the last second to the bar. He could feel his feet dangling freely in the air above the moat and he heard the gasps of people staring at him.

"Out of the way," Charlie yelled. He jumped over the rail like Steven and both of them dropped.

Steven broke most of the fall with his shoes scraping against the sloping concrete. His hands drew blood but he landed upright and immediately started climbing toward the hippo. In a few seconds he grasped one of the iron spikes and pulled himself up to level ground. Charlie was right behind.

The hippo's eyes were glazed. A thin white film covered his cornea and the seepage from his tear ducts was gelatinous. He lay like some fallen tree stump keeled over in a thunderstorm. His whole body spastically contracted; the waves of rippling jerks spread from his belly outward and jiggled rolls of fat. He squealed. He tried to bleat but the blood filling his throat only allowed a choking gurgle. His tiny tail whirred, beating the water in the pool to a froth. His eyes saw Steven's dark shape and with the energy of maddened fury, he roared, snapping viciously.

"*Steven!*" Charlie yelled.

Charlie grabbed Steven's belt and yanked him back just as the hippo's mouth slammed shut. The force of the pull knocked both of them down and as they scrambled to their feet Steven saw the crowd. It was the first time he noticed them—really noticed them. There were over a hundred bodies, each face squeezed over the rail and staring, staring. They packed tightly together and a growing surge from the rear pressed them forward.

"Charlie!" Steven yelled. "*Charlie!*"

"Get out of the way."

Steven screamed. His face twisted with pain. There was a pounding in his head and he felt like gagging. "Charlie—" he screamed, grabbing his uncle's coat and shaking like a dog. "*Someone is killing my animals.*"

Charlie broke Steven's hold and pulled him farther away from the hippo's mouth. The huge animal sneezed, spraying mists of blood over their shirts. Then the behemoth began to move.

"Steven!"

The hippo painfully rose on his feet and inched forward, toward the spikes and the moat. His huge mouth leaned over the row of bars. Then his shoulder caught on one of the dull points. But instead of retreating, the hippo shoved forward like a tank. The spikes were normally enough to keep him from the moat but in his crazed condition they hardly deterred him.

"Keep him out of the moat," Steven shouted. "If he falls in we'll never get him out."

Charlie ran to the animal's rear. With a studied lunge, he grabbed the short tail. The hair was coarse and sharp; it cut into his hands. Charlie braced his feet and yanked. The hippo bellowed. With a gurgling choke, it stopped its forward push and struck out with its hind leg. Charlie saw the muscles tense and he jumped out of the way as the stump of a leg missed his skull only by inches.

Steven saw the kick coming. He was on the other side of the hippo, staring at the moat. The only thing on his mind was keeping the beast from falling into the trench. If he did, there would be no way to pull him out alive. But now as he stared at the hippo, Steven felt his stomach twist even tighter. One of the spike points was rubbing against the hippo's throat. Steven cursed at the row of bars. They had been installed decades ago, long before his father took over. At the time they were the cage designer's dream, beautiful and cleanly functional. Now, they were deadly.

The hippo moved forward again. His entire throat leaned over the spikes. The rods were starting to bend; one of them broke loose from its cement anchor. If he falls, Steven swore, he'll spear himself on those goddamn spikes.

Steven furiously searched the exhibit. His eyes ran over the pool, the stonework, the back walls. He didn't know what he needed but he knew he had to do something, and fast. At the far end of the pool a dead oak tree was bolted to the floor of the exhibit. Its bark had been chiseled off; most of the branches were sawed away to allow a smooth surface for the hippo to rub against. Steven ran to the tree and grabbed at one of the remaining limbs. It was about the diameter of a baseball bat and Steven tested it with a jerk. It wobbled slightly. He threw all his weight on it and pulled as hard as he could.

The dead wood gave a little but it was still attached solidly. Another yank. It started to crack. Then the limb suddenly split and Steven pulled it away.

He ran back to the moat and crept as close as he dared to the hippo's mouth. Lifting the limb high in the air, he brought it down smartly on the beast's ear. The hippo choked again, yawning his jaws and gurgling blood. Its eyes gave a brief flurry of activity, of white terror, but it stopped crawling.

"Here!" Steven yelled to Charlie. "Take this. Hit the sonofabitch again if he moves."

Charlie took the branch and held it high. The end of the club dripped with blood. "He's going to fall in," he yelled.

"Hit him again. Keep him away from the moat."

Steven ran toward the back of the enclosure, toward the exhibit gate, but it was locked. He began to climb over the top, over the cement landscaping, and dropped behind the exhibit. It took twenty steps to sprint inside the supply tunnel and reach the phone. He spun the dial with bloody fingers.

"Yes?"

"Harriet!" Steven yelled. "The hippo—"

"I know," she cut him off. "I just got word. I sent Dr. Lewis over two minutes ago. He's on his way."

"A crane," Steven yelled. "Call maintenance and run it over as fast as they can. I mean *now*. We need the flatbed, too."

"Right."

"Get some keepers, pull in as many as you can. Get them down here and get the people away. Bring rope, some barrels— just tell them to get the damn people out of here."

"Do you want a message over the public address?"

"Hell, no," Steven shouted. "I don't want any *more* people."

"Steven?"

"Yes?"

"Get off the phone, will you? I need it."

Charlie! Steven slammed the receiver down and ran back to the hippo. The scene hadn't changed. Charlie wielded the club high over the quiet, immobile hippo. The air was tense and heavy. In the seemingly endless time before the vet came, Steven had a chance to study the crowd. He glared at the people packed together across the moat. They stared back eagerly. For an instant he felt like an animal himself, being spied on. Their faces were like rows of cardboard caricatures, their eyes wide and bulging, their mouths tight and grim, their hands rigid and set.

They were aware of being in the midst of pain, but a rare and unusual pain. They didn't scream anymore. They just waited. Steven ran his eyes over the crowd's faces. One of them, he knew, some one of them had done this. But which one? The one eating popcorn and staring hungrily? The one taking photographs? The lady with the binoculars coldly focusing on the trickle of blood seeping from the hippo's throat? Steven again ran his eyes over the crowd. Nobody had a brown coat. Nobody was wearing sunglasses.

Dr. Lewis and two assistant keepers unlocked the service gate and hurried over to the hippo. The crane and the flatbed truck arrived and began to honk their horns for the crowd to make a path. Keepers in uniforms began to appear one by one from across the grounds, alerted by Harriet's phone calls and also by some unexplainable sense of disaster akin to telepathy. The crowd began to murmur and even grumble as they were slowly herded back, away from the sight.

Steven stood next to Charlie. Both of them watched Dr. Lewis lift the hippo's eyelids, run his hands for broken bones, and check the color of the freely flowing blood. Finally, the vet stood. He looked at Steven while wiping his hands on a cloth.

"I'm sorry, Steven."

Steven's face grew puzzled. "What do you mean?"

"The hippo," Dr. Lewis said. "He's dead."

"Dead? He can't be. Damn it, you just got here. Five minutes ago—"

"He's dead now," Dr. Lewis said slowly.

"That's impossible . . . Charlie! Charlie, do you—"

"Easy, Steven," Charlie said. "After you left, it didn't move anymore. It never moved."

Steven stared at the mountain of flesh that had been the hippo. The sun already had begun to stiffen the hide. "But how?"

Dr. Lewis's face grew grim. "I'm not entirely sure. My first guess is that he choked to death."

"But he doesn't get fed until the zoo closes," Steven protested stupidly.

"He choked," Dr. Lewis said softly, "on his own blood."

Steven nodded numbly. "I want an autopsy," he said through gritted teeth.

"Of course," Dr. Lewis said quickly. "No question about that."

"I want an autopsy *today.*"

Steven walked away from the vet and stood close to the dry moat. He waved the crane operator nearer and ordered the heavy leather slings rolled under the carcass. It was to be several hours before the hippo was finally deposited on the straining flatbed truck and hauled to the veterinarian's compound.

■ ■ ■

Dr. Lewis stepped into his small laboratory from an adjoining building. The main operating room was much too cramped for the hippo and the autopsy was performed in a converted feed barn. The procedure had been swiftly carried out with the help of three volunteer medical students—the organs removed and bottled, the teeth pulled, various bones scraped and prepared for boiling. Every animal in the zoo had an "obit" file—a list of tissue samples or organs that were to be removed and saved upon its death. These were then sent to the various scientists in the area who requested them. For most of the researchers, it was a once in a lifetime chance to study exotic species.

Dr. Lewis carried a small bucket. After he rinsed the contents, he thoroughly scrubbed his arms up to his shoulders. His pipe had gone out. Drying his hands on a towel, he relit it and turned to Steven, who had been waiting three hours.

"My first guess was right," Dr. Lewis said. "His throat and nasal cavities were completely flooded with blood."

"From what?"

"Throat lacerations, all the way down the gastrointestinal

tract. You might be interested in these." Dr. Lewis took the bucket and flipped its contents onto a stainless steel table. He picked up the objects as he continued his report. "These were in the stomach. One plastic wallet. Sixty-five coins, roughly five dollars' worth. Two lipstick cases. One cigar holder, plastic. A metal thimble. Half a pair of eyeglasses. A squirt gun. And this." Dr. Lewis held up a blackened mass.

"What the hell is that?"

"I couldn't tell either at first. One of my assistants finally identified it. A track shoe."

"Christ," Steven muttered, sinking back in his chair. "It makes me sick."

"It might make *you* sick," Dr. Lewis pointed out. "If I had that junk inside me, I wouldn't feel too chipper either. But it didn't bother that hippo. That junk took years to collect. Here. You can see with these pennies most clearly. See that? Encrusted with deposits, like a small gallstone. But they have huge stomachs. None of this really hurt the beast."

"Something did," Steven said. "What was it?"

"These," Dr. Lewis said. He unscrewed a sample jar and spilled out several dozen pieces of metal bands. "Razor blades. I was pulling them out of his mouth, his throat, all the way down. Look at them—bright and shiny. They're new. Double edged, platinum coated."

"Oh, God."

"The vehicle was probably an apple. I found undigested pieces in the teeth and throat."

Steven felt weak. He put his hands together, then rested his head in them. The vet began recording the objects on a chart. Both of them nodded wordlessly at Charlie, who came in and walked over to the table. He stared at the pile of junk and the mound of razor blades.

"That's one hell of an appetite," Charlie said softly. Picking up one of the razor blades, he softly whistled.

The room was silent. Steven glanced at the two men. Dr. Lewis was perched on a high stool, his face studying the floor as he sucked his pipe. Charlie stood near the table. His hands were jammed in his coat pockets and he scowled. They were waiting, Steven knew, for him to say something. But what could he say? Nothing had prepared him for this. He was supposed to be baby-sitting the animals, giving them bottles of formula and putting them to bed at night. Having them murdered in the crib was not part of the plan. It was no unexplainable crib death—it was as bloody and premeditated as any murder. The letter proved that.

"Thank God this is over," the veterinarian breathed. "I don't think I could stand it again."

"What makes you think it's over?" Steven asked leadenly.

"Because it's so horrible," Dr. Lewis muttered. "Nothing this disgusting could happen again."

"I wish I could agree with you," Steven said. "But I can't. Not until we find out who did it."

"I know who did it," Charlie muttered. As the two men whirled around, he cleared his throat. "I mean, all of us know who did it. Don't we?"

"Who?"

"It was some kid," Charlie said, shrugging. "Or a gang of them. Punks. Every year or so something like this happens. Gordon told me."

"Hippos killed?"

"No," Charlie admitted. "But other things."

"What things?" Steven demanded.

Charlie stirred uncomfortably. He wished he hadn't brought up the subject. The memory hovered painfully in his mind, not all the time, but rather it bobbed in his head like a guilty reminder whenever he felt his control slipping. The limey Percival had taught him control; Africa and five continents had made him lose it.

"A few years ago," Charlie stuttered.

"Go on," Steven broke in. "What are you saying?"

But he couldn't. Charlie's memory swirled like fog, clouding over the spots he wanted to see. Had it been two years ago? Of course it was. Charlie strained his mind toward the spot, keeping it clear of mist. He had just returned to San Francisco from Hong Kong after the unsuccessful panda bear kidnap fiasco with the lying Chinese. He hadn't seen Gordon's zoo in years. Everything had changed. The carnival had gotten a new owner and gaudy rides were being built. There was a new deer pasture. Yes, the deer pasture. Gordon had acquired four rare Père David deer and Charlie was standing by himself admiring them from the outskirts of their enclosure.

"What's the matter, Charlie?" Steven's voice broke through the mist.

Charlie didn't hear. Instead, the memory swirled in a denser fog and his voice crackled in the laboratory. Without control, he spoke to himself, ignoring the two men now exchanging worried glances. Control, Charlie muttered to himself, he had lost it. "Père David deer," Charlie murmured. His eyes locked on a cloudy bottle of formaldehyde gathering dust as thick as his memory. "Two years ago I was at the deer pasture, ten yards from the carnival fence where the brush thickens. I heard this plink-plink coming from some bushes. I came up on it, carefully, and stuck my hand in the bush. I grabbed this scruffy kid by his neck and he started screaming bloody murder. A little BB gun dropped out of his hands. He couldn't have been fourteen years old. Ugly as sin, he had these cauliflower ears. Like a boxer I knew in Chicago that—"

"Forget the cauliflower ears," Steven broke in. "What happened?"

Charlie heeded the demand without acknowledging Steven's presence. His voice droned at the bottle of formaldehyde. "The kid was shooting BB's into the antlers of the deer. The BB's were sticking in the antlers, *sticking*. I heard him laughing; the little bastard was laughing."

"Did you take him to the police?"

"No," Charlie answered vacantly. "They wouldn't have done anything."

"But what did you do?" Steven asked.

Charlie stirred, then he smiled proudly. "What do you *think* I did? I rolled down his pants and shot him in the ass with his own BB's. That was the only thing to do." A frown creased his temple. "Nobody saw me, don't worry. I told him that if I ever saw his ugly cauliflower ears *near* the zoo again, I'd throw him in the rhino pit and watch him get gored to death. And I'd laugh at *him.*"

"That was stupid, Charlie. Stupid and dangerous."

"He never came back," Charlie said.

"Then who killed the hippo?"

Steven's voice shattered the air with its intensity. Startled, Charlie whirled around. His eyes blinked rapidly, his nose twitched as if testing the air for dangerous scents.

"Damn it, Charlie," Steven thundered. "Do you know what could have happened? How could you even think of shooting him?"

"Charlie's right," Dr. Lewis blurted. His face reddened. "I mean about the vandalism. Most of it *is* done by children. They do it on the spur of the moment. Something evil takes hold of them and they decide to do it. But only once. A dare maybe. A challenge. Like Charlie said, they never do it again."

They don't understand, Steven thought to himself. They're grasping at straws. He didn't know who was worse. Dr. Lewis was ready to sweep the death under the carpet. Like a horse fitted with blinders, the vet kept his eyes from the hippo's razor blades, as if by not seeing them they ceased to exist. Was that what he did with the antelope? The antelope was murdered. Steven was sure of that now. Did Dr. Lewis also blind his eyes then, refusing to believe what he had seen?

And Charlie. Because two years ago he had seen a kid do something wrong, he was eager to blame anything on children. Steven shuddered. Did Gordon know what Charlie did to the kid? What would have happened if his parents had brought suit against the zoo? It could have been catastrophic.

And as he thought, Steven's hands tightened around the letter in his pocket. Why couldn't he tell them about the man with the brown coat and sunglasses, the letters? Why couldn't he prove to them how wrong they were?

"I'm going to the police," Steven said finally. "None of us know what to do and I need help. I want both of you not to leak even one word about the real cause of the hippo's death. We need time to think. The police will tell us what to do."

"Under the circumstances," Dr. Lewis softly murmured, "I think that's the wisest thing to do."

"The police aren't going to do a damn thing," Charlie blurted.

"And what would *you* do?" Steven countered heatedly. "Find the person who did this and shoot BB's into him?"

"No," Charlie said. "A magnum slug."

■ ■ ■

The lieutenant stared out the window from his twelfth floor office. There was nothing to see except skyscrapers. On a good day, without fog, it was possible to stand in a certain spot and see half a tower of the Golden Gate Bridge and a wedge of the Bay. But it was summer now; there weren't any good days. He was staring out the window because he didn't want the other man in his office to see him working a toothpick against a few bits of calamari wedged in his teeth. He had just returned from lunching at a restaurant in Fisherman's Wharf owned by the Mayor's nephew. The calamari could not have been very fresh.

"From what you've told me," the lieutenant said, turning around, "you have a serious problem."

Steven winced at the man's choice of words. "It's more than a problem, Lieutenant Tadich. It's an emergency."

"It's . . . serious," Lieutenant Tadich agreed. "Have you called the ASPCA?"

Steven stared icily. "The zoo doesn't call the ASPCA. They call us."

"Who else have you talked to about this letter?"

"Nobody."

"Not even your staff?"

"No."

"And what would you like us to do about it?"

Steven hesitated, startled by the question. "I'd like the police department to take charge, of course. It's way out of my hands."

"Take charge?"

"I can't have another single animal murdered."

"I understand that. You want us to prevent another animal killing."

"Yes, damn it. Why do you think I came here?"

Tadich clasped his hands behind his back and began to pace around the room. Passing a waste basket next to his desk, he flipped the used toothpick in and continued his stroll. This was either going to be a difficult job or an impossible one. "Let me tell you something, Mr. Cooper, something about this building. Basically we do one thing. We process people, usually criminals. They pass from one part of town into jail, a few more are squeezed through the courts, still fewer are sentenced and chilled for a while. We're always behind."

"I don't need a lec—"

"I'm sure you're wondering what this has to do with you. What I'm trying to tell you is that we can't *prevent* a damn thing, Mr. Cooper."

"I don't want any more animals killed."

"Neither do I. Again I ask you, what do you want us to do?"

"How do I know? Put some cops on the grounds. Undercover. Check people out—goddamn it, I don't know. That isn't my job."

"But you're beginning to see the problem. You have this witness who said she saw a man with a brown coat and sunglasses in the vicinity of the first animal's cage near the time of its death. You have a letter with a vaguely threatening tone. You have a second animal dying. Did you see anyone with a brown coat and sunglasses then?"

"No."

"I didn't think you would. Now suppose we sent six officers to the zoo, suppose a dozen. *What would I tell them to do?*"

Steven began to quietly fume in his seat.

"I hardly think he's going to put on his brown coat uniform

again," Tadich speculated. "He will probably never set foot in the zoo again. That's just my feel of the case. But would you stop and search every visitor with sunglasses? And what would you be looking for? A knife? Everyone has a pocketknife. It's no crime. An apple with razor blades? Again, I'll bet you, you won't see another one. There's no pattern, Mr. Cooper. If it *is* one person responsible, he's changing his methods. Do you see the problem now?"

"I see your problem, you don't see *mine*. Are you telling me you're not going to do anything?"

"On the contrary. I'm trying to tell you we will do anything that is *possible*. This letter, for instance. We'll dust for fingerprints but I'm not too hopeful after your handling. *If* you get another one, don't under any circumstances open it. Call this number and we'll send a man out to look at it."

"You're not going to send police now?"

"I'll ask for an increase in the car patrols around the zoo neighborhood. What kind of a security system do you have?"

"What do you mean?"

"Burglar alarms, sensors, that sort of thing."

"None."

Tadich shrugged. "I don't think that's crucial anyway. They're always broken when you need them. The feel I get from this case is that it's basically a coward acting. He needs the safety of a crowd and daylight. You have guards?"

"A night watchman. A security guard for the daytime shift, but he mainly stays at the entrance gate."

"Armed?"

"Hell, no."

"Good. I wouldn't want anybody hurt. There's always that chance in public."

"I don't give a damn, Lieutenant Tadich, if anybody gets hurt. But I don't want my animals touched."

Tadich grinned unexpectedly. "I'll pretend I didn't hear that."

"I'll pretend you didn't say that."

"In the meantime," Lieutenant Tadich continued, "I would not mention the letters to anybody else. There, I think I've about covered everything. Is there anything else that you want to ask?"

"Yes," Steven said. He stood and eyed the lieutenant coldly. "What are you going to *do?*"

■ ■ ■

Steven returned to the zoo from police headquarters with a growing sense of dread. Charlie had been right. The police weren't going to do anything. As he crossed the plaza a bitter anger began to burn inside him. It wasn't fair. This was supposed to be a snap caretaker vacation. But already one antelope and a hippo were dead. And Steven blamed himself. Whoever wrote those letters, Steven thought, wrote them to *me*. He's taunting me. And how can I face Gordon and tell him the animals are dying? How can I explain? He's not going to believe I'm trying.

It was nearly closing time and the few scattered visitors dawdled near the exit gates. Suddenly a man hurried up to Steven and held up a camera. He snapped a picture and reached in his pocket for a notebook.

"Director Cooper?" he asked, pencil in hand.

"What do you want?"

"I'm from the *Chronicle.* The city desk sent me down to ask you some questions. Can we talk in your office?"

"I'm sorry. I can't talk right now."

The reporter moved to cut off Steven's attempted escape. "Maybe you'd rather talk in front of the hippo exhibit. I understand there's a lot of room suddenly available."

Steven stopped. He looked carefully at the man. "What do you mean by that?"

"Look, I'll tell you what I know if you tell me what you know. Fair enough?" When Steven remained silent, the reporter shrugged and continued anyway. "We got a dozen calls yesterday afternoon about this hippo dying at the zoo."

"So?"

"That's what I'm asking you," the reporter explained. "Did it die?"

"Yes."

"How much was it worth?"

"Eight thousand."

"What was its name?"

"Harold."

"Harold the hippo? It's getting more interesting. How did he die?"

"Stomach problems," Steven said.

"Can I quote you on that?"

"Yes."

"What kind of stomach problems?"

"I haven't read the veterinarian's final report yet," Steven said truthfully.

"But you said stomach problems? That's what I'm going to quote you. What's your statement on torture?"

"Huh?" Steven cocked his head.

"The phone calls said they saw the hippo bleeding like a stuck pig. Something about spikes in the cage. Cruel and unusual punishment. That you were beating it, torturing it."

"That's not true."

"We'll see."

"Look, I'll tell you what happened. The animal died of stomach complications. Our vet tried to save it, but couldn't. The animal's cage had nothing, I repeat, *nothing* to do with its death."

"Then you won't mind us publishing this picture? It was taken by a visitor. She was pretty angry about the hippo's treatment."

The reporter pulled out a folded eight-by-ten of the exhibit. It had been taken from across the moat and the yawning bloody mouth of the hippo made Steven cringe.

"It's not very pretty," the reporter said.

"You can't publish that."

"Why not?"

"Don't you realize? It could trigger every nut in the Bay Area to start killing animals. You can't print stories like this. It's irresponsible."

"It's news."

"I'm asking you for the sake of the zoo not to publish that picture."

"I've got a job to do. Just like you. Only I hope I'm doing mine better than you are yours."

"What do you mean?"

"You said killing, I didn't. Are you admitting you killed the hippo?"

"I don't want that picture published," Steven snapped. "All photos taken in the zoo have to be cleared by us for nonprivate use. I'm not authorizing that picture for release."

"Too bad."

"I told you, you don't have the zoo's permission. Do you want me to drag in a lawyer?"

"We've got lawyers, too. But if you did beat the hippo to death, I'd understand why you wouldn't want publicity."

"If you publish that picture, it will be pure irresponsibility."

"I might believe that, if it came from a responsible director. How long have you been on the job?"

"One week," Steven answered testily.

"Then you must have a lot of experience to be taking care so well of the city's zoo. You see, I did a little background work and found some interesting quotes. Your students at Berkeley were pretty cooperative."

"What do you mean?"

The reporter read from his notes. "Quote—'Dr. Cooper? He hates zoos. He thinks they should be abolished. Everyone knows that?' Unquote. Tell me, Dr. Cooper, did the hippo know that?"

"Get out of here."

"Are you kicking me out?" the reporter asked almost eagerly.

Steven brushed him aside. "The zoo's closed," he muttered. Steven never looked behind as he strode quickly away. At one point he glanced down and saw both of his hands clenched tightly in fists. He consciously loosened them and put them in his pockets. The meeting with the police had gone far worse than he ever expected. And the reporter's obnoxious insinuations had put the whole situation in a different light. Steven was beginning to feel trapped, as if various strings were being pulled, ensnaring him in a grasping, inescapable noose. What had started out as a despicable case of vandalism was threatening him with an ominous, foreboding disaster. He needed time. He needed time to think.

Steven's shoes hit the asphalt thickly. He didn't notice the chilly wind that seeped almost to his bones. His head was low; he forged ahead.

"Hey!" someone yelled in his ear. "What do I have to do to make you stop?"

Steven's eyes blinked and he raised his head, puzzled. Amanda was half walking, half jogging beside him. Her face bore a curious mixture of a grin and a worried frown.

"Hi," he said weakly.

"Hello yourself. What's the matter? I've been yelling at you for a hundred feet. Didn't you hear me?"

"No," Steven said truthfully.

"Well?"

"Well, what?"

"I threw away my padded shoes. I forgot all my crummy jokes and I'm itching to herd little people around little animals. How about my transfer to the children's zoo?"

"Transfer?" Steven asked blankly.

"I knew it." Amanda scowled. "You forgot, didn't you?"

"I'm sorry."

Amanda stopped, putting her hands on her hips. "What do you do as a director? I've been watching your office all afternoon from the tram because they said you left. Is that a way to run a zoo?"

Steven was still trying to get his bearings. The run-in with the reporter had left him shaking. Why had he yelled at him? God, what a mistake. He couldn't tell the truth about the hippo's death but he hadn't been lying about the reaction the photograph would provoke. Why couldn't the reporter understand? He should have told the *Chronicle* everything, maybe that would have stopped the story. Damn it, he *wanted* to tell that reporter. He had to tell someone. It was spreading like poison inside him.

"Look, maybe I'm the one who's slipping," Amanda said, "but

have I been talking for the last five minutes to a stone wall? Do I have to wave a cracker in front of you and yell speak, speak?"

Steven blinked again and he stared at her for a long minute. "There's something I have to tell you," he said quickly. He was surprised at how relieved he felt once the words had been spoken.

Amanda drew in a worried breath. "The lecture is finally coming?" she asked grimly.

"Yeah," Steven said, nodding. "A lecture."

"Can't wait? Like next summer?"

"No, right now. What are you doing for dinner?"

Amanda gulped. "I thought I was going to get roasted over coals."

"Can we talk?"

"I know a place on Geary," she said, suddenly grinning. "They serve great buffalo burgers. My car's this way."

"No," Steven said, continuing his assault down the path. "I have to stay on the grounds. Let's eat at the house."

"What house?"

"Come on."

It had been a stable once, when the zoo was first built. The draft horses were kicked out and the first director moved in. The second patched-in plumbing and the succession that followed added Victorian scrollwork, a captain's tower, bay windows, and a fireplace. In the early days of the century, it was the custom for all directors to live on zoo grounds and although the tradition was now fading, Gordon promptly reinstated it. The small cottage was hidden in a jungle of live oak and eucalyptus, and unless you looked closely, quite invisible.

"You live *here?*" Amanda asked. "I don't believe it."

"Why?" Steven asked, unlocking the front door.

"Because houses like this don't exist. It's too beautiful. Can I eat it? Is it gingerbread?"

Steven led her into the foyer and took her coat. She brushed past him and inspected the room with shameless curiosity. Gordon had rather Spartan tastes. Steven's mother had died within a year of giving birth to him and the organized blending of a household did not rank high in his father's hierarchy of talents. An ancient horsehair couch reigned in one corner; a huge rolltop desk squatted like a communal weaverbird nest crammed with letters and notes. Files were everywhere; reports, clipboards, and magazines littered the chairs, rugs, and tables.

"What are these?" Amanda immediately asked.

"Pictures," Steven said. "Just pictures."

There were literally hundreds of photographs on the walls, pictures that Steven had seen all his life but which now assumed a different quality with his father across town in a hospital recovering from a heart attack. Here on the wall was a younger Gordon, a strong, healthy, mustached fire of a man. There Gordon was with Uncle Charlie (was it forty years ago?), smiling beneath their newly painted sign ANIMALS UNLIMITED. There they were, standing at the rail of a miserable-looking scow, chugging up the Limpopo on their first collecting trip where Gordon nearly died from dysentery. A picture of him behind the desk of the animal import business, surrounded by cages of animals Charlie was now shipping back as fast as his vast hordes of native hunters dragged them squealing out of the steamy jungles of the Essequibo, the vast stretches of the Kalahari, the French forests of Vietnam. Mombasa, Old Delhi, Sydney, Peiping—the names jumped out of Steven's head in the only way he had seen them, postmarks on letters or addresses on cables. There was his father's second office, in a warehouse on Long Island. This was the height of the business; it would never again be as crowded until the postwar boom, when trading routes reopened. Steven remembered the brick building; he had been born there.

"Is that you?" Amanda asked. "That can't be you."

A picture of his mother, standing on the lawn of the house in Oyster Bay—his father had an arm around her and beneath them on the grass, a chimpanzee was cradling the baby Steven in its arms. Then there was a lapse of a few years, the gaps which make the absence of photographs loom into significance as they both represented and hid the personal pain, the loneliness, the financial setbacks, the bad times. There were pictures of those, but they were not on the wall and Steven could see them only when he closed his eyes.

Amanda's eyes widened. She ran from one spot on the wall to another. "Look," she said.

More photographs. Steven's father in his first uniform as junior cage attendant at the Bronx Zoo. Then the photos shifted westward, with different uniforms and different archways—Chicago's Brookfield Zoo, St. Louis, San Diego. All the while, mixed in between, Charlie still smiled with his triumphant lips proudly exhibiting a pair of chipped teeth suffered early in his career at the hands of an orangutan and which he swore by oaths of Jesus he would never repair. Charlie was always the same, his arms around a Catholic missionary, a ferocious savage, a British traveler, or a sultry native woman with bare breasts and lithe, supple legs. There he was shaking hands with "Bring 'em back alive" Frank Buck, who later would bribe officials to confiscate Charlie's best shipment from Java. There were Charlie and Phillip Percival thundering across the plains in a Land-Rover, with Kilimanjaro's peak capped by snow. A leopard was tied to the hood, which they were going to bury on the peak as a joke on one of their clients.

"You don't have to laugh," Steven said grimly. "I bet you didn't look so great in high school either."

Amanda giggled. "Actually I was a knockout. But *you—*"

There were pictures of Steven: the child standing with his father and uncle donating a great bear to the American Museum of Natural History; the boy on the lawn in front of the Vermont boarding school; the teenager in warm clothes at a winter break from a Massachusetts academy; the young man at Princeton; the graduate student at Harvard. And in between the formal poses of school pictures was Steven, kneeling by a cage and feeding animals, cleaning animals, watering and exercising animals. They were informal snapshots, candid moments that were more representative of his life than any of his educational regimens. For while Uncle Charlie was always in some far-off land catching the animals and while his father was muddling through paperwork trying to sell them, Steven—the connecting link of the triangle—quietly and dutifully loaded hay and scraped dung heaps. When the animal business failed and his father started to climb the ladder in the zoo world, there was always Steven in the background scrubbing the back of a snapping turtle in the bathtub, applying a hot pad to an ailing ocelot, filing the toenails of a baby elephant. Everybody seemed to leave those things to him. The photographs, the frozen moments, were the real furniture in a house of people's lives.

When Amanda turned away from the pictures, her face seemed muted and distant, as if she had turned a dusty dictionary page and found someone else's pressed memory. But she felt the memory. Why?

"You know," she said slowly, "I would have given anything to have done what you did. To be around animals all your life."

"It's not what it looks like," Steven started to say.

Amanda didn't hear him. "I was born in Los Angeles. The only thing I learned how to tame was a car. A cherry red Mustang convertible and the only reason I wanted it was because I liked its name. I used to drive up to the LA Zoo every chance I had. I went twice every time to the circus when it came. I dreamed of animals, of someday being with them."

"So did I," Steven said, shrugging.

"You didn't dream," Amanda said, shaking her head. "You did it."

And Steven felt the familiar sensation growing again. It was always the same. He felt it whenever someone brought up the subject of animals. How could he tell them, *prove* to them, what it was really like, how it was nothing like they imagined? He always tried, but he always found that people heard what they wanted to hear. He had always given up; he always fell back on the stories. And what stories he could tell. Was that what Charlie did?

Steven snapped out of it. "Let me cook something," he said. "You're probably starving."

They ate dinner mostly in silence. Steven had burned the

hamburgers and food was the only subject he felt he could talk about. It was after dinner, when Steven was burning the coffee, that Amanda started it.

"That was some lousy dinner," she said suddenly. "And I wouldn't turn around and deny it."

"Look—"

"I'd rather listen. You haven't said a thing and I'm getting tired of answering my own questions."

"There's something . . ." Steven bit his lip.

"Well?" Amanda demanded. "Why did you stop? Are you going to tell me?"

Steam hissed from the pot and Steven grabbed it. It scorched his hands and he threw it, clattering, in the sink. Whirling around, he barked, "Someone is killing my animals."

Amanda's face showed no expression at first. Then her eyes grew puzzled. "What do you mean?"

"You don't know about this."

"Which animals? You mean the hippo? Everyone's gossiping about that. I heard that it choked on something."

"That's the story I put out. But the hippo was murdered. Someone fed it razor blades in an apple."

"But who—"

"The same person who killed the antelope last week."

"I didn't hear about that."

"Only the vet, a keeper, and I know about it. The antelope was caught in the fence out of sight. There was a gash across his throat. I think somebody started to cut him but stopped."

Amanda's face drained of color. "Antelope?"

"Yes."

"Oh, my God!"

Each of them realized what the other was thinking. Steven said it first. "It was probably the guy who got on your tram."

"I don't believe it."

"Neither could I at first. But I got two letters. One of them threatened the hippo *before* he died."

"Have you gone to the police?"

"I was there this afternoon. They're no help. I have to tell someone. Amanda, I need help."

"What can I do?"

Steven stopped, looking at her closely. Of all the people he had talked with, only Amanda had said those words. *What can I do?* He realized those were the words he had wanted to hear. All the rest had either refused to recognize the threat or belittled its horror. Only she had offered the kind of help he needed.

"I don't know," Steven said numbly.

And then he told her the recurring nightmare, the dream that started years ago. It made him scream and jerk awake with the covers wet with sweat. The same dream. The zoo was burning. The cages were on fire and the animals clawed to escape. The animals. Some kicked and struggled to squeeze through the bars while others trembled from exhaustion and fear. Some were petrified in a catatonic trance, mesmerized by the crackling flames. He tried to unlock the cages but the keys melted in his hands and dripped like molten wax. The flames rose higher and the animals screamed. That was the point when he always awoke, his body cramped and his throat dry.

Steven felt embarrassed from her silence. He walked to the stove and tried the coffee again. "I'm sorry," he said. "I don't know why I said that. I just needed someone to talk with."

Amanda nodded. "But what are you going to *do?*"

Steven paused. It was the same demand he had made to Lieutenant Tadich. "There isn't anything I can do," he said, turning his head.

"What if the killer tries again?"

"He probably won't."

"But what if he does?"

Steven frowned. "I told you, I don't know. What would *you* do?"

Amanda didn't hesitate. "Let's catch the sonofabitch."

Steven groaned to himself. "Let's not talk about it anymore. Just forget it."

"What are his motives?" Amanda said, ignoring him.

"Motives? The guy's crazy. It's too complicated."

"Maybe it's too simple."

"What do you mean?"

"We know he doesn't like animals."

Steven shook his head. "In his letters he said he likes them."

"You're going to take the word of a crazy person?"

Steven began to pace. So this is what happens when you trust someone, he thought. They come up with wild ideas. Catch the killer?

"Forget this," Steven blurted. "Forget everything I told you tonight. I don't want you mixed up in this. I'll handle it somehow."

"I want to work at the zoo," Amanda declared. "If there aren't any animals left, it doesn't make much sense, does it?"

"Do you want some more coffee?" Steven asked, walking toward the sink.

Amanda glanced at her watch. "I can't. I'm late already."

"For what?"

"Dance class. I've got to run."

"What about the coffee? It's finally burned enough."

"Tomorrow. I haven't paid for tomorrow yet but I sure did write a check for that dance class."

"I'll walk you to your car."

"You don't have to. I know the way. I work here, remember?"

"I have to take a walk anyway, to make the night rounds."

They put on their coats, Steven slipping a tiny flashlight in his pocket. Outside the cottage, the zoo was pitch-black, lit only by dim lamp posts every hundred yards. The cage bars gleamed in unpredictable slivers. Their footsteps clopped loud in the darkness as Amanda shivered.

"Are we going the right way?" she asked.

"Some guide you are."

"I still don't know where I am. Everything's different at night."

"We're passing the koalas. There's Monkey Island up there." Steven pointed to a looming mass even blacker than the night. "Watch out for wasps."

· 74 ·

"How come there aren't any lights?"

"What for? Do you want to give them insomnia?"

"I didn't think of that. Where are we now?"

Steven smiled. He knew the paths like the back of his hand. "Let's go this way. Next to the carnival. They've got plenty of light. Plenty of bills, too."

Steven led her across a strip of grass through a small grove of pine trees, and found the path that followed the boundary of the zoo grounds.

"Well?" It was Amanda who broke the silence. She turned her head to Steven.

"Well what?"

"Well, we just passed the children's zoo and suddenly you're not saying much."

"Oh?" Steven realized it was true. "I forgot," he said sheepishly.

"I've noticed," Amanda dryly commented.

"There's a problem," Steven began.

"I'm glad you see it my way for once. I can't stand that tram."

"About the children's zoo," Steven corrected. "There's already a keeper working there and he won't be transferred for another month."

"I'm leaving next month," Amanda said. "I've got a movie shooting in Los Angeles."

"What's it about?"

Amanda shrugged. "I don't know. Some police story. Lots of blood and action."

So that was it, Steven thought. His bubble burst. That was why she had offered to help, that was why she wanted to catch the killer. She was an actress, damn it, how could he have forgotten it? To her, catching the killer was just playing another stupid role.

"I'm sorry the zoo can't fit in with your schedule."

"Not as sorry as I am," she replied just as curtly.

"I'm offering you a transfer next month." Steven's voice grew suddenly cool. "I can't do anything more."

"Forget it," Amanda said brusquely. "Just forget it, will you?"

Steven burned inside. Why was she trying to take advantage of him? If she wanted the job, she could have it. Was it his fault she worked only summers? Unconsciously, his step quickened as he silently led her down the path.

There was a little more illumination now, colored lights from the ferris wheel and carousel. The reds and blues danced over the links of the chain fence. It was eerie. The closer they approached, the noisier grew the faint squeals—the piping organ, the popping shooting gallery, the blare of toy trumpets. The sounds echoed among the trees before dying abruptly in the bushy foilage. It was Amanda who heard the other sound first.

She moved closer to Steven and put her arm around him. "Shh," she ordered. "Keep walking."

In surprise Steven looked at her, trying to see her face in the pale light. He kept on walking under her whispered urging.

"There," Amanda whispered again. "Did you hear that?"

"No."

"It was a noise, I tell you."

"There's nobody around."

Steven kept silent. He put his arm around her, more to keep his balance than anything else. He concentrated on listening, removing the sounds of the carnival from his ears. Then he heard it, too. A dull snap, like a twig being stepped on. A few moments later, it was a very soft scraping of a bush. Without a word, the two of them walked faster.

"It's probably a peacock," Amanda began. Her voice strained to sound confident.

"No. They sleep at night."

"I'm trying very hard to believe it's a peacock. You're not helping."

"It's not a peacock."

"How can you be so damn sure?"

"Because ever since we started to walk faster, it did, too."

"Don't peacocks do that? If they're hurrying?" She shivered involuntarily at some dark thought. "What do they eat, anyway?"

"Bugs," Steven said quietly. An unmistakable footstep followed his answer. "Crickets. Seeds. Popcorn. Anything."

"What are we going to do?"

"I'm open to suggestions."

"How about running?"

"That's one idea. But—"

"But what?" Amanda objected. "I think running is an excellent idea."

"We'd never find out who it is," Steven said.

"I think," Amanda said, "I can live with that."

"I thought you—"

"I know who it is," Amanda breathed, slowing down. "It's the night watchman." She relaxed in a slouch of relief.

"No," Steven said.

"Why not?"

"Because I see him at the gate ahead."

Amanda lifted her head. The path was crooked but a hundred yards ahead, under a lamp post, a solitary figure stood. He had on a guard's cap and leaned against the fence.

"If it's not the watchman," Amanda hissed, *"then who's following us?"*

Steven didn't answer. He pulled Amanda closer and felt for the flashlight in his pocket. Withdrawing it slowly, he nudged Amanda.

"You see that tree where the path curves?"

"I think so."

"Let's walk a little faster. Not too fast. Right. Now when we pass it, you go on alone—I'm going to wait. He won't know for a minute you're alone."

"I'll know," she muttered.

"I want to get one good look at him. He knows the grounds, I can tell. He's following too well. I might not be able to catch him but at least I'll see what he looks like."

"What do you want me to do?"

"Keep walking. He mustn't suspect anything. If you hear something going on, run like hell for the guard."

"Steven?"

"Yes?"

"Is it brown coat and sunglasses?"

"Maybe brown coat. Forget the sunglasses."

"I'm scared. This is no joke."

"You won't miss your dance class, I promise."

They lapsed into silence as an occasional snapping kept pace with them. Steven judged the sound to be twenty yards behind and to the left. When they turned the sharp corner, Steven slipped away and took three quick strides to a bush. He faded into the leaves and watched Amanda continue alone. She didn't look back.

For a moment, there was only the sound of Amanda's shoes on the path. Steven hoped that her steady beat would make up for the loss of his footsteps. Finally only a whisper of wind shivered pine needles far above him. He strained his ears. Nothing. Then the carousel began another rotation, sending a raspy screech of organ fugues across the fence. A faint squeal of a child. A back-fire from a go-cart.

A twig snapped behind the bush and Steven froze. His eyes forced their way into the darkness and his hand clenched the tiny flashlight. A few leaves shivered against something and then Steven saw a man pass the bush. He was walking carefully, easing his feet down and pushing branches away with care. His back was to Steven and his head followed the trail of Amanda's foot-steps.

Steven yelled and flicked on his weak penlight. The dim light barely had an effect. For an instant, he could see the man's face but hands shot up to cover it. There was a muffled curse of surprise and the man lifted something heavy in his right hand.

Steven still couldn't see. He took a step forward and held out his penlight like a dagger stabbing the blackness. Then the man blinded him.

Steven was hit by a blast of light from a powerful torch, stunning him into immobility. He felt his knees lock and his arms freeze like a deer on a road caught by a car's high beams. The puny plastic penlight dropped from his hands and vanished into the grass.

The light shone stronger as the man moved closer. He thrust it into Steven's face, sweeping it back and forth like a blade. Then he began to laugh—short, gasping things that wheezed from his nose. He was silent for a moment, then he snorted quickly, "You're Gordon's son, aren't you?"

Steven's ears flicked. Where had he heard that voice before? It was smooth, oily smooth and jeering. The man moved back a bit and began to play his torchlight over Steven's clothes. Steven brought his hands up against the glare but even with his eyelids tightly shut, the light still burned. Where had he heard that voice before?

The light flicked off. Steven became aware of the darkness as a cool, sudden force. He opened his eyes and although still partially blind, now he could make out the shape of the man. He was about Steven's height and build, with a puffy face and ugly ears.

"What are you doing here?" the voice demanded.

Steven's mind clicked, he remembered. It was Curt Shacker, the owner of the carnival. "You can start explaining first, Shacker," he said.

"I heard your father got sick," the voice said.

"I'm in charge of the zoo now," Steven said. "And I'd like to know what the hell you're doing following people at night."

"It's too bad about your father. Heart attack, was it? Probably worrying too much. He was always worrying. Sticking his nose into other people's business and worrying."

"I'm sure you're concerned," Steven said bitterly. "What are you doing on zoo property?"

The man paused, as if deciding on what to say. "Chasing a kid," he grunted. "I saw one climb over the fence."

"Into the zoo?"

Shacker laughed. "That I wouldn't give a damn about. But nobody crashes my gate. I came over here to see if there were any more, to teach them a lesson."

"What did you find?" Steven demanded.

"Nothing. Just a few chickens walking around."

"Get out of here, Shacker. I don't want to see you here again, ever."

"A little touchy, aren't you?"

"You know what I mean."

Shacker laughed. "You're not holding that little argument I had with your father against me, are you? That was a long time ago."

It had been several years ago but the memory was still fresh for Steven. There had been a pickpocket operating on zoo grounds, sometimes up to a dozen complaints a day. The man was finally spotted and followed to the carnival, where he vanished. An employee was suspected; Steven's father wanted Shacker to help. He refused. The next day the man was gone, tipped off by Shacker. There had been other incidents, none of them peaceful.

"You're beginning to worry too much," Shacker said. "Just like your father. Take it easy."

"I try," Steven said dryly.

"You have a good job, don't rattle the cages. You have nice animals, they're a good gimmick. The best. All I have are some broken-down rides and a few candy apple stands. But we do the best we can, right?" When Steven didn't answer, Shacker continued. "I think we can both help ourselves. Your father never could see it my way."

"What are you talking about, Shacker?"

"Like I said, I like your animals. A good gimmick. They're a good draw. That's all I need—something to draw the marks in. Something to make them walk past the bally. That's all. What I don't like is the fence." Shacker jabbed a finger at the carnival's chain link.

"If it was up to me," Steven said, "it'd be a wall."

"The fence is going to come down," Shacker continued, "one of these days. Both of us need to expand. It's going to be better business for both of us."

"Not as long as I have anything to do with it."

"Maybe, maybe not. But it could be worth your while. Think about it. I'd really like for you to see it my way."

Steven's eyes were normal now. A movement down the path caught his attention. He moved his head slightly and saw the glimmer of a badge on someone's coat. Amanda and the guard were running. Shacker must have seen them too because he began to edge away. Steven didn't want him to leave before Amanda had a chance to see him.

"Wait, Shacker."

"You know where to reach me."

"I want to talk."

"Think about it first," Shacker said. He moved toward his carnival.

Amanda and the guard burst into the clearing and stopped, chests heaving from the run. They stared at Shacker, then glanced at Steven for an explanation. He was about to gesture for Amanda to get a closer look when Shacker grunted in surprise.

A twig snapped behind a bush and then footsteps hit the asphalt. Out of the black underbrush a small figure had fled from the sudden appearance of the guard's uniform. Taking gazelle-like leaps, a young boy dashed for the nearest escape—the carnival fence. From the way he handled the climb, it seemed as if he had had much practice. He was almost over when Shacker resumed his chase.

"You little runt," Shacker yelled. "I told you not to come here. I'll teach you." Shacker lumbered into a clumsy jog and shook his flashlight menacingly.

"I'll get him," the guard said, making a move to follow.

"No," Steven ordered. "Let Shacker take care of it. If he catches him."

The boy had now dropped into the carnival madness and they watched Shacker flounder among the tents like a hound dog with the scent lost. Steven urgently turned to Amanda. "Was that the man on the tram?"

Amanda frowned. "I couldn't tell. He's the same height."

"Is there any chance, any chance at all?"

"I don't know," Amanda cried.

■■■

The newspaper story was worse than Steven had expected. Harriet silently brought it in and laid it on his desk. He didn't have to unfold the paper to read it; it leaped off the front page. The hippo's picture was a little grainy but the way it had been cropped showed Steven's hands holding a club over the gaping mouth, as if he were caught in the act of bludgeoning it to death. The caption was short and blunt—ZOO TERROR!

The calls began coming in at eight o'clock. The first was from another professor in Berkeley who offered a "chance to get away if it got too rough" at his ranch in the hills. The next four calls were television editors demanding film interviews. Then Charlie got through with a garbled, profane denunciation of the *Chronicle* in general and certain reporters specifically. At nine o'clock, the "concerned citizens" began their attacks and fifteen minutes later Steven had to tell Harriet not to accept any more calls.

"Can you hold them off?" Steven asked wearily. His voice was already rough and the morning had just started.

"I can stall most of them," Harriet said. "But the ones outside are going to be tough."

Steven peered through the curtained windows and saw the print reporters gathered en masse outside the office door.

"They're not going to last long on 'no comment,' " Harriet said. "All of them look pretty lean and hungry."

Steven nodded his head slowly. "How is the attendance this morning?"

Harriet made a call and when she put the receiver down, her face was long. "Down," she said. "By more than half."

"I figured it would be. Today it'll be deserted. Then the rumors will sink in. And tomorrow—tomorrow's going to be the crush. Wall to wall."

"Why do you think that?"

Steven stared idly through the windows. "People," he explained.

Harriet busied herself with making a pot of coffee. "You talk as if you knew them better than the animals."

"No," Steven said. "But I wish I did."

Harriet poured the coffee and Steven sipped his slowly, as if he were trying to decide something. Then he said softly, "All right, Harriet, here's what you tell them. I'll hold a news conference at eleven o'clock. I'll have a statement and they can ask questions afterward."

"You're going to go it alone?"

"No," Steven said, deciding on something else. "Dr. Lewis will be there, too. Have someone clear the Visitors' Building, that will probably be big enough."

▬ ▬ ▬

At eleven-fifteen, Steven glanced at Dr. Lewis again. The look he received in return had not changed for an hour. On the other side of the door, Steven could hear irritated cameramen buzzing, gaffers taping microphones to a stand, and the growing rumble of people's anger at the delay.

Dr. Lewis and Steven were alone in a tiny office of the Visitors' Building with two folding chairs, a spindly desk, and an overhanging bare bulb that erupted sporadically in fitful spurts of light. Steven began to pace again, circling the stone-faced and rigid Dr. Lewis.

"I can't do it," Dr. Lewis repeated. His voice was strained.

"And I'm not going out there without you," Steven said. His voice was low, to prevent eavesdropping.

"I told you I'd give my full report. That's all I can do."

"No," Steven said, shaking his head. "It's all you want to do."

"It's not a question of wanting. I can't lie, that's all."

"I'm not asking you to lie. All I want is for you to walk through that door, step up to the microphones, and tell them that in your professional opinion the hippo died from internal injuries, period. The exhibit enclosure had nothing to do with its death. The hippo was in perfect health at the last regular monthly check-up. Where in those statements do you see a lie?"

"You're twisting words, Steven."

"You're damn right I'm twisting words. I'll squeeze them like a sponge. But I'm not going out there and tell them the hippo was killed by a razor-blade-stuffed apple."

"It's the truth."

"Is *this* the truth?" Steven demanded, thrusting the *Chronicle* under the vet's face. He shook the paper to make his point. The vet glanced at the photograph and sucked his pipe.

Steven was almost frantic. The vet had proved as stubborn as he was scared before. At the autopsy he had not wanted to admit the murder, now he was loath to deny it. But he *had* to, Steven swore to himself. The facts about the hippo had to be kept from the papers.

Dr. Lewis murmured distantly. "You should tell them what really happened. That's the only choice I see."

"And that would be signing a death certificate, giving away a free license to kill, an incentive—"

"I don't see it that way."

"I *have* to see it that way. It's my job."

"Catching the killer is the job of the police. Have you told them?"

"Yes," Steven said irritably.

"And they don't approve of telling the truth about the murders?"

"They don't think he's going to move again."

"I don't think he will either if the publicity gets out. He'll be too afraid."

"Or he might," Steven said, "feel justified."

Dr. Lewis stirred in his seat. "Frankly, I don't see your point,

Steven. I really wonder, I have to wonder, what Gordon would do in a situation like this."

"It's a little pointless right now, isn't it?"

"I think Gordon would—"

"The point is we don't know," Steven interrupted. "He's still not able to receive visitors."

Dr. Lewis stared ahead, vacantly examining the wall and seemingly absorbed in its featureless textures. Steven heard the murmur of the reporters grow louder.

The vet stirred again. A hand reached up and weathered fingers tugged at an earlobe. His face took on a curious look, as if clouded. "I'm a doctor," he began. "I just happen to have strange patients. Do you know how I became a zoo vet? I don't think I ever told you. I became involved with zoos really as an accident. I was in agriculture school, firmly committed to spending my life driving from one farm to another, worming cattle, whelping piglets, and manhandling colic. It was winter. Someone brought in a timber wolf with a steel trap still clamped to its paw. The wolf had almost succeeded in chewing off his toes and I remember thinking at the time that no domestic animal could ever have the brains to do that. It made sense, don't you think? To chew off toes rather than be captured? Well, after that there was no way I could look at sheep or chickens or hogs and be interested; they had already made up their minds a long time ago on what they wanted to be. The wolf—the wolf was once removed."

"What happened to the wolf?"

"Oh, it died. We hardly knew anything about anesthetics in those days and I almost gassed him to death with chloroform. I put a cast on him, a splint. When he woke up during the night and saw all the plaster and bandages, he thought it was another form of torture. He chewed it off and literally bled to death. It was the first of many deaths I've seen since."

"Zoos are about the only places you can find wolves now."

"Oh, I don't concern myself with arguments like that. That's for other people to worry about. But that wolf, you see, would have been quite alive had he gnawed off his toes from the trap and hobbled off without my interference. When I look back at the animals in the zoos I've known I see a lot of interference."

Steven was silent for a few long minutes. He was about to say something else but instead he shrugged. "How long ago did the wolf die?"

Dr. Lewis paused. He scratched the stubble that was just beginning to grizzle his face. "Too long."

Another silence.

"They're waiting outside," Steven said.

"You know, Steven, you're going about this the wrong way."

"Maybe."

"You should be letting the police handle this."

"They won't."

"You're just as stubborn as your father."

"They're waiting outside."

Dr. Lewis nodded. "Yes. Well, then, what do you want me to read?"

■ ■ ■

For a few seconds nobody noticed them making their way to the small stage. Then the floodlights hit and Steven squinted. Dr. Lewis followed behind. None of the reporters came up to them as it was plain from the look on Steven's tight-lipped face that he wouldn't be interrupted.

There were chairs behind the microphone stand but neither of the two men sat. Steven looked at the crowd in front of him and immediately started to speak. His voice boomed through the speakers.

"Thank you for coming. Later I'll answer any questions you have. But first I want the zoo's veterinarian, Dr. Arnold Lewis, to give you very briefly some information on the hippo's death. Dr. Lewis?"

The vet moved stiffly to the microphones. He blinked once, cleared his throat, and leaned slightly forward. The cameramen moved closer and focused first on his hands clenched on the sides of the rostrum, then up higher, at his smoke-spewing briar.

"The hippopotamus," Dr. Lewis said slowly but without hesitation, "died at approximately eleven-forty-five in the morning, from a throat and intestinal irregularity. The animal had been given a normal examination by me a month previously. At that time, there was no indication whatsoever of any disorder caused by his quarters at the zoo. As you are probably aware, every animal in the zoo is seen by its particular keeper at least twice every day and, in the hippo's case, there has never been any report of physical incompatibility with its enclosure."

Dr. Lewis pulled his head slightly back, to indicate that he was finished. One of the print reporters immediately fired off a question.

"What kind of irregularity?"

"Hemorrhaging. Internal bleeding."

Another shouted, "What about the spikes?"

"The spikes were in no way related to the animal's death."

There was a slight pause and Dr. Lewis chose the opportunity to step backward. As Steven passed to take his place, a quick glance passed between them.

"I was going to ask," the last reporter said in an exasperated tone, "if the spikes didn't have anything to do with the hippo's death, then why were they sticking in his throat?"

Steven couldn't see the man, but he faced the direction of his voice. "If you'll look a little more carefully at the photograph in the *Chronicle,* you can see for yourself that the iron rods are bent forward. They broke loose from their anchors when the hippo fell against them. He was already bleeding before he came into contact with the rods."

"Why did they break?" another man quickly broke in. He added sarcastically, "What about the lions? Is their cage going to break, too?"

Steven breathed easier. He had prayed that he wouldn't have to bring up the spikes himself. It was the only card he held and the reporter had played into his hand. The spikes were on their minds; none of them had thought to pursue further the cause of the "irregularity."

"I can't answer that question," Steven said slowly, as if wringing out a confession.

There was a stunned silence in the room that lasted exactly as long as it took for two dozen people to shout the next question.

"Are you saying the lion cage isn't safe?"

"No," Steven said, shifting his feet. "What I said was that I couldn't answer that question with any certainty."

"What *can* you say?"

Steven lifted a brown volume he had been carrying. "This is a copy of the zoo's proposed budget for this year. It contains a request for capital improvements, including renovations for several groups. Specifically the big cats. As you know, my father prepared this budget. A few days ago I received an indication from the Mayor of a mandatory rollback of ten percent in the Parks and Recreation Department, on which the zoo is dependent for funding."

"Are you saying the Mayor won't give you money to keep the lions safe?"

"All I'm saying is that I have every confidence the Mayor won't continue to allow lions to be housed in faulty, antiquated cages."

"Are you blaming the Mayor for the hippo?"

"If you'll excuse me, I have to get back to the job of running the zoo."

Steven left the building quickly but not before he noticed a figure standing motionless in the shadows at the far end of the hall. The man reached into a coat pocket, withdrew a toothpick, then stuck it in his mouth. It was Lieutenant Tadich.

■ ■ ■

The landlady was out of breath from the four flights of stairs but she held the shoe box in her hands as if it were treasure. She rapped lightly on the door of 4-B.

At first there was no reply. Then a voice responded in a hesitating, uncertain tone. "Who is it?"

"It's me."

"Who is that?"

"Mrs. Richards, your landlady."

"Hello," the voice grudgingly acknowledged.

"Good afternoon. I've brought you something." She smiled in anticipation but the door remained closed.

"What is it?" the voice asked after a pause.

"A kitten," Mrs. Richards said. "A poor little kitten I've found."

"A kitten?" the voice questioned eagerly.

Immediately there was a scrape of locks being worked and a moment later the door cracked open. Two eyes peered out.

"She's in the box," Mrs. Richards said, holding it up for proof. "A darling little calico without a home."

From the apartment a definite scent of soiled ammonia hit her nostrils. A hand reached out to take the box, barely opening the door. The eyes returned.

"Thank you," the voice said.

"It's you who should be thanked," Mrs. Richards said, "for taking in a homeless creature. I found her in the street without a mother."

"You're very kind."

"How is my other kitten doing?"

"That one is not very energetic."

"Has she grown? Would it be all right just to take a peek at her?"

The eyes furrowed. "I'm afraid not just now. Perhaps another time."

Mrs. Richards nodded. "There's one more thing?"

"What is that?"

"About the rent—"

"Didn't you get my envelope?"

"Yes. But I was a little bit nervous to get cash. I live all alone since my husband died."

"I don't believe in checks."

Mrs. Richards nodded sadly. "I still haven't had a chance to put your name on the mailbox. Could you tell me again how you spell it?"

"Don't trouble yourself. I won't be getting any mail here. I just do my . . . work here."

Mrs. Richards smiled shyly. "A painter? You have wonderful light in there. On the top floor and the view. You can see the ocean, the beach, and even part of the zoo."

"If you'll excuse me . . ."

"Yes, of course. Goodbye. And I hope you like the kitten."

Mrs. Richards turned away and clucked sympathetically as she descended the stairs. The poor man had seemed so lonely when he moved in, hardly talking at all. No friends visited him. All he had were his pets. . . . A pot of tea, perhaps someday she'd bring a piping pot of tea and they could discuss Rousseau. Of course she'd insist on opening a window of his, that musty smell was simply intolerable.

Mrs. Richards was unaware that two eyes followed her descent. They studied her with a slight frown. Then the door was bolted. The man held the box carefully and turned around in his kitchen.

It was green. The entire kitchen was suffused with a bluish green subterranean light that trembled on the walls. The light seeped from a tiny window and passed through a huge fifty-gallon aquarium. Radiating out, the greenish glow eased through yet another row of aquariums stacked along sinks, cupboards, stove, and counters.

There was a time when gurgling air bubbled through plastic

tubes but the pumps hadn't worked in some time. Overgrown plants literally reached out like algae-covered arms from the thick murky water. A mossy scum plated the upper reaches of the tanks, casting verdant shadows. Occasionally near the edge of the glass, slowly moving dark shapes could be seen finning erratically.

The man paused by one of the tanks and frowned. He reached his hand into the soupy water and green scum collected on his cuff. His fingers closed around a dark shape and withdrew. He frowned again, this time sadly.

"There, there," he murmured, ambling toward the bathroom. He dropped the dead guppy into the toilet and flushed. The gurgling maelstrom whirled and sucked the bloated corpse into a watery grave. He would have to get those air pumps working again. How long had it been? He couldn't remember.

He walked past a closet and into the living room. It was dim, grey dim. Blankets had been draped against the windows and only a low level of grey paleness seeped into the apartment. When he passed under an arch, two fluttering shapes swooped low, nearly grazing his head.

"There, there," he scolded, ducking. He held out his free hand, extending a finger, but the birds did not land.

The furniture was spotted with bird droppings. A huge beam supported the ceiling and upon it roosted several dozen sleeping canaries, macaws, robins, and long-tailed cockatoos. The floor directly underneath was covered with an inch-thick layer of bird dung and empty seed husks.

The man made his way very carefully across the room, not wanting to disturb the birds. A few of them drowsily opened their eyes and cocked their heads, but none took flight. The man made his way toward the wall where nine or ten bird cages were lined up. Penned inside nearly every tiny wire home was a cat.

Placing the shoe box in front of an empty cage, he held the gate and opened the landlady's box. The ball of fur meowed, a tiny pink tongue lapped hopefully. The man shook the kitten into the cage, taking care not to touch it. His lips curled in unspeakable disgust as he snapped shut the gate. The noise woke the other cats and now their skinny paws scraped in nervous, exhausted hunger.

The man raised his head toward the wall. There were drawings there, crude figures drawn thickly with tubes of laundry markers. Every one was a face, flat and frontal view, of animals. He stared for a long time with his hands in his pockets.

■ ■ ■

When Steven entered the office, he found Harriet smiling for the first time in a week.

"I've been waiting for you to come in," she said. "I was going to ring the cottage this morning."

"Why?"

"The hospital called. They said Gordon asked for you."

"How long ago?"

"A few minutes. Visiting hours start at twelve."

"I'll be there. Can you juggle my schedule?"

"I already did. I got you two hours starting at eleven."

"Thanks."

The smile on her tired face started to lose a little of its strength. "I put this morning's *Chronicle* on your desk," Harriet said. "We're front page again."

"Have we heard from the good Mayor's office?" Steven asked ruefully.

"Nothing yet," Harriet said. "But I imagine he'll want to get in touch."

Steven nodded. "When he reads the paper this morning I hope he doesn't choke. Did you see the broadcasts last night?"

"Yes."

"They cut out Dr. Lewis."

"They left in enough of you." Harriet paused. She leaned back in her chair and eyed Steven. "I hope you know what you're getting into," she said slowly.

"If I did," Steven said, disappearing into the inner office, "I wouldn't be doing this."

Standing before his desk, Steven stared at the front page. He felt a little strange as he looked at himself in the photograph, standing at the podium and waving a hand in the air. His tie was crooked, the tie he wore two times a year. Steven winced at the article's headline: INTERIM ZOO DIRECTOR BLASTS MAYOR. He skimmed the paragraphs but didn't find much difference from the television reports last night. Time, Steven thought, that's all I need. Time to catch this murderer before anyone finds out. Especially Gordon.

As he read further, he was interrupted by a tapping at the window. Amanda rapped her fingers and Steven let her in.

"Did you see the paper?" she asked.

"I was just reading it."

"You've got to get rid of that sorry tie. It doesn't make it."

Amanda picked up the newspaper. Without asking, she began to read aloud the reporter's account of the meeting. It was several minutes before she glanced up and saw that Steven wasn't listening. He wasn't even looking at her; his body was rigid and he stared at the desk top.

"Hey," Amanda protested, "I was reading your best lines."

Steven didn't answer. He looked at a pile of mail Harriet had put under the paper.

"What's wrong?" Amanda asked, coming to stand next to him.

"That envelope," Steven said, pointing at the top of the mail.

"What about it?"

"It's the same kind he sent me before."

"This one?" Amanda asked, picking it up. "From Mr. Brown-coat?"

"Don't touch it," Steven snapped.

Amanda looked at him, but still held the envelope. "I'm just looking at it. You can open it first."

"No," Steven said, shaking his head. "I can't."

"What do you mean?"

"The police have to check for fingerprints. They said not to open it. I have to call them first."

Amanda scowled. "Sounds stupid to me. If you open it, they can tell your fingerprints. What do you think's in it?"

"I know what's in it," Steven said slowly. "He's telling me the next animal he's going to kill."

Amanda's eyes widened. Her voice was unbelieving as she held up the envelope. "And you're not going to open it?"

"I can't."

"When there's a chance you can do something about it? You're going to wait for some policeman to crawl over here and paw over it?"

"That's what they said."

"When you got the last letter—the letter about the hippo—how soon after was it attacked?"

"The same morning."

"Then you've *got* to open this. You've got to do it now."

"I can't."

"There's no time."

"I'll call the police," Steven said.

"To hell with the police."

"Give me the letter," Steven ordered.

Amanda moved backward. "Maybe they told *you* not to open it," she said. "But they didn't say anything about me."

Steven lunged for the letter but she ran behind the couch. He jumped toward her and both of them fell. Amanda tore open the envelope. The letter dropped on to the carpet with the writing plainly visible.

Direktor,
Why aren't you telling the people why the animals are *really* dying? The longer you keep quiet, the more the animals will suffer. Do I have to do it? Remain silent and you will force me to help them free themselves.

An Animal Lover

PS When a King of the Jungle can't breathe anymore, which jungle is he king of?

Amanda's voice quickened. "What does he mean 'when the king of the jungle can't breathe anymore?' "

"I don't know."

"Well, it's obviously a lion he's talking about."

"Yes," Steven agreed. "Or a big cat."

"How many jungles do we have in the zoo?"

"None," Steven admitted. "He's talking about the big cats. But which one? They're all in the same kind of exhibit the hippo was in. Outside. Concrete-lined. A few bare logs. A wading pool."

"No jungle," Amanda said.

"No jungle," Steven repeated. "But it's a big area. A hundred people could be around the exhibits and anyone can disappear in a crowd."

"That's a big help."

"Wait a minute," Steven said. He paced again. "The big cats."

"What's the matter?"

Steven suddenly stopped and faced her. "All the cats are grouped around one building. Gordon exhibits them outside most of the year but a few months during the winter he keeps them inside the main hall. They really hate it then—there's hardly any room to exercise in—but it's heated. The smell is unbelievable; it takes until May to air it out every year."

"So?" Amanda asked.

"So inside the hall, there are only two doors. One of them is always secured, except for emergencies."

Amanda began to see his point. "You mean there's only one way out."

"Exactly. If you have to leave in a hurry, you *have* to pass through one set of doors."

"And there's no reason to be in a hurry unless you're doing something you shouldn't be."

Steven began to walk around the office again, thinking out loud. "The hall is big, but not that big. A person can stand at one end and see everything that's going on."

"But wouldn't the killer spot any keepers?" Amanda objected.

"Of course," Steven said, nodding his head. "But he wouldn't notice a woman in regular clothes, standing around with a camera around her neck."

"Just a minute," Amanda said. She matched his pace around the office and fell into step. "Who said I was going to do this?"

"You did. At my house, remember?"

"*Let's.* I said let *us* catch him."

"I can't do it."

"Why not?"

"He'll recognize me."

"How?"

"My picture in the *Chronicle.*"

"Oh," Amanda said, almost sullenly.

"Wait a minute," Steven said. He walked over to the couch and bent down. Studying the upper-right-hand corner, he could barely make out the date on the faint postmark. "June twenty-fifth," he read.

"Today's the twenty-sixth," Amanda said. "That means he must have seen the article in yesterday's *Chronicle.*"

"But not today's," Steven continued. There was a frown on his face.

Amanda guessed what he was thinking. She went over to the letter and read the first two sentences. "Why aren't you telling the people why the animals are really dying? The longer you keep quiet . . ."

"Go on," Steven said. "Finish it."

"The longer you keep quiet, the more the animals will suffer." Amanda held the letter in her hand and raised her head. "The news conference was *after* he mailed the letter. You didn't say anything about the killer."

"I know."

"What do you think he's going to do now?"

"Whatever it is," Steven said quickly, "he'll do it fast." Steven flipped on the intercom switch. "Harriet? Call the cat house and tell them I'm coming right over."

"You have an appointment in ten minutes with the Members' Society."

"Sorry, this can't wait. Round up three keepers for emergency work and send them over. Make sure they're in uniform."

"Trouble?"

"No. Just a little roundup. And one more thing. I want a messenger sent immediately to the police department with an envelope I'll give you."

Steven flicked off the intercom and stared at the letter. He opened a drawer, took out a manila folder, and approached the letter with a pair of tweezers.

"Wait," Amanda said. She was staring under the letter where it leaned against the couch leg.

Steven joined her. On the other side of the letter were three drawings, very tiny and poorly done. It seemed as if the person had used a dull pencil with soft, thick lead. There were three bodyless heads, tilting at an angle. They were heads of cats.

"They don't look much like kings of the jungle," Amanda said.

"They don't look much like anything."

Amanda shivered. "They're horrible."

■ ■ ■

The three keepers Harriet called were already waiting at the cat building when Steven and Amanda arrived. Steven led them inside where they crowded into a side room used for food preparation. The head keeper for the cats was there, supervising the chopping of the hanging sides of beef and horses. Piles of sawed bones and weighed meat waited for the sorting buckets.

Steven took the cat keeper aside and quickly explained what he wanted done. He decided not to tell him about the killer's threat but rather let the man think the Mayor's budget cut was responsible. This the keeper readily agreed to, even offering to "touch things up a bit at night" if a decrepit-looking exhibit would get rebuilding money.

The cages inside the hall were prepared—hosed down, sprayed with disinfectants, and the bars tested. Meanwhile, Steven had the uniformed keepers continually strolling around outside, passing conspicuously through the crowd. Steven counted on their presence to stop any attempts on the cats, at least until they were moved inside.

Within seconds, the cats started to stir. Their accustomed routine was being rudely broken by the sound of hoses inside the hall, unfamiliar footsteps, and strange smells. The Siberian tigers were the first to object. One whiskered old monarch coughed and rumbled at the bars. The high-strung jaguars paced faster. The two pumas flicked their tails but the black-maned lions remained motionless—only their ears twitched sporadically, flickering.

Barely an hour later the first group was shunted indoors—two black panthers who bounded inside as soon as the gate was lifted. One by one each cage was filled. The cats explored the cages ceaselessly, barely concealing their contempt for the cleanliness. After urinating in all corners to make the concrete floor more homey, they growled at the close scent of horse meat from the kitchen.

Steven ordered the head keeper to open for the public in the next hour.

"What do you want me to do?" Amanda asked.

They stood in front of the locked doors as Steven checked his watch. "Change out of your guide uniform. I'll tell the tram tour you're being reassigned. Come back here when it opens and wait. I'll come as soon as I can."

"What do you mean? Where are you going?"

"I've got to go to the hospital for a little while."

As Steven turned away, Amanda grabbed his shoulder. "Hey! What am I supposed to *do?*"

"Make sure nobody gets too close to the cats."

"And what's too close? When fingers go through the bars?"

"You can see anybody that tries to throw something in. Anything. Apples, hot dogs, anything. Get a look at him. That's all. Take his picture if you can. You have a camera? Don't go after him. He'll want to get out of here as fast as he can but if you follow him outside, I don't know what he'll do."

"I'm not sure about this."

"Neither am I. Look, I'm late."

Steven left her there, standing in front of the hall with her hands in her pockets and her shoes scraping the ground. She was giving him a dirty look. He wasn't sure about the plan either, but he had to do something.

"Hey!" he yelled back over his shoulder. "You look pretty when you're terrified."

■ ■ ■

The doctor in charge of Gordon's case laid a hand on Steven's shoulder. "Before you go in," he said, "I'll have to tell you that five minutes is the most I can let you have."

"I understand."

The doctor frowned. "Was your father under a lot of pressure before his attack?"

"He has been all his life."

"He needs rest."

"Is he going to recover?"

"It was a minor attack. He should recover fully if he just rests now."

"Will he have another one?"

"After the first, the odds automatically increase. But his arteries are in fine shape. Cholesterol count low for his age. If it wasn't for the heart, I'd say his condition is good, extremely good. He's been active all his life, he's taken care of himself."

"Except for this," Steven said.

The doctor shrugged. "He's a very strong man. I think he's going to come out of it okay." He nodded encouragingly and turned to leave.

"Wait," Steven said. "I need something."

"Oh?"

"Gordon *was* under a lot of pressure. Can you help me keep it off?"

"How do you mean?"

"I'd like you to restrict his visitors to my uncle, myself, and people who work at the zoo. I've already told them not to talk about certain . . . pressures . . . at the zoo. We have—"

"Yes," the doctor interrupted. "I read the *Chronicle.*"

Steven took in a breath. "I'd like you also not to allow newspapers, television, or radios in his room."

"I think I understand," the doctor muttered somewhat coolly.

"There might be reporters trying to see him, or friends who don't understand. I don't want Gordon to—"

"Yes. The situation is rather unusual, isn't it?"

"Will you do it?"

The doctor nodded. "I think that in this case, the measures you suggest would be beneficial. I'll instruct the nurse in charge of this ward."

Steven nodded his thanks and the doctor left. It was with shaking hands that he opened the door of the private room and walked to the bed.

Gordon lay immobile, wrapped cocoonlike in a blue cotton hospital gown. The stiff sheets were tucked securely around his torso and a pillow propped up his head. There was a stir under the sheets and Steven realized his father was trying to lift a hand in greeting. The movement quit, aborted, and Gordon lay still. Only his eyes watched Steven.

And Steven saw the eyes of Boss-Man. He saw the helpless confusion of a mind ordering a body to move but finding stillness. The mind was alive, the mind commanded, but the eyes saw only defeat. Steven looked at Gordon's face and saw the folds of skin creeping under his chin just like Charlie, and the uneven stubble of whiskers from a bad hospital shave.

"Steven," Gordon tried to say.

"You're going to be all right," Steven murmured. "You're going to be okay."

"The zoo . . ." Gordon said thickly. He tried to raise his head. "Somebody has to—"

"Don't worry about the zoo. Everything's being taken care of. Charlie . . . Charlie and I are handling everything."

"Charlie—"

"I know," Steven interrupted. He decided not to tell Gordon he had read the letter. "We're keeping the zoo for you. We're just waiting for you to get better and come back. You know Charlie, sometimes he needs a little help."

There was silence in the room. Both of them listened to the sound of a cart outside being wheeled down the hall. A faint whine of an elevator seeped through the walls. Steven swallowed.

"The animals?"

"The animals are fine," Steven said convincingly.

"There was—before it happened, an okapi was—"

"I took care of it. Dr. Lewis is treating him. He's coming along nicely. Don't worry."

"Good," Gordon breathed.

"Harriet and Charlie are coming to see you later. The zoo people want to visit, too. I'll be here as much as I can."

A nurse appeared at Steven's side and motioned him to leave. Steven started to turn away.

"Steven?" Gordon rasped.

"Yes?"

"Thanks . . ."

"Charlie said somebody has to do it."

"No," Gordon said. "You're doing it for me."

Steven followed the nurse out of the room. A roar of noise was screaming in his ears.

■ ■ ■

Steven checked in with Harriet the minute he walked on to the grounds. "Anything happening?" he asked, trying to sound casual.

Harriet turned away from her typewriter and shook her head. "Nothing much. The chairman of the Members' Society wasn't too happy. That was the second appointment you've canceled."

"Reschedule it as soon as you can."

"Tomorrow morning."

"Good."

"Oh," Harriet added. "The girl called. She seemed a little upset."

"Girl?" Steven gave a start.

"Yes. The girl who works for Dr. Lewis."

"Oh," Steven said, not a little relieved.

"Her mother died and she's taking emergency leave to fly out to Boston."

"So?" Steven asked, puzzled.

"Mr. Roberts," Harriet said, as if explaining the problem.

There was a blank look on Steven's face as he stared at Harriet. Then the name struck him. Mr. Roberts. He was a two-year-old chimpanzee they were sending to the Milwaukee Zoo. Before the transfer took place, Mr. Roberts was assigned a human companion. Constant care and attention were given, loaded with toys and special food. The idea was not to spoil him but rather get him reused to human contact to make his arrival in Wisconsin less traumatic. The assignment was a plum, everybody wanted it. Mr. Roberts was hairy and cute.

"When does he leave?" Steven asked.

"Wednesday."

"I'll take him," Steven said.

"You?"

"Why not?"

"No reason. It's just that you haven't looked exactly paternal the last week."

"Maybe Mr. Roberts can cheer me up. He's at the vet's?"

"Yes."

"Call them. I'll be over later to pick him up."

"Right." Harriet paused and looked at Steven. "How is Gordon?"

Steven smiled. "He's doing fine. His doctor said he's going to come out of it fine."

Harriet nodded, sighing in relief. "Has he heard what happened?"

"No," Steven said. "And when you see him you can't mention anything about the hippo. That goes for anyone who visits him. I'll tell Charlie."

"Of course."

"Doctor's orders," Steven said truthfully. He walked into his office and rummaged around in a filing cabinet he had brought from Berkeley. He found what he wanted and stuffed two small packages in his coat pocket as he prepared to leave again.

"Where to now?" Harriet asked.

"I'll be at the cat house."

"To keep them from escaping?" Harriet asked with a sardonic smile. "Should I call the Mayor and ask him to help?"

"Don't bother," Steven answered. "His kind of help I don't need. How's the attendance so far today?"

"Up," Harriet said. "Like you said. Can't you tell?"

Steven could. As he crossed the crowded plaza he had to thread his way past the curious throngs. Just by glancing at them, Steven could tell they were not normal visitors. From their dress, it was evident that they lived in the city. No tourists, no white shoes, no leisure suits—they milled around in the peculiar layered San Francisco blend of sweaters, shawls, and vests, expensive loafers and jogging shoes. They had been drawn to the zoo by the *Chronicle*'s inflammatory articles but they still weren't sure exactly what they were supposed to look at.

On the whole, Steven wasn't displeased to see them. As far as he was concerned, every person who paid for a ticket was a potential ally against the Mayor's critical attack against attendance figures. The fewer tourists, the better the zoo's situation became. It was time, Steven thought, that San Franciscans woke up and realized that they had a zoo. What they were going to do about it was another problem.

The crowds increased as he approached the cat building. Steven used his passkey to slip into the food preparation room and he peered into the main hall through a cautiously opened door. There were maybe a hundred or so people milling around in front of the cages; most of the cats were sleeping. Amanda was a dozen steps from the door, leaning against a railing.

Steven hissed to attract her attention and she walked quickly toward him. He pulled her partly inside so they could talk without being seen.

"How is it going?" Steven asked anxiously.

"They stink," Amanda said, wrinkling her nose. "They stink very bad."

"Can you see everything?"

"Oh, sure. There's not much to see, though. One of the lions woke up from a nap and coughed some. The jaguar's still jogging around his cage trying to catch his tail. He's a big pussycat."

"You ought to see his food bill."

"Well, did you come to relieve me?"

"I can't. Look, I got you off the tram, didn't I?"

"Sure," Amanda said, scowling slightly.

"I brought you this," Steven said, bringing out one of the packages he picked up at the office. He opened a little box and removed a small rectangular object the size of a cigarette pack. He gave it to her.

"What is it?"

"It's a transceiver. I have one just like it. Push this button here and mine will buzz. If you want to talk, use this switch. You can hold it up to your ear to listen but it's loud enough if you keep it in your pocket, too."

"Why do I need it?"

"Because I can't stay here. If something happens, I want you to call me, fast."

Amanda slipped the cartridge in her pocket. "I'm getting bored."

"We're going to open the building at one o'clock from now on. It's just four or five hours every day."

"Four or five *hours?*"

"I knew you'd understand. I've got to go back to the office. Do you want to come over for dinner? Keep up the good work."

Before she had a chance to object, Steven kissed her on the cheek and left the same way he had come in—ducking his head between rows of meat hooks and hanging carvers' knives. If he had looked back, he would have seen someone watching him with arms crossed, foot tapping, and an exasperated look settling on her face.

■ ■ ■

A half-hour before the zoo closed, Steven entered the hospital compound. Mr. Roberts was waiting.

Steven reached behind the cage high on the wall for a key. Then he took the key across the room to a box which he unlocked. Inside was another key which this time worked the lock on Mr. Roberts's cage. In Gordon's zoo nobody took any chances with chimps; they had learned from painful experience.

Mr. Roberts started jumping up and down at the sound of the locks being worked. He smacked his lips quite satisfactorily and his gleaming white teeth shone to advantage. His chubby fingers grasped the bars of the cage and he rocked back and forth. A whistle of pleasure screeched from his lips and if there had been room, he would have turned a cartwheel.

Steven opened the gate and Mr. Roberts shot out, landing with chirruping and lip-smacking at his favorite spot, around a shoulder with one long arm clasping Steven's neck.

"Okay, Mr. Roberts," Steven said. "I've got a pile of bananas at home I want to get rid of."

The few visitors hurrying toward the gates were not a little surprised to see a man walking slowly with a twisting mass of hairy arms and legs tugging at his ears and occasionally rising, fists clenched in excited victory, toward the sky. Mr. Roberts, Steven thought as he walked up the pathway to his cottage, wait until you see what snow in Milwaukee is.

Once inside, Steven put Mr. Roberts down in a chair and told him to sit still. Then Steven went from room to room, searching carefully for objects he would mind having destroyed. There were few: a favorite ink pen, a small tobacco jar, three or four crystal wineglasses. Then he locked up all loose matches, a lighter, and a sharp bone letter opener—a previous owner had taught Mr. Roberts to smoke and Steven didn't want to encourage him. When he came back to the living room, Mr. Roberts was quite still and content, surveying the cluttered walls and floors with ill-feigned rapture.

"Okay," Steven said. "You're a guest now. You can do whatever you want."

Mr. Roberts waited politely for a few seconds, smacking his lips in an attempt at well-meaning small talk. Then he put his fists down on the chair and turned over, springing into the air and landing upright. He clasped his palms together over his head and stormed into the kitchen.

Steven could hear him rummaging around in the fruit bowl and a few shrill cheeps of delight. Then there was a curious rattling sound and he guessed it to be Mr. Roberts's hands swirling inside a bowl of nuts.

A half-hour later, Mr. Roberts staggered out of the kitchen and Steven led him into a spare bedroom. "Take a nap," Steven suggested. "Coffee will be ready in a few hours." Mr. Roberts meekly climbed onto the bed and immediately curled up into a tight ball, clutching his stomach and moaning. Steven shook his head sadly and backed out of the room. He locked the door, fastening a bolt, and left the chimpanzee to sleep off the stomachache alone.

With a gin and tonic, Steven began to read through a stack of journals that had been accumulating. The sight of the articles made him think of the completely different world he had left across the Bay only a short week or so ago. He took another sip of the drink and wondered if it would ever be possible to return to his nice, quiet life teaching undergraduates the mysteries of life.

At first the knocking on the door went completely unnoticed. Steven was deeply into an article on the eating habits of Komodo dragons and he couldn't hear anything. When the knocking turned into pounding, he raised his head in puzzlement.

He walked over to the door and opened it, still reading the journal. After a moment he glanced up. "Hello," he said. "Do you know that Komodo dragons—"

"No, I don't," Amanda said, storming past him into the hall. "Well, they're locked up. Snug as a bug. I'm starving."

"Good. I . . ." Steven's voice slipped away.

Amanda stared at him, her eyes suddenly narrowing. "What are you doing?"

"Me?" Steven said. His nose was twitching. "Nothing. I was just—"

"So what if I smell like lions?" Amanda attacked with a scowl. She crossed her arms and glared at him. "Wouldn't you reek, shut up in a dingy hall all afternoon?"

"Sure," Steven said, backing away. "Let me just check the steaks."

"You have a shower in this place?" Amanda muttered.

"Down the hall, first door on the left," Steven said over his shoulder. "Towels inside."

"All I wanted was a transfer to the children's zoo," Amanda muttered, stalking off down the hall. She stopped and sniffed the air. "Smells like a zoo in here."

Steven busied himself in the kitchen, setting out plates, steaming vegetables, and scrounging around in a cabinet for a forgotten bottle of burgundy. When everything was simmering on the stove and under control, he poured himself a glass of wine and returned to the living room. He could hear the splash of the shower against the curtains and a faint murmur of singing. Sitting in a comfortable chair, he picked up the Komodo dragon article and resumed his reading. The wine tasted good.

It was five minutes later when the scream hit him.

Steven jumped to his feet, dropping the glass of wine. Another scream, louder, from the bathroom. *The window!* Since he moved in he hadn't checked the lock on the outside window. As he sprinted down the hall Amanda cried again in terror. There was a sound of something hitting against the bathroom wall and a sickening rip of the shower curtain being torn from its rings.

Steven tried the bathroom door. Open! He burst inside and stopped. Amanda's hand was coming out of the shower stall, clutching the sides and slipping down. Water poured over the floor. Steam hovered like a murky fog. Above Amanda's arm, a different hand appeared. It found her wrist, tightened like a vise, and began to force it back. A horrible gurgling, like someone choking, sputtered in the steamy room.

Steven moved closer, clenching his fists. His eyes searched quickly for a weapon and he grasped the end of a shampoo bottle. He raised it high and approached the shower stall.

"Get out of here!" Amanda screamed at someone in the shower.

There was the sound of more struggling, the beating of arms against the shower, and suddenly a dark shape lunged out of the stall and slammed onto the floor. Steven raised the bottle and Amanda screamed again.

Two white eyes blinked rapidly and Mr. Roberts smacked his lips.

"What the hell?" Steven muttered, dropping the bottle.

Mr. Roberts had wrapped the plastic shower curtain completely around his torso like a robe. Only his head and arms stuck out. He began to hop on his feet, dragging the curtain across the floor. High in the air he jumped, smacking his lips and shaking his head to get rid of water droplets.

Steven grabbed an end of the monkey's plastic cape and dragged the screeching chimp away from the shower.

"It's okay now," Steven said. He aimed his assurance toward the figure huddled in the stall.

"What *was* that," a cold voice slowly demanded.

"That was Mr. Roberts," Steven replied carefully. "I guess I should have told you. He's staying with me for a couple of days."

"I see."

"I thought he was locked in the other room," Steven said, puzzled.

"I have never been more scared in my life," the voice stated mechanically. "I am in a state of shock. I am cold. I am wet. I have no clothes on and I am—"

"They're not supposed to like showers," Steven said, trying to explain.

"I now realize that fact," the voice said. "He was trying to turn off the water."

"He probably thought he was saving you."

"From what?"

"From that horrible lion stink," Steven answered truthfully, sniffing at Amanda's pile of clothes lying in a corner. "If you want to put your things in a bag, I think I can find something of mine that'll fit you."

"Thank you," the voice stated. "And will you please be so kind as to choke that sonofabitch ape with a bicycle chain on your way out?"

Steven dragged Mr. Roberts out of the bathroom and locked him up again. The bolt had been jiggled loose and this time Steven fastened it more securely. He found a pair of slacks and a shirt in a drawer and knocked on the bathroom door.

"Come in," Amanda said.

Steven walked in and laid the clothes on a stand. Amanda had wrapped herself in a towel and was rubbing another cloth against the mirror to get rid of the steam.

"I brought you some clothes," Steven said. "I'm sorry about—"

"Don't worry about it," Amanda said. "Happens all the time. Did you choke him for me? No, forget that. I guess he *was* trying to save me."

Steven nodded. "Sometimes you have to look at it from their point of view. If you need anything else . . ."

"I could use a mirror," she said, rubbing harder against the glass.

"Here, let me do that," Steven said. He took the cloth from her hands and started to move it around the mirror. Then he stopped. The cloth dropped from his hands but neither of them picked it up. Steven looked at Amanda for a moment and then leaned slightly. He kissed her lightly on her lips.

He could smell her cheeks, the faint trace of soap and the dampness. Then his arms were around her shoulders. Her long hair brushed against his hands and felt cool where it touched.

"That's nicer than Mr. Roberts," Amanda said after a moment.

"Is that a compliment or not?"

They kissed again. Amanda's hands went around Steven's back and he could feel her lightly pressing him. He moved closer and felt her legs against his.

"Do I still smell like a cage?" she asked.

"What's the matter with smelling like a cage?"

"Don't get so defensive. You've been around zoos too long."

She began to run her fingers along his neck and then kissed him. A drop of water fell from her forehead, ran down her nose, and was transferred to Steven's chin. The droplet spread between their cheeks like a coating of oil.

"Did you bring some clothes?" Amanda asked.

"Behind you."

Without breaking her embrace, Amanda picked up the shirt and pants. She brought the hand with the clothes to rest again behind Steven's back. When she blinked he could feel her eyelashes touch the sides of his nose. Then he felt the clothes drop and hit the back of his calves before landing in a crumpled pile at his heels.

He kissed her again but the towel wrapped around her was loose and when he brought her neck closer, it fell to join the clothes on the floor. Steven passed his hands down, lightly, along the ridges of her spine, feeling her still moist shower skin. He felt the curve of her belly, the growing roundness of her buttocks, and the point where her thighs became firm.

"I'm cold," Amanda said.

"Probably because you don't have any clothes on."

"They fell," she defended.

Steven smiled at her and nodded. He passed his hands over her breast and pulled her closer. She began to unloosen the buckle on his belt. When she slipped her hand inside and felt him, she stopped.

"That's better than Mr. Roberts," she said.

Steven drew back. "What was the bastard trying to do?"

Amanda frowned as she concentrated on the memory. "I was singing in the shower. I was rinsing the shampoo out of my hair and I heard these sounds. Cheeps. I thought it was the shower head squeaking or something. For some reason it reminded me of Fay Wray in *King Kong* and I began to imagine myself blond and helpless and ravishing."

"Yes?"

"And then this great hairy arm comes in through the shower curtain and at first I didn't see it. There was some soap in my eyes and I was rubbing them. Then I saw the hairy hand, the fingers wiggling, and I *still* thought I was Fay Wray. But I stopped singing and began to think some more."

"That's a lot of thinking."

"Then I thought it was your hand."

"I knock first."

"Then the whole monkey jumps inside and starts pounding on the faucet, trying to turn the water off. He was screaming his head off but if it was a screaming contest, I wanted to win that one."

"He was trying to help."

"I'll never do that again."

"Dream you're Fay Wray?"

"No. Take a shower with a monkey."

They walked out and Steven led her to the bedroom. Amanda sat on the bed, leaning against the pillows while she watched Steven undress. Her legs stretched out and her toes played with the bedspread.

"What are you looking at?" Steven asked, unbuttoning his shirt and tossing it on a chair.

"I'm watching you take your clothes off."

"Am I doing it right?" he asked, throwing a sock at her.

"You have nice arms," Amanda said.

"You have nice ears," Steven said, sitting beside her on the bed. He laid a hand on her thighs and squeezed. "And you have legs like a dancer."

A smile crept over Amanda's face. "I'm glad you said that."

"Why?" Steven asked, surprised.

"Well, I thought for a second you'd say I have legs like a gazelle, or an impala, or some other graceful animal. And then you'd say I have a nice neck, like a deer, or a swan, or a rabbit. And then nice eyes, like—"

"I get the point."

"It doesn't matter. You didn't say it."

They kissed again, stretching out side by side on the bed. Amanda's hand ran over his arms and across his chest. Steven moved closer and felt her breasts against his ribs.

"Why would I do that?" Steven asked with a start.

"Do what?"

"Say things like that."

"I don't know," Amanda said. "How do I know? I'm just an actress who works a tram tour in the summer. You're a zoo director. You look at animals all day. Who knows what you see when you're off duty."

"Who knows," Steven agreed.

"All day long," Amanda continued, "you look at naked animals."

Steven kissed her breasts, feeling her nipples between his lips. Amanda stirred and ran her legs between his.

"Are you still cold?" he asked.

"No."

They moved closer together, Amanda lifting her legs and tightly locking them around Steven's calves. They kissed harder, Steven smelling the shampoo, the soap, the sweat on her upper lip.

"I smell something burning," Amanda said.

"Dinner."

She thought for a second. "No. I don't think so."

There was a slight sound in the room, a faint rustle, and both of them looked at the other side of the bed. Sitting comfortably in a chair, legs crossed and toes curled, was Mr. Roberts. In his right hand was a lit cigarette and as if to show his pleasure at being noticed, he expelled a voluminous cloud of smoke. Then he cheeped his approval.

"He smokes," Steven said to Amanda.

"How long has he been watching?" Amanda whispered.

"I don't know. Do you want me to get him out?"

"No. I like you where you are."

"Why are we whispering?" Steven asked.

"Oh, let him stay where he is," Amanda said. "It just feels weird, that's all. Stark naked, making love in front of a monkey. What do you think he's thinking about us?"

"I don't know. Do you mind?"

"No," she said finally. "As long as he doesn't spread rumors."

Both of them turned slightly, so their bodies hid them as best they could. Amanda's legs lifted higher, around Steven's back, and both of them began to move harder as a billowing cloud of cigarette smoke gently filled the air above them like a canopy.

■ ■ ■

The morning went normally, as normally as zoos went. Three woodpecker chicks began to break out of their shells at ten o'clock. Steven kept in touch with the incubation room by phone. One of the penguins came down with a cold and the keeper asked Steven for permission to isolate him. Harriet ushered in the president of the Members' Society and they finally agreed on a date for the annual social function—a night party on zoo grounds. The menu was discussed and approved. Steven was thoroughly bored with the man, but the annual party was necessary for a money pitch. There were always rich widows or fat businessmen hankering to underwrite an animal purchase or a new exhibit. They put up the money and their names were painted on a plaque. Steven hated the patronage system, but he knew Gordon was forced to depend on it for extra income.

Harriet brought him lunch—a couple of hot dogs and potato chips—as he read more keepers' reports. Afterward he dictated letters: to nurseries asking for bids on some landscaping work, to other zoo directors listing San Francisco's surplus "barter" stock, and a nasty note to a grain supply company complaining about sprouting barley in the last feed shipment.

At exactly two o'clock he was standing by the coffee warmer eying what appeared to be less than half a cup left when his coat beeped.

It beeped again and Steven dropped the cup. The coat was buzzing like a switchboard. Steven grabbed the transceiver and flicked the button.

"Steven?" the voice crackled with a tinny sound.

"What!" Steven demanded.

"Are you there?"

"Yes, damn it. What's wrong?"

Amanda's voice was faint. He had to strain to hear above the static.

"He's here," she said.

"What?"

"What should I do?"

"Watch him," Steven yelled. "Don't let him out of your sight. I'm coming."

Steven didn't wait for an answer. He threw on his coat and ran out of the office, jumping completely over the hedges in the courtyard. He landed, feet pumping, and flew down the path toward the cat house. It took less than two minutes to reach the building; he let himself in the food preparation room and stopped to get his breath back. Right in front of him was the door. Taking deep breaths to calm himself, he grasped the handle and opened it a crack.

There were maybe fifty people inside the dim hall. He looked for Amanda and saw her in the same place as last time. She noticed the door open and saw him peek through at the same time. Amanda began to ease backward toward the door, trying to appear casual. Her attention was kept on one place across the hall and her hands were around her camera.

Steven waited for her to stand in front of the door, blocking him from sight.

"Where is he?" he said, his breath still short.

"There," Amanda said in a low voice, nodding with her head. "In the corner. All the way across the hall in front of the jaguar."

Steven looked far down the hall. Three sailors and a girl were strolling past the cage, laughing at something. They had their arms around each other, blocking the cat from sight. Then they passed, and Steven saw the man. He was standing a little to the side, his back to the wall and one hand resting on the railing. His other hand was inside the pocket of a wrinkled brown coat, lightly soiled and bulky. A pair of dark sunglasses rested on the bridge of his nose. His head moved back and forth, following the jaguar's incessant pacing. He was quite ordinary looking.

"He's been there for fifteen minutes," Amanda continued.

"In front of the jaguar?"

"Yes. I didn't notice him at first. But then I saw those sunglasses. He was walking slowly around the hall, but always touching the railing with that hand."

"What about the other hand?"

"In his pocket? It's been there ever since I spotted him. What do you think he's got in it?"

"I don't know," Steven said. "But we're going to find out."

"He's looking this way," Amanda warned. She turned quickly to her left and made a show of snapping a picture of a puma stretching.

"Do you think he's spotted you?" Steven whispered.

"I don't think so. What do we do?"

Steven thought quickly. "Wait a few minutes, give me a chance to go around and come in the main entrance. When you see me come in, start walking toward him. Make some noise with your shoes. Attract his attention. I'll try to get behind him."

"Then what?"

"When you get close enough, take his picture. We need proof for the police. He's not going to like that. If he starts to run, I'll try to get his sunglasses off or trip him or something. We've got to find out what he's got in that pocket."

"Then what?"

"We can't have him arrested for standing around. But if we can show his picture to the police, they'll believe us. Are you ready?"

"I think so."

"Okay. Give me a couple of minutes."

Steven closed the door and sprinted out of the kitchen and around the building to the main entrance. He stopped, getting back his breath, and prayed feverishly. He turned up the collar of his coat, hiding his face as much as possible, and walked in.

Damn it, he cursed to himself, why didn't I wait to get my eyes adjusted? The darkness of the hall after the intense sunlight outside made him squint in confusion. He turned left, relying on his memory, and made his way as inconspicuously as possible.

A minute later he reached the position he wanted. The man was barely a dozen steps away. Then he saw Amanda coming across the hall. Her heels beat a clip on the cement floor and she was whistling horribly off-key.

The man started to watch her, his hand still hidden in his pocket. Amanda walked directly at him and as he became aware of the fact, his feet stirred nervously.

Steven moved closer to him, slowly, and from behind. Finally he was just a couple of feet away and he could hear Amanda saying hello.

"Can I take your picture?" Amanda was saying. "I'm in art school. Class project," she blurted. She raised the camera and snapped a picture before he could protest.

The man moved away from the jaguar and stopped. His hand stirred inside his coat pocket. Amanda took another picture and his face locked on hers.

Amanda stopped. "Do you mind?" she asked.

"Who are you?" the man asked suddenly.

"Art project," Amanda said. "Could you take off your sun-glasses?"

The man was very still. He studied her carefully. Then he

grinned. "Of course," he said, briefly smiling again. He removed his sunglasses with a quick gesture.

Amanda snapped his picture again. She bobbed the camera and smiled nervously. Steven saw her hands shaking.

"Who are you?" the man repeated. The smile suddenly faded from his face.

"Photog—"

"I don't think so," the man interrupted. "There's not enough light in here for a picture and you don't have a flash."

Steven groaned silently. He had completely forgotten about the flash. The pictures were useless. He inched closer.

"Maybe outside," Amanda stuttered. "Maybe I could take your picture outside."

"I've been watching you," the man said.

"Me?" Amanda gulped.

"You've been standing across the hall, staring at me."

"I don't know what you're talking about."

"Yes, you do. Maybe you should tell me why."

"I—I don't know," stammered Amanda, as the man moved closer.

"Maybe we'd better find out," the man said harshly. His hand moved inside his pocket. As he brought it out, Amanda screamed.

Steven jumped. He grabbed the man's coat at the shoulder and yanked. He jerked hard; the coat pulled down, pinning the man's arms before they had a chance to move.

The man gasped. As he turned he kicked Steven in the shins with a vicious heel thrust.

Steven howled with pain. He swung his fist but was too slow as he felt his legs buckle. He fell on the floor of the lion house and cracked his head on the cement.

The man's hands were out of the raincoat by now. His left hand grabbed Steven's throat and squeezed tightly. His right hand held something heavy and ugly. A .38 revolver. The man pressed the cold muzzle against Steven's temple and shoved hard.

"Make one move," the man snarled, "and I'll blow your brains out."

He was going to say more but he grunted as Amanda's camera

slammed into the back of his head. The lens broke off, clattering to the floor, and blood began streaming down his neck. Still pressing the gun against Steven's head, he turned and cursed at Amanda.

She drew back her arm, trying to wind up another swing of the camera remains. The man snaked out his free arm, grabbed her ankle, and yanked her off her feet. She fell as quickly as Steven, thudding against the floor.

The whole incident had taken only seconds. One moment there had been three people standing in front of the jaguar cage; the next saw two of them flat on their backs with the third kneeling above and brandishing a gun. The man waved the pistol in the air, shouting at the people in the hall.

"Get out of here," he yelled. *"Go away."*

The people needed no second warning. They ran toward the doors, screaming and packing the exit in a mass of flailing arms. The animals in the cages began to wake up; a lion pushed his nose between the bars and roared. The deep-throated thunder vibrated the bones in Steven's ears. Steven stared at the gun; he felt the metal freeze against his temple.

As the hall emptied, the man began to go through Steven's pockets. He kept a wary eye on Amanda, lying frozen with fear.

"What do you want?" Steven choked.

"Shut up," the man grunted. "You're under arrest."

"What?"

"Shut up," the man repeated. His free hand began to touch the wound on his scalp. He felt for the gash and looked at the blood on his fingers. "Attempted robbery, assaulting a police officer— you two run a pretty good racket, don't you? I get sent down here to watch some goddamn fleabitten lion and look what I catch."

■ ■ ■

Two o'clock, the maintenance man noted on his watch. His hand rested on one of the main water valves inside the supply shed. The valve controlled the water flow to a large exhibition pool that had just been drained for cleaning. He was waiting for the keeper's signal to refill it. Outside, the keeper waved his hand and the maintenance man began filling a cement pit where the filtered water sparkled clear and bright just before the pumps shot it into the animal pool. Since it took half an hour for the pool to fill, he ambled outside to grab a cup of coffee with the keeper. As he walked out of the shed, he didn't bother to lock the door.

Someone was, however, taking the bother to watch him. Standing by a marmoset cage, eating popcorn from a gaily decorated box, was a medium-built man with a brown coat and sunglasses. He mechanically placed the kernels of corn into his mouth, but when the maintenance man left the shed the half-full box was dropped quickly into the nearest garbage can. A hand began to pat his thin-lipped mouth with a handerchief and he walked slowly forward.

Seeming to be interested in the shrubbery, he in fact studied the darkened interior of the shed. When he was satisfied that it was empty, he strolled through the open door.

Lifting his sunglasses to get a better view, he ran his eyes over the valves, dials, and pipes. He gave no indication that he recognized any of the mechanical functions and in fact he frowned at the complicated machinery. Eventually he stared down at his feet where the cement pit's water sparkled as it was sucked by a thirsty pump. He studied the gurgling pit for a moment and a connection was made in his mind with activities he had observed outside. For the first time he appeared pleased.

Reaching in his pocket, he took out a tiny amber medicine

bottle. It was a common type, the kind used by drugstores to dispense iodine solutions. He carefully shook the bottle. Holding it away from his face, he unscrewed the cap from the bottle and dropped both into the pit of water. They landed near the pumping tube and were immediately sucked against a wire filter screen. Lowering his sunglasses, he strolled out of the water shed.

It was three minutes after two o'clock when he emerged. He cocked an ear toward the pool and heard the splash of the hoses gradually raising the water level. He was about to stroll away when he heard a voice address him.

"Young man?"

He whirled around. An old woman was sitting on a bench and staring at him with a quizzical expression on her face. Her grey hair was held in place with amber barrettes.

"Haven't I seen you here before?" she asked. Her face was cocked to one side, like a curious hen.

"I don't think so," the man said, smiling nervously. He shifted his feet and looked about him for some reason to leave.

"I come to the zoo very often," she continued. "Almost every day. I get to know all the regulars after a while."

"Regulars? Well, I don't think you can call me a regular. I just come here when I feel I have to."

"I understand completely," the lady said, bobbing her head in total agreement. "Sometimes the world outside gets too complicated and it's so peaceful in here."

The woman's words triggered a facial tic and he pawed his cheeks to rub the spasm away. There was something about the woman's words—this old woman on the bench *understood*. The world outside the zoo was all an illusion, a mirage maintained by power-mad manipulators.

"It's complicated everywhere. Everywhere you look," he gasped in a feverish choke, "there's tyranny and subjugation, lies, deceits, hypocrisy, and poisonous despotism."

"Dear me," the lady sadly confided, "I'm afraid I don't keep up much with politics. I just watch the animals."

"So do I," the man agreed. He nodded his head in consent but the movement was exaggerated, mechanically and rigidly overextended. This woman *knew* about the animals. She possessed the secret. But how much does she know? "Sometimes," he ventured discreetly, "I think I can hear the animals talking."

"Of course you can," the old lady tittered. She beamed and clapped her birdlike hands together. "All of us regulars have learned the language."

She knew! The man relaxed, but along with the lack of tension he felt the surge of excitement in finding someone at last with whom he could share his secrets. This woman knew about the animals. She knew everything, even—he gratefully accepted— about his mission. The only thing left to do was to ask her if she had seen his friend.

"Do you know Francis?" he whispered. Perhaps he was too bold with this old woman but he couldn't help himself.

"Who?" the lady asked.

"A . . . a friend of mine," the man explained. "I come here to meet him. You must have seen him. It's very important that you must have seen him."

"What does he look like?"

The man paused and reconsidered. He was telling far too much and risking everything. Why had he suddenly lost his control? This was becoming dangerous.

"Won't you join me?" the lady asked, indicating her empty bench with the point of her umbrella. "Now I remember you, young man. I met you before on the tram ride. You wanted my advice on joining the Members' Society. I'm Mrs. Fleisher."

"How do you do." The man returned her smile and sat beside her.

"Your name is . . . ?"

"Oh, well," the man said, waving the air in front of him. "I'm—"

"Yes?"

"Pleased to meet you," said the man uneasily. When he said the words, his hands trembled in his lap.

"Did you ever join the Society?"

"In a manner of speaking."

He paused for a moment, again unsure of what he had heard.

What was this Members' Society? Was it what *he* was thinking? Were there others like him in some secret fraternal order? Was he being singled out, tapped for membership? The strange questions of the old lady only made sense if she were recruiting prospective knights for the mission of mercy. But he must still tread lightly, say the correct things; he could not fail this test of holy faith. She was looking at him with celestial assurance. He must say the correct things.

The lady continued. "I hope you don't think I'm impudent, but we in the ranks of the Society take an active interest in the well-being of the zoo."

"So do I, Mrs. Fleisher," he muttered under his breath. "Intolerable conditions, restrictive environments, totalitarian—"

Mrs. Fleisher cupped a hand over her ear. "I'm afraid I didn't catch that."

He scowled to himself, despondent at his inarticulateness. "I said, the zoo is *like a zoo.*"

"Of course it is," agreed Mrs. Fleisher, puzzled. "Tell me, what other things do you like about the zoo?"

The man thought for a long time. For almost a minute his eyes silently studied the ground at his feet. He examined the popcorn kernels, the crushed candy boxes, the wrappers, and the ooze of melting cotton candy that caught his shoelaces. The question transported him to another dimension, another world. In his mind, images suddenly appeared, moved jerkily across his frame, and snapped down—like the metal targets of a penny arcade shooting gallery. An immobile pet turtle the size of a half dollar, lying quietly in a plastic bowl too close to an open window where the sudden freezing storm had caused ice to condense on the plastic palm tree. He tried to pick up the turtle but it was frozen to the plastic. A soft baby chick brought home by his father from a grocery store giveaway at Easter. So soft, so small. He had tried to hold it in his hands and love it as hard as he could but it was too soft, *too soft.* Why don't you move? Breathe! Why don't you *breathe?* He tried to help but the chick didn't move anymore. The image of another bird took its place, just as tiny, a robin nestling fallen from its nest. A gaping mouth. Fluttering, half-formed wings. He had hidden it from his parents in the garage and slipped away after dinner to feed it ground beef and milk. Walking down the stairs, he froze. There was the cat—the neighbor's cat—slinking away from the shoe box. Licking his lips, licking his lips. There was blood smeared on his whiskers. And then his best friend Francis who lived across the vacant lot told him what to do.

"I like to draw," he finally said.

"What do you like to draw?" the woman asked pointedly.

"Animals. All kinds of animals."

"Really? I have to say I'm a little jealous. I can't draw a line. Would you show me some of your work? Can you make a little sketch for me?"

"I . . . I don't have a pencil. Or paper."

Mrs. Fleisher rummaged in her purse. "Here you are. A number two pencil. I sharpened it this morning. And paper. How about this?" She handed him the pencil and a folded piece of notepaper.

He held the objects in his lap and stared at them. "What should I draw?"

"Well," Mrs. Fleisher said, "draw what we both came to see. In front of us. You were looking at them, I saw you."

"In front of us?"

"Yes," Mrs. Fleisher said. "There. The sea lions. Draw the sea lions."

He nodded, licking the pencil tip with his tongue. Then he glanced at the pool. He began to make short marks while studying the creatures. Mrs. Fleisher smiled contentedly and averted her eyes from the paper in a seemingly proper way.

The sea lion pool was large. It stretched in a huge oval for twenty yards, an island of smooth stone slabs surrounded by a trench for swimming. At the moment the trench was nearly empty; the dozen sea lions gathered at the lowest point in the moat barked at the hose. They clapped their flippers, coughed, and thrust their noses into the spray. Jostling for position, shoving each other aside, they frolicked in the deepening pool of water. One of them barked and opened his mouth wide to allow the spray to shoot into his throat.

Mrs. Fleisher settled back on the bench. She breathed in

deeply the warm afternoon air and seemed content. In front of her passed a keeper and a maintenance man, both carrying steaming cups of coffee and smoking cigarettes. The clouds in the sky sailed above the zoo like a flotilla of tall masted ships. Mrs. Fleisher gazed at the gathering sea lions and she smiled again, amused at their antics.

The man's face flushed as he worked the pencil across the paper. He was *seeing* things again. They were coming back again! His vision began to cloud and flashes of sparks, like lightning, streaked across his retina. Pale images floated in the storm of his sight. Great foggy spirals coalesced into grossly distorted human shapes—faces, most of them, leering and scolding, disdainful and punitive. There was his mother, leaning down to look at the dead turtle in his little hands. She was covering her mouth to hide her horror. Then there was his second-grade teacher, coming forward angrily to snatch away the mousetrap that he had brought to show and tell. A look of absolute disgust was on her face as she grabbed the trap with the still wiggling mouse clamped securely in the spring, rivulets of blood seeping from its tiny ears. There was his father, laughing, jeering, as he bent down to examine the frog his son had skillfully steered his bicycle toward and flattened with the treads of both tires. The guts had spurted from the frog's mouth and a greenish bile spread a glistening glaze as the curious man and boy poked the mess with a stick. There was an aunt, an ancient aunt, screaming and shrieking as she backed away from her flower bed. He was holding up the king snake he had chopped with the hoe and he thrust it in her face to show the severed spinal cord and how it could do no harm to her now. There were other faces, dozens of them, that he saw reflected in the paper. Some were nameless, some were indistinct; but all of them clutched at his vision with a relentless grasp until the next face overpowered the hold and asserted another clamp. And in between all of them was a pale ascetic face that struggled for recognition, his lips working hard but never quite being heard. Francis screamed, trying to attract attention, but the vacant lot was too vacant and then he moved away.

In front of him a sea lion began to cough, shaking his head

from side to side. He sneezed once, twice, and a last time. His flippers began to tremble, beating the rising puddle of water. He rolled over and tried to sneeze again. The sea lion's head and neck were the first to become still. His chubby sleek chest was next, and then his tail went limp. His snout sank and the rising stream of water began to twist his inert body clockwise.

His companions began to nuzzle him, pushing their snouts against his belly, trying to move him. The pool was filling up; some of them dove under the limp body and jostled upward, toward the air.

One of the pack barked, snorted, and opened his mouth to play at the stream of water. Then he too began to sneeze, blinking his eyes and grunting.

"Don't you like the way they play?" Mrs. Fleisher remarked to her companion on the bench. "Are you about finished?"

"Almost." He painfully scratched a few more lines but the tip of the pencil snapped off.

"Is it done?" she asked. "Can I see it?"

"Here." He handed her the notepaper.

Mrs. Fleisher looked at the paper with great anticipation. She studied it carefully, pursing her lips in concentration. Something began to trouble her.

"Do you like it?"

"It's very unusual," Mrs. Fleisher said slowly. "But there's something I don't understand."

"There's nothing to understand about it," he almost snapped. "It's a drawing."

"These animals," Mrs. Fleisher said, pointing with her finger. She frowned. "All of them look like cats."

Mrs. Fleisher stared at the paper again but there was no way that she could fathom a sea lion from the scrawls. There were whiskers, true, but there were also oval faces and thin, slitlike eyes. Or were they eyes? It was hard to tell among the smudges, erasings, and jumbled squiggles. It was only because the man had given her the paper carefully that she kept from studying it upside down.

Suddenly there was a movement in front of them. The keeper

who had been talking with the maintenance man dropped his coffee cup. The brown liquid spilled over the walkway; the cup rolled away. The keeper began to run toward the sea lions.

"Maybe it's not meant to be representational," Mrs. Fleisher commented. She was thoroughly engrossed in the drawing.

The man sullenly shrugged. "They're sea lions," he muttered stubbornly. He looked at the keeper, who was leaning over the pool's railing and shouting something at the sea lions. Half of the pack was lying under the water, quite still. The rest were sneezing and turning erratic, slow-motion somersaults.

"They don't look very happy, do they?"

"Eh? What?" the man snapped.

"These animals," Mrs. Fleisher said, pointing at the drawing. She still studied it with a frown.

There was a distant scream, then several screams. They came from beyond the sea lion pool, across the plaza. Both Mrs. Fleisher and the man raised their heads and covered their eyes against the sun's glare.

From beyond the plaza a crowd of people streamed out of the cat house. Their shrill cries carried far across the grounds.

"What do you suppose is happening over there?" asked Mrs. Fleisher.

"I have no idea," he answered truthfully. He was just as puzzled.

"Really," Mrs. Fleisher said, quite exasperated. "I've been coming here ten years for the peace and quiet. But in the past few weeks this zoo has been unbearably noisy. Don't you agree?"

The man yelled. A roar of terror issued from his white face and he pointed with trembling fingers at his feet. A bantam cock pecked at his shoelaces, rapping its beak against the eyelets but only succeeding in attacking the cotton candy. The shoelaces danced and the man leaped to his feet. The bird fled at the disturbance and scrambled for safety under a juniper bush. "Did you see that?" the man gasped, pointing a terrified finger at the bush. The woman had not noticed and the renewed shouts of the crowd made him temporarily forget his attacker. He stared at the distant cat house.

"I think I'm going to register a complaint," Mrs. Fleisher said. Her patience was clearly exhausted as she pawed through her purse. "I'm going to go all the way this time, all the way to the top. What do *you* think, Mr.—" Mrs. Fleisher stopped. She found herself speaking to an empty seat. Her former companion was already across the plaza walking quickly toward the lion house. Mrs. Fleisher shrugged.

She searched for something to write on but there was only the piece of paper with the man's drawings. She turned it over and began laboriously to compose her message. She finished in a few moments and, wrapping her shawl around her shoulders, began to walk toward the director's office.

She knocked firmly on the office door and Harriet let her in.

"Yes?" Harriet asked. "What can I do for you?"

"I wish," Mrs. Fleisher said firmly, "to see the director."

"I'm afraid he's rather busy at the moment. Is it important?"

"Extremely," stated Mrs. Fleisher.

"Oh? What is it about? Maybe I can help."

"It's about ambience," Mrs. Fleisher said. "That's all I can say. I'll wait."

"He might be late. Perhaps if you left a message," suggested Harriet.

Mrs. Fleisher frowned and reached into her purse. She took out the piece of notepaper and disdainfully dropped it on Harriet's desk. With an aristocratic sniff of her nose, Mrs. Fleisher turned and left the office.

Harriet picked up the paper and read it. The handwriting was neat, the i's carefully dotted, and the loops meticulously closed.

To Whom It May Concern,

As a long-standing member of the Members' Society, I feel compelled to formally protest the recent deterioration of the zoo's ambience. While it has been my habit to make my afternoons here, if the current level of inconsiderate visitor noise is not properly controlled, I will be forced to regretfully withhold my dues.

In good conscience,

Mrs. Margaret R. Fleisher

Harriet laid the paper down and shook her head, smiling as she did so. Strange woman, she thought. Harriet folded the paper once, twice, and tossed it into the trash can. A corner of the paper was exposed on top, showing the whiskers of a thickly drawn face, catlike. Harriet didn't notice.

■ ■ ■

"Hold it a second." Steven cupped his hand over the telephone receiver and walked over to the door. He opened it with a foot and nodded quickly at Charlie.

"What's that?" Steven snapped into the phone. "Yeah. Okay, I'll wait." Steven propped the phone between his ear and shoulder as he rubbed the back of his head. "What time is it?" he asked Charlie.

"Three o'clock," Charlie said. "Who's on the phone?"

"Dr. Lewis. He's checking on the goddamn sea lions. Seven of them. Seven goddamn sea lions are dead."

"When?"

"An hour ago."

"When you were jumping the cop?"

Steven grimaced. "How'd you find out?"

Charlie shrugged. "I smell trouble. And this one smelled bad. Why'd you do it?"

"Go to hell, Charlie. I didn't know the bastard was a cop. He didn't tell me."

"You could have told him who you were."

"Look, I don't need—" Steven broke off his answer as he held the phone tighter. "Yeah?" he muttered. "What kind . . . When can you find out? . . . Yes . . . Call me." Steven slammed the phone down. His hands were white as he whirled to face his uncle. "Poisoned."

"What?"

"The sea lions were poisoned."

"How?"

"I don't know. The pool was being filled up. Dr. Lewis is just beginning the autopsies but his first guess is rat poison."

"Rat poison? The zoo doesn't—"

"That's right," Steven interrupted irritably. "The zoo doesn't use it. But *someone* does. Rat poison. Goddammit, you can walk into any hardware store in San Francisco—"

"So it's the same one, eh?"

"Who?"

"Our friend who did in the hippo."

"Yeah," Steven said bitterly. "The same one."

"I just came back from the hospital," Charlie said. "Checking on Gordon. I didn't tell him about the hippo."

"How is he?"

"Okay," Charlie said, shrugging. "He wanted me to drop by and see how things were."

"They're fine," Steven almost choked. "Just fine."

"So the police are on the job, eh?"

Steven gave him a dirty look. "We were at the wrong lions."

"It's not your fault," Charlie said. "You didn't know what the bastard was going to do."

"I did," Steven said. "He's been writing me letters. Telling me which animal he's going to murder next."

Charlie looked up in surprise. "He told you he was going to kill the sea lions?"

"In so many words," Steven admitted. "If I had just read them right."

"The guy's crazy. Screwed up in the head."

"I know," Steven said irritably. "I've known that for a long time."

"What you ought to do—"

"I know what your ideas are, Charlie. Pump him full of lead. Come on, let's go."

"Where?"

"The sea lion pool. I want to talk to the keeper, maybe he noticed something."

Both of them walked in silence. Charlie marched in long strides as if he were again exploring some stretch of the veldt. He kept his head high in constant motion, testing the wind direction, the scents, the length of shadows. Steven kept his head bent to the ground, lost in solitary gloom. Although he knew it wouldn't solve anything, he blamed himself for bungling the whole affair, from the death of the antelope to the sea lions. It had taken half an hour and a dozen phone calls to straighten out the undercover policeman mess. By the time he was told of the sea lion catastrophe he felt the familiar sick feeling in his stomach. The timing had been incredible. Steven buried his fists in his coat pocket and trudged alongside his uncle.

When they reached the empty sea lion pool, the keeper hurried to greet them. He looked about as miserable as Steven, twisting his hands nervously and biting his lips. When Steven told him that the vet suspected poisoning, the keeper gulped.

"Did you see anything, anything at all," Steven asked, "that was different? Anybody hanging around?"

"No," the keeper said. "We just went for a cup of coffee."

"How long were you gone?"

"Five minutes. Less than that. My God, if I'd any idea this would happen—"

Steven nodded and led the three of them into the water shed. The maintenance man was checking the cement pit holding the filtered water. He was flat on the floor, his long arm completely immersed and working at something near the screen. He grabbed what he was looking for and rose to his feet, arm dripping.

"What is it?" Steven asked.

"A bottle," he said. "I don't know how it got there."

"The sea lions were poisoned," the keeper blurted.

When the maintenance man heard the words, his hand began to shake and he almost dropped the bottle. Steven took it from him and examined it. He sniffed but there was no trace of an odor.

"Do you have a garbage bag?" Steven asked.

"Yes."

Steven dropped the bottle inside a sack and stuffed the small package in his pocket.

"Do you normally lock the door when you go out?" he asked slowly.

The man shook his head. "Never. I never had any reason to. I only lock it at night when I go home."

Steven bit his lips. "You'll have to reroute the sea lion water. Dump it. Get it out of the zoo. Assume it's totally contaminated. Tomorrow I'll get you some help to scrub out the pool."

"Right away."

"But this afternoon," Steven said loudly, "I want that door locked if you so much as stick your head outside. I want another fence put up around the shed. The door's going to be reinforced and more locks put on. You'll lock it every time you leave. Is that clear?"

"Yes."

"It's not your fault what happened to the sea lions," Steven said to the two men. "I don't want you to feel responsible."

"They're dead," the keeper blurted indignantly. "How are we supposed to feel? They're *dead.*"

Steven looked at him. The man was standing with his feet apart and his hands jerked nervously. His eyes were wide.

Without another word, Steven walked out of the shed. Charlie followed silently, a half-step behind. When they rounded the end of the pool, someone jumped in front of them to block the way.

"The *Chronicle.* I need an interview."

Steven looked up. In front of him was the same reporter that had started the mess with the hippo. "Get out of my way," Steven growled. He started to walk around the man.

"Sea lions," shouted the man. "What happened to the sea lions?"

"Nothing."

"What about the shooting in the lion house?"

"I don't know what you're talking about."

The man reached out a hand and grabbed Steven's elbow. "Goddammit, you were *there.*"

"Let go of my coat," Steven said coldly.

The reporter fumed. "Look," he snarled, "you're a city employee. Who do you think you are? The public's got a right to know what's going—"

"Let go of my coat," Steven repeated.

"Shooting," the reporter snapped. "Tell me about the goddamn—"

He cut his question short as he felt something tighten around his neck. It was his own collar. He began to feel himself leaving the ground. His arms dangled at his side and he gulped. There was empty air between his shoes and the asphalt. Slowly twisting, he was turned toward the man who had clasped his collar.

Charlie stared at the reporter, fixing his gaze on the man's bulging eyes. "You don't understand," Charlie said slowly.

"Let me down," gasped the reporter.

"In Burma. Do you know what we did with people like you in Burma?"

"No," said the reporter, violently shaking his head from side to side.

"Nobody knows," Charlie concluded sadly. "Because none of them ever came back."

"Are you threatening me?"

"No," Charlie said. "I'm not threatening you. I'm just holding you up by the scruff of your sorry neck. And shaking you, like this."

"Put him down, Charlie," Steven said.

The reporter was lowered to the ground. He loosened his collar and picked up the fallen notebook. "Who are you?"

"He's my uncle," Steven said. "He's sixty-four years old. He's not very polite."

The reporter was about to say something but changed his mind. He looked at both men and clamped his mouth shut. Stuffing the notebook in his pocket, he scurried across the plaza.

"Charlie," Steven said. "I want to talk to you about Gordon. Can you stick around?"

"Sure."

"I'm going over to the vet's for half an hour. Meet me at the office in thirty minutes?"

"I'll grab a beer. Thirty minutes."

Steven turned away and headed for the veterinarian's compound. Passing a phone booth made him pause as a nagging suspicion grew stronger. Calling information for a number, he dialed it with quick, impatient strokes.

"Yeah?" a bored woman's voice answered.

"Is Shacker there?" Steven asked.

"Maybe," the woman answered evasively. "Who's calling?"

"The Mayor's office," Steven lied without a pause.

"Just a sec, I'll wake him up."

"No, wait," Steven interrupted. "Don't wake him up."

"Do you want to talk to him or don't you?" the voice demanded.

"How long has he been sleeping? I just realized that he works at night and this is probably a bad time for—"

"He's been dead since noon in the trailer."

"You're sure of that?"

"What is this? A bed check? Do you want me to wake him up or not?"

"No," Steven said. "It can wait. Thanks."

"You're a real saint," the woman grunted, immediately breaking the connection.

So much for that, Steven muttered as he resumed his slouching march toward the vet's compound. He couldn't see any reason for the woman to lie and even if Shacker *had* poisoned the sea lions, the keepers would have recognized him in the area. Nobody could miss Shacker and his ugly ears.

Steven hung his head and trudged along the paths. Bantam roosters flocked around his shoes and pecked hopefully at the laces, but Steven ignored them. The image of the sea lions burned in his vision—the floating carcasses looking for all the world like waterlogged punching bags. Why hadn't he deciphered the note? It was so obvious now the way it led him off the track, confusing him with the insane puzzle. He should have solved the message, put extra guards around the sea lions. Something *could* have been done. Now he'd have to construct another lie about the sea lions' death, another lie to cover up the biggest deceit of all. For swooping down like an avenging angel over the wasteland of his nightmare, he was seized with the ugliest thought of all—that but for the killing, he agreed with the notes. He *agreed* with them. Damn it, he choked, clenching his fists tightly in his pockets. The words in the notes were *his* words. The concentration camp, the screams of imprisonment, the suffering. He had used them all before. Steven shuddered. If ever there was a time he needed a miracle more, he couldn't think of it.

■ ■ ■

Licking his lips, Charlie bought himself a large mug of beer and sat down at an umbrella-topped table. In front of him was the duck pond. A small flock of pintails, grebes, and ruddys competed with a school of golden carp for stray bits of floating popcorn. Charlie sipped his beer with a steadied, measured purpose—as if anticipating a doctor's threat ordering it to be his last. When he tipped the mug to drain the last bit of foam, a shadow fell beside the table and another mug was set before him. Charlie looked up.

"How about another beer?" the reporter asked with a grin.

"What do *you* want," Charlie said, ignoring the cup.

The reporter spread out his hands, as if to show his innocence. "I just want to buy you a beer."

"Why?"

"Because," the reporter said, sitting in a chair beside Charlie, "I've never been picked up like a sack of beans by a sixty-four-year-old man. How do you do it?"

Charlie grunted and eyed the beer. "Practice," he snorted.

The reporter smiled. "Natural foods? Yoga? Pumping iron? What's your secret?"

Charlie shrugged and tested a sip of foam. "I've been around the world seven times. Seen everything. Done everything. Picking up . . . picking up a sack of shit is nothing."

As if to prove his point, Charlie upended the mug and drained the reporter's beer in one gulp. His throat bobbed as the liquid poured through. He put the empty cup next to the first and belched.

The reporter smiled. He reached inside his coat and pulled out a worn, silver flask. Inside was a liquid of tawny color. "Have you been to Kentucky?" he asked, unscrewing the cap and pouring out two shipmaster's measures in the beer mugs. "They make a very good product over there. Purely medicinal. Cures a lot of things."

"Mud in yours," Charlie grunted, upending the mug for a second time.

"Here's to you," the reporter said, sipping his whisky slowly. "Tell me," he added, "a little about yourself. You sound like a man with a few adventures to tell. Ever thought about writing a book?"

Charlie grunted again. "Never bothered. But one time in Newfoundland—"

"Yes," the reporter said, pouring another shot of whisky. "Tell me about Newfoundland."

For fifteen minutes Charlie related a hair-raising story of being attacked by a rutting moose, being lost in the tundra, and living off raw salmon and sphagnum moss. A similar incident was next, involving an attack by hippos on a placid stream in the Cameroons.

"Was life as an animal collector always so dangerous?" asked the reporter, refilling Charlie's cup again.

"Hell, no. I've just had bad luck. Animal trapping's no more dangerous than a picnic. Just as long as you don't make stupid mistakes. Stupid mistakes, they'll do you in every time. Like running out of Spam."

"Then hippos aren't really dangerous?"

"Hell, no. Tamest beasts you'll find. Except when they're in rut. But anything's dangerous when they're in rut. Even if they're sixty-four."

"But hippos," the reporter said, keeping his voice apparently unconcerned. "Like for instance the hippo here at the zoo."

"What about him?"

"He wasn't dangerous? I mean, he wasn't crazy mad or anything? Was there anything about him that would make somebody feel angry?"

"No," Charlie said, wagging his head. He took another sip. "That hippo was a gentleman, a real gentleman. Beats hell out of me why anybody would want to kill him."

The reporter, who had been concentrating on watching the ducks, gave only a hint of his interest by flicking his eyes at the word Charlie used. He emptied the whisky bottle in Charlie's mug. "Maybe he had a reason to kill him," the reporter speculated. "Maybe the hippo bit your nephew or something, I don't know. I'm sure he must have had a good reason to kill him."

Charlie's face clouded. His words began to slur. "Steven? Steven didn't kill him. What are you talking about?"

"You said the hippo was killed."

"Yeah, by some weirdo with an apple full of razor blades. But Steven didn't have anything to do with it. He tried like hell to save him."

The reporter gulped, then nodded quickly.

"No," Charlie said. "Steven's in a helluva mess. Zoos. Zoos are a pain in the ass. Take these sea lions."

"The ones that died? We just had a few calls at the paper about them."

"Didn't die," Charlie whispered confidentially. *"Poisoned."*

"Poisoned?" the reporter repeated. This time he couldn't help gaping at Charlie. "How?"

"Same sonofabitch with the hippo. He threw some rat poison in the pipes refilling the pool."

The reporter consciously fought an urge to reach for his notebook. Instead, he tried quickly to think of some way to keep

Charlie talking. "What is Steven, I mean, your nephew, doing about it?"

Charlie looked at him with a trace of suspicion. "Don't worry about Steven. Worry about the sonofabitch who's murdering the animals. I can't talk anymore about it. Only told you this much because it's true."

"What's true?"

"Animals. Animals are stupid beasts. It's humans, people, you have to watch out for. They're the ones, all right. Talk about danger? Once in Rangoon, almost got poisoned myself. Bastard who worked behind the counter didn't sterilize his bar glasses and—"

"But the zoo—" the reporter interrupted. He couldn't afford to let Charlie wander off again. "Have the police been—"

"Police," Charlie grunted. "Steven can tell you about the police. He just had a run-in at the lion house."

"Who would want to murder animals here? I don't understand."

"I told you all there is to understand. The sonofabitch doesn't like to give chances. Damn coward. Wait until we catch him, see what kind of chances we'll give him. The same chance he gives the animals."

"What would you do?"

"Well," Charlie said, and stopped. He looked down at the table. A feeling that he had said too much clouded his features. "What time is it?"

The reporter checked his watch. "Fifteen minutes past four."

"Late," barked Charlie. "I'm late."

"That's right," another person agreed. The voice was cold and flat. The two men jerked in their seats.

"I waited for half an hour," Steven said, eying Charlie. "Then I decided to come looking for you." Why had Charlie done it? Why did he talk about it? Steven knew he should have made sure the reporter left the grounds. Now it was too late, unless Charlie hadn't told all of it.

"What's your comment, Director Cooper, on the reasons the killer poisoned the sea lions?"

Steven felt sick. Charlie had spilled everything. "You can't publish that story."

The reporter stood. "That's what you told me about the hippo. You seem to have a one-track mind."

"I do when it comes to protecting my animals."

"You didn't have much success with the sea lions, did you?"

"I'm working with the police. We are doing everything possible to control this situation. If you publish that story, it's going to kill this zoo. Literally *kill* it."

"Either way, I don't see much difference," the reporter said dryly. "The animals are dying anyway."

"You could have buried that hippo story in the back page; you didn't have to use that picture. But when you blow it up three columns wide, you're *creating* madness. Can't you see that? You're planting seeds of madness. It's going to put the idea in that many more heads. Someone is killing my animals—don't make the *Chronicle* an accomplice."

"Sorry," the reporter said. "But I smell a lot of bullshit around here. That argument stinks and I'm sick of it. If there's a hijack, I'm going to report it. Same as a bomb threat. These things happen. This is a *real* world. And it's people like you who want to cover it up and keep everybody ignorant and happy that are living the fantasy. I don't put my ideas in anybody's head. I just tell them it's a real world out there, with real guns and real bombs and real murders and they better look at it. It's not going to go away by closing your eyes. You have your job—I have mine."

"Get out of here," Steven growled. "Both of you."

Charlie stood. He staggered and blinked his eyes. Then he cleared his throat. "I'm trying to help," he said. "Somebody has to do something."

Mrs. Richards tapped gently on the door of 4B. After a pause, she rapped harder and waited. The longer she stood, the more horrible the hall smelled. She frowned.

"Hello?" she said, aiming her greeting through the peephole. No answer. Mrs. Richards didn't know what to do. In the last week alone three separate tenants had complained about the smell. Disgusting, they had said, go there and smell for yourself. Mrs. Richards had checked and it was true; the odor was coming out of 4B and seeping through the hall. Even from the floor below you could hardly help but gasp.

In her mind flashed bits of television news broadcasts, the announcer detailing discoveries of gross suicides by recluses in apartment houses. Dead with no warning, with no friends, no mail, no telephone calls, just an unbearable smell that finally forced the superintendent to investigate. She shivered.

"*Hello?*" Mrs. Richards repeated, much louder. She rapped hard on the door with her key chain. Silence. Mrs. Richards wondered if she should call the police. But what if it was unnecessary and the other tenants saw them crashing through the door? The building had a reputation to uphold. Perhaps if she just took a quick look around inside. Normally she didn't use her passkey unless she was sure the person wouldn't be coming back for a while. But the smell, the smell was extraordinary.

Mrs. Richards knocked once more, as if to legitimize her decision. Then she eased the master key into the lock and turned. The door opened easily and she peered inside. It was dim but the darkness made the smell seem even more intense. The odor was horrible, a rich stench of decay and ammonia. Fetid and dank. Mrs. Richards coughed.

"Hello?" she asked without much hope. Only a musty silence

answered her. She could make out vague shapes in the kitchen—a humming refrigerator, a dark stove with four pale violet pilot lights glowing in the corner. Her footsteps clicked on the linoleum. Overgrown weeds in aquariums gave off a wretched stink. She passed an empty closet with unused brooms leaning inside.

At the short hallway connecting the kitchen to the living room, the smell became stronger. She gagged. The air was dead, heavy and thick, pungent like a rotting bed of amanita mushrooms.

A layer of white bird dung completely covered every square inch of the living room. It reflected a pale yellow glow like an arctic ice floe. Mrs. Richards sucked in her breath in an involuntary gasp but immediately regretted it as her throat began to burn.

"God almighty!" she cried. "Will you look at my couch!"

The naugahyde couch, the two Danish stick chairs, the imitation maple coffee table, all were covered with the foul-smelling excrement. Mrs. Richards wavered as she walked further into the room; it was all she could do to keep from bursting into tears. What caused this, she murmured to herself, who on earth would do such a filthy thing? She felt weak. Her head scanned the room, rotating as if on a fixed track. Then she heard the cries.

They were low at first, faint murmurs. But as Mrs. Richards's shoes squished through the muck, the cries grew as if awakened. Mrs. Richards frowned and cocked her head. The murmurs increased. Now they were plaintive, high-pitched whimpers. They came from the far wall.

She walked across the room and saw them, the cages stacked by the wall. Four of the kittens had died. Their stiffened bodies, shrunken and dried, lay on the wire racks of the bird cages like forgotten biscuits. One of them had stretched out his paw through the space between the wires in a vain attempt to reach out. In death, the tiny twig of a paw stuck out with a desiccated, withered hope. A fly worked its way over the footpad and Mrs. Richards recognized the calico kitten as the one she had found in the street looking so hopeless and so lost.

The rest of the cats were barely hanging on to life. Only their pitiful whimpers set them apart from their stiff companions. One kitten was grossly swollen; her bloated belly puffed up with an accumulation of gas until her pink skin could be seen between the matted tufts of fur. Her grey tongue lolled from a set of grey gums.

Mrs. Richards felt weaker. Her knees failed and she reached out to steady herself on the sticky back of a filthy chair. She closed her eyes and worked her lips in silent prayer. It was during this muted supplication that she heard the kitchen door open and something strike the linoleum floor.

Mrs. Richards's eyes fluttered open. Had she really heard the door? The footsteps had sounded once, twice, and then stopped. She tried to remember, had she left the door open or not? Could the sound have been another door down the hall? But the footsteps . . . She strained to listen, focusing all her powers trained by years of being a landlady. But there was no more sound.

Mrs. Richards shivered again. The tingling wave passed across her flesh like a convulsion. Her eyes blinked furiously; the pattern of the bird cages filled with starving kittens flashed across her retina in a blinding stab of horror. Her legs wobbled and she pressed her knees together to keep them from buckling. When a kitten whimpered unexpectedly, she jerked and the small chair toppled over, falling with a smart crack on the floor. Mrs. Richards groaned. She felt her chest heave as her heart pumped what seemed like streams of ice through her arteries. Her breath was coming now in great gulps.

It must have been the door down the hall in 4C, Mrs. Richards thought. She wished very hard that it was 4C and she finally began to believe it. Slowly, very slowly, she eased out of her frozen position. Still on guard for the slightest sound, she ever so slowly crept toward the kitchen.

She reached the dividing hallway. Three more steps and she would be in the kitchen. Mrs. Richards took a deep breath and tiptoed into the dim room.

"There!" Mrs. Richards breathed a sigh of relief that fled from parched lips. Nobody! The kitchen was empty. The door was open and it was 4C after all. She ran toward the door, thankful for her answered prayers.

■■ ■■ ■■

A man buried his head in the collar of his coat as he crept up the stairs. His feet silently brushed against the treads. He purposefully used the extreme side where it didn't creak because the pesky landlady was always spying on his comings and goings.

He reached the fourth floor and took out his key. Inserting it into the lock he was astonished to find that it turned easily. He frowned. He never left his apartment without locking the door. Lifting his sunglasses, he stared at the keyhole. Didn't I lock it? I must be going crazy, he laughed to himself harmlessly. A mistake like this—he shuddered when he considered.

He pushed open the door and took three steps into his kitchen before he stopped. *Wrong!* There was something awfully wrong. He stood still, straining his ears to listen.

The kittens, his little kittens, were stirring but they should be sleeping for good and very still by this time. But there was something else; something else was wrong. He shivered. The tiny hairs on the back of his neck stiffened and rose. An uncanny sense was warning him of something. But what was it?

Suddenly there was a muted breath of air, like a gasp, and then a sharp smack—like a chair falling over. The silence that followed was dead, heavy and dead. He shivered again. The sound had come from the living room and there could be no doubt now. A sense of dread seeped into his mind; his face became cold and dry. He felt as if he had been violated. Someone had trespassed and violated his privacy. Someone was in his living room touching—*touching* his things. He fought back an urge to retch. It was inconceivable that another person could be only feet away and looking at his things. God almighty, he murmured under his breath, those are my private things. Who could do such a thing?

Then the blood rushed into his face, the warm blood. It heated his flesh as the full consequences of the violation were realized. If somebody was looking at his things, then they could look into him. His sunglasses were no protection. Nothing could ever be concealed again after they gained the power. His knees felt weak. His arms trembled as the overwhelming sense of nakedness shuddered his body.

He blinked, took in several deep breaths, and realized that he must do something. He stretched out his hand toward the nearest drawer and silently, slowly, pulled it open. His fingers slipped over the cool hickory handle and they gripped tightly.

The blade sparkled when it first exposed itself. The polished stainless steel collected every stray particle of light and shot it back, gleaming. He pulled further.

A final tug and the carving knife sprang free. It was alive! It swung in the darkness like a glowing force, an extra long Henckels blade, Solingen steel, designed for replacing a cleaver when light weight and sharper penetration were needed. He hefted the steel to remember its balance. Then he began to slide his feet lightly across the linoleum. When he passed the closet with the curtain strung on a rope across the opening, he slipped inside and waited. He raised the knife above his head, pointed the tip beyond the curtain, and waited.

For five minutes there was no sound. Only the occasional cough of a car's engine struggling up a hill made its way into the kitchen. The knife eased down. But when someone's footsteps pattered, the blade jerked to attention and his breath came in short, uncontrollable spurts.

Mrs. Richards poked her head into the kitchen and let loose a sigh of heartfelt relief. She briefly crossed herself and murmured another prayer of thanks. She began to walk.

Just before she reached the closet, she paused for some unexplainable reason. She heard a sound. A peculiar sound like a rustle. A fluttering kind of sound, a beating of something in motion. Then Mrs. Richards moved forward, in front of the closet. Her sleeve brushed against the blanket. The sound rose louder.

She screamed! The sound, which had been growing louder, suddenly exploded around her head. The air above her hair cracked and thundered, swirling in cyclonic windstorms.

A swarm of flying bodies turned the corner of the kitchen and aimed their packed flock toward the open door. The barrier of Mrs. Richards's head confused them at first. In the wavering instant of indecision they flapped their wings about her hair. The parrots extended their claws, dug into Mrs. Richards's hair and yanked, yanked. She screamed again and the parrots clawed at the blanket. Long tail feathers fluttered to the floor, bright scarlet and iridescent green. The powerful beak of the macaw clamped the blanket and began to grind. The noise was deafening. Shrieks issued from every throat as the birds' collective hysteria unleashed itself in fury.

Mrs. Richards's hands rose above her shoulders, trying to protect herself from the onslaught. Her waving fingers further confused the birds. They slashed at her arms, trying to regroup in another attempt toward the kitchen door. Mrs. Richards uttered a piercing scream.

Inside the closet, muttering with a fury all his own, the man struggled. His carving knife still rose in the air, the tip pointing at the carotid artery in Mrs. Richards's neck. As she jerked, the blade jerked to follow.

The man was apoplectic. His arm muscles screamed for permission to plunge the blade into her neck. Her fat white neck was inches away. Only the blanket was between her and a just punishment for her crime. The blade quivered in anticipation of the thrust.

But the birds! He had heard them like a mother hears her children, with a supernatural sixth sense. He heard them take off from the beam in the living room and round the corner into the kitchen. At the same time he realized that the kitchen door was open. He stifled a cry.

He might hurt one of his children. He twisted into a hundred positions in the cramped closet, trying to find a path to the landlady's neck. She was screaming. It irritated him. Not so much because it made her movements erratic, but rather because he knew it alarmed his children and confused them. He wished she would stop. The more she screamed, the more his children flapped their wings and cried.

There was a pause. Mrs. Richards froze. The man's arm rose high in the air. He plunged the knife and Mrs. Richards screamed.

The landlady howled. The birds parted and she could see the beckoning door! She dashed for it. She was deaf to the sound of ripping cloth behind her, the sound of tearing threads.

Mrs. Richards and the birds made the hallway at the same time. She immediately fled down, toward her apartment, while the flock rose high, up the stairwell. The sounds of her thick shoes hitting the stairs thundered through the building.

The man emerged from the closet, shaking. His face was livid. His hands trembled. Everything was gone. He looked around the dim kitchen to find a silence more empty than any he had ever known. His birds were gone. The dry carving knife slipped from his sweating fingers and clattered to the floor.

▪ ▪ ▪

Steven's hands touched the television switch as if it might have the power to electrocute him. When the wavering image of the Mayor appeared on the screen, the effect of electric execution was complete. The reporters' microphones were thrust at the Mayor like primitive stakes cornering a fearful beast. The Mayor fought for dignity, unleashing his attack with honorable outrage bravely controlled.

A steely-voiced woman reporter raced ahead of the pack. "What's your comment on this morning's *Chronicle* report on the zoo?"

The Mayor scratched his chin. "I found it most disturbing, as did I'm sure all the people of San Francisco."

"Do you think it's true that there's a killer loose at the zoo?"

"I have no way of answering that."

"But the article quotes an interview with Lieutenant Tadich of the police department. He gave the *Chronicle* copies of drawings made by the killer."

"I have every confidence in the ability of the police department to handle any crisis situation."

"How much confidence do you have in the zoo's director?"

"Less," the Mayor said, arching his eyebrows to make his point.

"Crisis." The woman picked up the word. "What do you mean by a crisis situation?"

The Mayor stirred and warmed to the question. He searched for the woman's face and made a note of her. If in the future he ever wanted to leak something, she would definitely be the most promising sponge. "I'm talking about an emergency, something that's been building up for years. Something that the people of San Francisco have been cheated from. And that is their right to a first-class zoo; one that's run efficiently. The present management has allowed the zoo to deteriorate, to lapse into fiscal mismanagement, and to lapse into its duty to . . . to the children especially of San Francisco." There, the Mayor paused, thinking rapidly. Did he leave anything out?

"What evidence do you have?"

The Mayor furrowed his brow and assumed a grave tone. "What more evidence do you need than the dead animals? What were they?"

"Sea lions and a hippopotamus."

"Sea lions, hippopotamus," the Mayor continued without breaking stride. "What's next? What other precious animal is next? An elephant? A gorilla? A giraffe?" The Mayor paused. Those were just about all the animals he knew and since he hadn't been to the zoo in twenty years, he wasn't even sure he should have mentioned the gorilla. Did the zoo have a gorilla? He decided to have his secretary check on that.

"What steps are you going to take?"

The Mayor looked shocked. "Whatever is necessary will be done. My advisers have been looking into the overall situation for a long time. An extremely long time, I might add. I have stressed over and over again to the elder Mr. Cooper that he would have to tighten his belt on zoo budgets."

"Yeah, but what are you going to do?"

"Fiscal responsibility," the Mayor said, slapping his hand into his palm forcefully. "I want to see more cost-effectiveness. Why should the taxpayers of San Francisco continue to pour in money for more animals when the zoo can't even take care of the ones they have? Pure irresponsibility."

"Are you going to announce your plans at the next Council meeting?"

"Why not here? First—" the Mayor jabbed a finger into the air—"I want to limit the powers of the zoo's director to squander his budget. Second, I'm going to propose the formation of a committee to control the awarding of construction and maintenance contracts integral to the zoo's operations. In my office we already have a list of contractors willing to bid for such services. I've worked with these men before; they are all honorable men. Third—" The finger jabbed again in the air—"I've been in contact with a consultant on public theme parks, Mr. Curt Shacker, who operates an amusement concession next to the zoo. He has expressed a willingness to expand his operation and donate his expertise in these matters for the benefit of the people of San Francisco. I need hardly add that his experience would greatly aid in balancing the zoo's budget with the addition of more facilities for the public. Income-generating facilities, I may add."

"You mean more rides?"

The Mayor spread out his hands. "Whatever the people want. Whatever they decide. After all, it's in their own best interest."

"You're talking about expanding the zoo?"

The Mayor continued heatedly. "Not in so many words. Expansion, yes. Expansion of the land's true tax-generating potential. I would like to see it shoulder more of the city's burden. I want to see it carry more weight. As to *actual* expansion—the land the zoo sits on is very choice property. Some of it is ocean-front. Might it not be wiser to relocate some of the animals to a less expensive area? The savings realized would be enormous and I really think the animals would be much happier down the coast somewhere. Somewhere in the hills. More natural down there, lots of trees and things."

"Thank you, Mr. Mayor."

"Thank you, ladies and gentlemen of the press. Thank *you*."

Steven flicked off the television. The Mayor's beaming face wagged from side to side, exuding a patriarchal radiance. But the smile faded then; the lips curled into a distorted leer. His face collapsed in shallow greys that washed his pale afterimage like a charcoal sketch left in the rain.

Collapsing himself into his cottage horsehair couch, Steven stared at the blank screen. His head dropped to his lap, dissolving again into painful half-sleep.

The evening news broadcast had done it again, making him just as sick in his stomach as the morning's newspaper had made him nauseous. The new article in the *Chronicle*'s vendetta had confirmed Steven's worst fears of Charlie's loose tongue. The glaring headlines exposed the killer's methods of operation to every newsstand in the Bay Area. The reporter had even tracked down Lieutenant Tadich, who released a copy of the drawing on the last letter.

All morning the reporters had descended on the office like a plague, camping outside the trailer with their film units like mounts before a fox hunt. It *was* a hunt, and Steven was the prey.

The switchboard lighted up all morning with incoming calls; Harriet's hands were wrapped in spaghetti cords at the ancient terminal board that Gordon couldn't afford to modernize. She had drawn the curtains to keep people from staring inside but the incessant knocking at the door kept her usually calm face scowling.

Before noon, Steven couldn't stand it any longer. He threw a coat over his head, told Harriet to walk out the front door as a diversion, and he dashed out the side exit. He ran like a criminal across the crowded zoo grounds and slipped into the cottage among the quiet eucalyptus. He kept in touch with Harriet by phone but there was nothing much to discuss. The business of the zoo had ground to a halt. The keepers had retreated close-lipped under the reporters' barrage; they avoided Steven's office. The creditors and contractors had ceased their clamoring, as if they knew which side the odds favored, and readdressed their schemes to the office of the Mayor.

And Steven waited in his cottage, exiled like a pariah. Running home across the grounds, the visitors had recognized his face and pointed with accusing fingers. Only the keepers, silent and tense, communicated their loyalty with grim eyes.

He made lunch and stared at it in disgust before pushing it back untouched. Sleep was no better. He rolled and tossed on the couch with a layer of sweat breaking out in icy shivers.

As he watched the Mayor's press conference, he realized that the cover-up had been an impossible idea, doomed from the start. It was just too big. He couldn't blame Charlie for spilling the story, too many people knew bits and pieces and all it took was someone to round them up. Steven couldn't have hoped to keep a lid on it forever. His only chance had been to catch the killer before someone dragged the deaths into the open. He tried to nod off in another fitful attempt at a nap when the rock hit the door.

Steven jerked upright, immediately alert. The stone was still clattering against the wood as his face turned grim. He leaped from the couch and ran across the room. Flinging the door open, he stared at the porch railing and stopped short.

"I figured," Amanda said, "that you wouldn't answer a knock."

She perched on the railing, resting her back on a corner post and dangling her legs wearily. Her shoes had been kicked off and her socks drooped limply. "I'm beat. Fourteen tramloads and you wouldn't believe the crowds." She pursed her lips and blew upward to remove a strand of damp hair irritating her eyes. "My feet . . . are not feet anymore."

Steven nodded, still standing at the door. "I thought tonight was your dance class."

"It is."

Steven leaned against the doorframe and stared at her. She gazed up at the eucalyptus trees where the tall crowns still caught the blazing setting sunlight and reflected it down like a golden flush into her face. The zoo was quiet. The visitors had left long ago and only an occasional screeching hoot or muted trumpet drifted through the cottage forest.

"You don't look so good," Amanda said to him. She stated the fact casually, examining her toes and wiggling to resume the circulation.

"The zoo," Steven began. "A lot of things are—"

"Not tonight." She broke through his attempted explanation. "Not tonight. Tonight you're not going to think about a god-damn thing."

Steven dropped his eyes. He felt the cottage behind his back, the ridges of the cedar shingles and the angle of the window frame. His head rose and his eyes slowly passed over the red-wood planking of the porch and settled on the figure now strad-ling the fence beam with her knees bent and arms wrapped around her ankles. She leaned her chin on her knees, watching the last rays of the sun battle the eucalyptus.

"I brought a bottle of cheap wine," she said. "And the last four hot dogs the wagon had. You'll like them, they're burned."

Steven saw a struggling sea breeze flap her blue-and-gold uni-form windbreaker. Her checkered shirt had a button loose and a glimpse of bronze tanned belly flashed through. The sea breeze surged again and held; Amanda's long auburn hair shivered and danced across the redwood post. He didn't know why he was staring at her. All he knew was that he couldn't stop.

"I think the wallaby's pregnant again," she said through locked knees. "At least it looked like that from the tram."

Steven nodded, resting against the wall. A minute passed and he straightened up. Taking slow steps, he crossed the porch and stood by Amanda. She looked up, still holding her knees to-gether, and stared back. Steven bent down and kissed her.

He smelled the sweat above her lips and he swore he could smell each exhibit she had passed on the tram. But the smells were familiar, he had grown up with them and they evoked a thousand memories, good memories. That was what made it so strange, Steven thought. The smells, the memories, the familiarity—but they drifted from this woman he had known for less than a month.

"I have to leave soon," Amanda said slowly. She stared up at him, the look in her face searching more intently than ever. "The movie I told you about? My agent told me this morning they speeded up the schedule. I only have a week left."

"I need you," Steven said.

Amanda lowered her eyes. She rested her chin again on her knees but faced out, toward the zoo. As Steven's hands found her hair and stroked gently, she stared at the eucalyptus.

■ ■ ■

Steven rolled over and the ticking of his watch raised an eyelid. Five o'clock in the morning. Steven rolled over again but this time a black hairy hand pushed him back. A series of grumpy snorts snuffled from a curled-up ball of fur and Steven scowled. Lifting his foot, he not so gently shoved the sleep-elastic chimpanzee away from its nest between Amanda's breasts and toward the foot of the bed. Mr. Roberts grumbled, but kept his eyes tightly locked in sleep. His chubby pink palms lingered across Amanda's belly and traced a drowsy pattern down her thighs before Steven's heel firmly wedged his bald behind against the bedframe. Steven frowned. Not taking any chances, he stuffed a blanket around the chimp to keep him from crawling back.

Leaning over, he kissed Amanda's eyelid. "Wake up," he said.

Amanda groaned. "Why did you move away just now? I was just getting comfortable.

"Wake up," he repeated softly.

"Why?"

"I want to show you something."

Amanda groaned again. "What time is it?"

"Do you want to see it or don't you?"

She opened one eye but immediately shut it. "It's dark," she said. "Don't talk dark to me. Talk to me sunshine. Okay?"

Through one cracked eyelid, Amanda watched Steven get out of bed and slip on a bathrobe. He put his feet into a pair of moth-eaten slippers and Amanda opened both eyes. "What do you want me to see?" she asked curiously.

"Suppose you find out."

"Give me a hint."

"It's outside," Steven said. "And very noisy."

"That's not much of a hint."

"You're not much of a guesser. Are you coming?"

Amanda groaned again and Steven threw her a spare bathrobe. She found another pair of slippers and scooped up Mr. Roberts. The chimp wrapped his arms around her shoulders and snuffled happily.

"You can leave him," Steven said.

"Not on your life. This is the second time I've found him stuffed in a crack at the foot of the bed and he must have been lonely there all night."

The mist was rising in the hour before dawn. Steven picked his way through the dark shapes for a couple of hundred yards and then stopped.

"Where are we?" Amanda asked. She rocked Mr. Roberts back to sleep on her shoulders and strained her eyes into the blackness. "What do we do now?"

"We wait," Steven said.

Amanda shifted her feet, peering intently at the strange forms now beginning to shift from black to purple. She knew they were in front of a cage, a large and tall one, but the walk through the gloomy mist had completely disoriented her. She leaned against a rail like Steven and like him, stared forward patiently. For over half an hour they remained silent, shifting their feet and waiting, one expectant, one bewildered, and one snoring with a grunting contentment.

Just before dawn the gibbons began their howl.

Amanda snapped open her eyes and Mr. Roberts stirred awake. Steven stared into the flight cage. At first it was the old female who began with a series of low guttural urgings. She stood in front of the head male and expanded her throat sac, wailing impatiently. The male blinked his eyes and stood. Though less than a yard tall, his arms spread outward twice his body length. He whooped.

Amanda jerked back, startled. Steven smiled and Mr. Roberts's jaw dropped.

The whoop grew into a whoop-whoop and then a series of screams and calls issued forth as the chorus rose in a shattering cacophony. The entire pack was now awake. The male called again and the pack answered. More than a dozen gibbons were now screaming through straining lungs and the leader vanished.

Effortlessly, he snaked an arm toward a bar and took flight. He ascended the ropes like a spider dancing over a web and he flew. The pack left the ground in unison like a graceful flock of teal. Their throat sacs expanded like grapefruit and the whoop-whooping boomed with furious intensity.

It had always been the gibbons that for Steven started mornings. Without their tremendous howls, there was no signal, no division of weeks into days.

"What are they doing?" Amanda yelled above the roarings.

Steven cupped his hands over his mouth and shouted back, "They're raising the sun."

"What?"

"The sun," Steven yelled. "It's their job to get it up."

"What?" Amanda repeated. "I don't—"

"There!" Steven shouted.

He lifted an arm and pointed to the east. The first wedge of the sun peeped over the horizon and the gibbons boomed with earth-shuddering intensity. They circled madly at the top of the cage, brachiating wildly among the ropes and suspended tires.

When the sun finally eased its width into the sky, the leader boomed a last whoop-whoop-WHOOP and descended the ropes with the swagger of a difficult task competently done. One by one the rest of the pack quit their calls and joined the leader on the floor of the cage to await their payment.

Steven grinned as Amanda stared in disbelief. She was about to say something when a movement at the edge of the cage caught her eye. She huddled closer to Steven, gathering Mr. Roberts in her arms.

"I think somone's watching us," she warned in a low voice.

Steven glanced up and waved at the figure standing silently by the wire screen.

"It's the keeper," Steven said to Amanda. "Do you want to talk with him?"

"Talk?" Amanda gasped. "Will you look at me? All I have on is a bathrobe."

"If you haven't noticed, so do I."

"But it's your zoo," she hissed. "I'm going back for my clothes."

"Suit yourself," Steven said, grinning. "Say hello to everyone on your way." He gestured with his head at the path back to the cottage. Amanda looked and saw a line of keepers ambling along the asphalt track. They were sipping cups of coffee and trying hard to keep straight faces.

After an agonizing moment of indecision, Amanda hurried toward Steven and joined him with a scowl. She pulled the bathrobe tighter around her neck and held the chimpanzee formally in front of her face.

Steven led Amanda down the paths and trails. Their bare ankles flashed beneath the flapping robes and Mr. Roberts climbed on Amanda's shoulders and beat his chest with clenched fists.

And Steven followed the paths as he had once followed Gordon in the traditional morning walk to inspect the grounds. As Steven greeted the keepers and exchanged words of advice, Amanda gradually relaxed. She lowered the chimp in front of her face and smiled. She threw back her head, ran her fingers quickly through her hair, and began to listen.

■ ■ ■

Steven bent down and flicked the intercom button. "Yes?" he muttered. Amanda was just leaving for the first tram tour.

"Gordon just called," Harriet said.

"Why didn't you connect me?"

"He wanted to leave a message."

"Yes?"

"He wants to see you. As soon as you can get down there."

Steven checked his watch. "Visiting hours don't start until noon."

"I'm just telling you the message. He said as soon as you can get down there."

"Did he sound okay?"

"He sounded fine," Harriet said. "Just fine."

"Thanks."

"Steven?" Harriet added. "The mailman just dropped the morning batch. Do you want me to sort it?"

"No. Bring it in, will you?"

Steven walked to the door connecting the two offices and Harriet handed him the large canvas sack. While he was sorting through the pile, Amanda came over and watched.

Steven noticed her hand reach into the bottom of the pile and pluck out a familiar-sized envelope. He froze and stared at the letter.

"Give it to me."

"Here," she said, passing it over.

Steven held it in his hands, cradling it as if it could explode at any moment.

"Are you going to call Lieutenant Tadich?"

"To hell with Lieutenant Tadich," Steven said. He ripped open the envelope. A thick sheet of paper, folded once, fell out and slowly began to rise from its single crease. Their heads nearly cracked together as they leaned over the desk to read the handwriting.

Direktor,
    One of your hunters and spies found my nest and fouled it with her filthy human smell. I had to abandon it. I fouled the sea lions' home to warn you. Why do you continue to imprison the creatures of this earth? Where is your sense of justice? Why are you forcing me to take action, to liberate my brothers and sisters from your torture and your sick experimentation?

—A Freedom Fighter

PS If you were betrayed by your only brother, wouldn't you cry for the comfort of the moon?

They finished reading and their heads rose at the same time.
    "What does he mean about one of the hunters and spies?" Amanda asked. "Do you think the police caught him?"
    "They would have told me if they knew something. At least I think they would."
    "Unless," Amanda said, "they don't want him caught."
    "What do you mean?"
    "The longer this killer is free, the more pressure you're under. The Mayor knows that; that's why he didn't criticize the police. After all, it's none of the good people of San Francisco being murdered and avoiding taxes."
    Steven quickly scanned the note again. "He admitted he poisoned the sea lions. Every letter follows the same damn formula. He's taunting me. Pushing me. Almost as if—"
    "As if he wants to be caught," Amanda finished the sentence for him.
    Steven pointed at the postscript and read aloud. " 'If you were betrayed by your only brother, wouldn't you cry for the comfort of the moon?' "
    "Who betrayed him?" Amanda asked. "How could anyone like that have a brother?"
    "He's talking about the next animal he's going to kill. He's not talking about himself."

"What about crying for the moon? What's that? It sounds like bats. Do you have bats?"

"No." Steven rubbed the back of his neck and stared at the wording. "I can't think. The answer is *there*. Every other time he told me."

"What are you going to do?"

Steven slipped the letter into a manila folder and put it in his pocket. "I've got to see Gordon. I can't think anymore."

Outside, Steven strode across the plaza toward the main gates and stared at the packed crowds. He was the only one walking against the flow and he had to dodge and weave. Steven studied their faces. They were wide-eyed, curious, hesitant in their footing. Steven wondered why they descended upon the zoo. Was it morbid curiosity? Had the newspaper articles jolted them out of the habits of marching to football games and ossifying in front of television sets? Had the zoo suddenly become a hot ticket? Steven turned up his coat collar and walked faster toward the parking lot. He couldn't help but look at each face he passed to match it against what he imagined a killer to be.

He drove across town to the hospital with sweat on his hands. The words rang in his head. If you were betrayed by your only brother, wouldn't you cry for the comfort of the moon?

■ ■ ■

Gordon sat up in bed and Steven was amazed at how swiftly he was recovering. The tone in his flesh had returned. His eyes were strong and he moved his hands in the old familiar ways. Steven smiled to himself as he recognized the feistiness. His father was back.

"So what are you staring at?" Gordon's voice rasped. "Haven't you seen a sick person before?"

"Having a heart attack isn't just being sick."

"I don't see much difference. They still stick things in you."

"How do you feel?"

"Sick."

"You're looking better," Steven said.

"Is that supposed to make me feel better? It doesn't. All it does is remind me when I didn't look good. You've got a lot to learn about visiting people in hospitals."

"Sorry," Steven said. "You look terrible."

"This place is a goddamn institution," Gordon complained. "They have me on a *feeding* schedule, Steven. Zoo food. Orange juice at noon, boiled beef at twelve-thirty, calcium-fortified milk at three. At four I get recreation—some volunteer from Pacific Heights comes in and plays Parcheesi for an hour."

"Do you win?"

"I don't know a tinker's damn how to play Parcheesi. I just move things around on the board but she won't let on that *she* knows I don't know. It would crack her face. Of course I win. When we first started I told her I'd have a heart attack if I ever lost. She said that was okay but in that case we wouldn't play for money."

"And what did you say?"

"I said okay, no money. Let's play for my life."

"I don't think that's very funny."

"Neither did she. You never saw someone lose games so fast."

Steven grinned. "It's good to see you."

Gordon asked the question for which he had summoned his son to the hospital. "How is the zoo?"

"It's still there," Steven said offhandedly. He tried to sound a little surprised, as if the question was unnecessary.

"The elephants okay? Keeping them out of must?"

"Elephants okay," Steven said.

"Checking the heater in the hummingbird house? The thermostat's okay?"

Gordon continued without a pause. "Hippo's still flapping shit all over the cage with his propeller tail?"

Steven took in a breath. The old man was watching him closely. Too closely, Steven decided.

"Before you answer," Gordon said, licking his dry lips, "could you get my glasses? They're in that drawer over there."

"Sure," Steven said, grateful for the delay. It would give him time to think of an answer. He walked over to the nightstand and slid open the drawer. The glasses were in plain sight, resting over a copy of the *Chronicle*.

"Someone," Gordon growled, "forgot to tell the Parcheesi lady."

Over. Everything was over. Steven looked at his father. Gordon's face started to color as hot blood filled his cheeks. His lips were tight, his teeth were exposed to the canines.

"*WOLF!*" Steven yelled.

Gordon snapped his mouth shut in surprise. His eyes blinked as he cocked his head toward his son.

"*Wolf,*" Steven shouted again. He jumped on the balls of his feet. "How could I be so stupid?"

"Take it easy," Gordon muttered, eying Steven nervously.

But Steven was heading away from the bed. Gordon fell back on his pillow, stunned, and watched his son jerk open the door. Steven vanished, running down the hall. Gordon shook his head, muttering again.

When Steven reached the hall, he increased his speed and sprinted to the elevator. He pounded on the call button, beating the plastic disk with his fist. *Wolves.* They had exhibited a wolf pack for six years now. Timber wolves. One prime male and seven females.

Betrayed. Betrayed by domesticated dogs, their only brother. So easy, so plain.

Steven swore at the elevator and ran to the emergency stairs. He flew down the steps four at a time, almost breaking his legs. The other animals had been killed right after he received the letters. Was there time? He had to get back in time.

◼ ◼ ◼

Lieutenant Tadich pressed the manager's buzzer of the apartment house on Lombard Street. As he waited, his head rose and he counted the number of floors in his usual habit. Four. There was no answer and he tried the hall door. Open.

Scanning the list of names on the mailboxes, he searched for the manager's. Mrs. Richards. Tadich stepped inside the hallway and held the door open for the evidence detail, two fingerprint men and a photographer. With the lieutenant in the lead, the troop made their way down the short hallway.

Tadich knocked loudly on the door and fixed his eyes on the wide-angle peephole. There was a sudden darkening and then a quavering voice floated through.

"Who's there?"

"Police department. Lieutenant Tadich."

"Do you have a badge?"

"Lady," Tadich said, "you called the department. We said we'd be right over. Who else do you think we'd be?"

A pause. There was a scrabble of a door chain being released and then a procession of bolts disengaged. Finally the door cracked open and Mrs. Richards's beady eyes peered out. "Yes?"

"I'm Lieutenant Tadich. Do you want to show us this room you called about?"

"Upstairs," Mrs. Richards croaked. "Four B."

"I'm sure it is," Tadich agreed. "Would you please come up with us?"

"Do I have to?"

"It's better," Tadich said. "You might be able to help us. You might notice something."

Mrs. Richards nodded silently. She clutched a small ring of keys and stepped into the hall. Carefully she locked the door behind her. Her face was pale. Traces of a cheek tremor still lingered. The nervous tic made her face twist to one side. Without a word, she led the policemen up the stairs.

"He left yesterday," Mrs. Richards whispered hoarsely, standing in front of 4B. "I saw him leave. He was carrying a grocery bag."

"Did you notice anything in it?"

"Clothes," Mrs. Richards said. "Filthy pajamas."

"Why didn't you call us then?"

"I couldn't—I couldn't move."

Lieutenant Tadich nodded as the landlady unlocked the door. Immediately the stench hit their faces. The lieutenant's nose twitched.

"Do I have to go inside?" Mrs. Richards asked.

"Please," Tadich said. "If you could just show us the drawings. The drawings are most important."

Mrs. Richards nodded reluctantly and walked through the green wavering kitchen. She tried to ignore a small pile of loose feathers in front of the closet. Wordlessly, she led the men into the living room.

"There," Mrs. Richards said. Her arm rose and she pointed a finger at the wall. The smell was bringing tears to her irritated eyes.

"Yes," murmured Tadich. He took a couple of steps toward the wall and stopped. Looking down at his shoes, he saw a whitish slime oozing over the laces. He turned to the print man and held out his hand for two plastic bags which he slipped over his polished black shoes. Then he marched toward the wall and stopped again.

The entire wall was covered with cat drawings. Ten feet by sixteen feet. A black pasty substance had been used to mark the figures over the dingy grey wallpaper. In parts it dribbled and streams of the inky paste oozed down the wall like drool. There was no order to the position of the cats; they were completely random in their distribution. Neither was there an attempt at proportion—huge drawings had incredibly tiny cats inked between paws. Parts of each cat had been worked on in preference to the rest. Teeth sprang from jaws like reptilian monsters. Claws shot out like rows of sabers.

The hideous eyes were the first to attract one's attention. Buried in the crude heads, they leered from every angle. The eyes were flat and oval, catlike, and burrowed into your sight wherever you stood. The bodies, or the scrawny caricatures meant as bodies, were outlined by a dripping laundry marker. Lifeless, awkward, and puffy, they seemed like the efforts of a grade-school child to draw something he had read about but never seen.

The limbs were grotesquely executed, alternately extending or contracting in frozen constraint. Intertwined among all the feline figures were the tails, roping together like coiling lariats. Long tails, hairy tails, and drooping tails. Some curled restfully around necks, some dangled free in space, and others stuck straight up, rigidly at attention, electric with hair.

There was something covering the mouth of each figure and Lieutenant Tadich started forward to examine it. In the dim light there was only a difference of shade but, as he moved closer, he ordered one of the blankets removed from a window. When the shaft of clean light struck the cats, the lieutenant touched the stain dabbled on the mouths. He immediately removed his finger and wiped it on a handkerchief. He had never seen blood used as paint before. The dried, darkish clots had confused him at first.

His foot nudged something on the floor. He looked down and saw the row of bird cages. Inside each was a stiff fur-covered object. Tadich turned and picked his way carefully to Mrs. Richards.

"When did you first find out about this?" he asked her.

"Yesterday. Yesterday it was."

"You had no idea before?"

"He never let anyone in his apartment."

"How did you find out yesterday?"

"I let myself in with my key. The smell . . ."

"Yes—go on."

"And I saw the drawings. The same drawings that were in the paper."

"I don't understand. You were in this apartment, and then you saw him leave?"

"That's right. I was trying to find the copy of the paper when I heard him go past my door."

"Yesterday?"

"He . . . he must have been hiding inside when . . ."

"When you were here?"

"It's so horrible."

"What is his name?" Tadich asked.

"I don't know. He never said."

"The lease?"

"He wanted it month to month. No lease. It's twenty dollars more that way. I thought he was an artist."

"How long did he live here?"

"Just this month, thank God. You don't think I would have put up with this much longer, do you?"

"I'll need a description of him. What did he look like?"

"I don't feel very well. Can we talk somewhere else?"

"Of course."

"I feel very ill."

"I understand."

Tadich noticed her eyes trying to keep from looking at the wall but she couldn't help it. The woman was hypnotized.

"Lousy artist, wasn't he," Tadich remarked. "Messed the place up pretty good. It'll take days to scrape it off. It's all dried."

"It's horrible."

"Hell of a mess," Tadich agreed. "Hope we can get some prints out of it."

"What kind of a person would do such a thing?"

Tadich shrugged again. "I don't make guesses. This is the first solid lead, I'll tell you. The track is warm. But we have him now."

■ ■ ■

Steven bounded up to the tram and hopped onto the lead car next to the driver. He almost tripped and as he stood up, six carloads of people stared at him. Amanda flicked off her microphone and helped him to his feet.

"What are you doing?" she hissed at him. "I'm in the middle of a tour."

"I know what animal it is," he hissed back.

"What animal?"

"The animal he's going to kill next."

The driver kept his eyes on the road, staring straight ahead. He knew Steven by sight and anything the director wanted to do was all right with him.

"What is it?" Amanda demanded.

"The wolf. It has to be the wolf."

"Are you sure?"

"As sure as anything. Let's go."

"I can't leave the tour; it's halfway through."

Steven grabbed her microphone and thrust it at the driver. "Say something," he ordered. Then he pushed Amanda off the tram and jumped after her.

"What are you doing?" she yelled at him.

"You wanted to get off the tour, didn't you?" Steven yelled back. "I'm letting you."

The six carloads of people craned their necks out of the tram and stared behind. Their faces bore a curious mixture of puzzlement and a vague, uncertain concern that they should do something but weren't quite sure what.

Amanda brushed off her jacket and straightened her blouse. She looked at the departing tram and tried to keep a stern face. "Keep your hands and arms inside," she yelled. Immediately the army of faces, elbows, and necks vanished inside the cars as the tram rounded a corner and slipped into a eucalyptus grove.

"I have to tell you something," Amanda said.

"Can it wait?" Steven asked, hurrying toward the wolf den.

"It's important."

"So are the wolves," Steven said, almost irritably.

"Goddammit!" Amanda flung away the hand that Steven had been dragging her with. "Will you just listen?"

Steven stopped. His head turned from the direction of the wolf den to Amanda's face, and back again. "We don't have time."

"To hell with it," Amanda said. She passed Steven and started to jog toward the wolves.

"What's the matter with you?" Steven asked, catching up with her and matching her pace.

"Nothing's the matter with me," she said through the side of her mouth. "It's you who should have his head examined. You can't see a damn thing around you."

"What are you talking about?"

"If you can't see it by now you're hopeless."

Steven was going to ask her more but, at the set look on her face, he changed his mind. Instead, he put his mind back on the wolves. The plan he was turning over had too many chances, too many sides. The advice of Charlie rang in his head. The dismal prophecies of Lieutenant Tadich tolled in his ears. And now Amanda was giving him the strangest look.

By the time they neared the wolf den, both of them slowed to a normal walking pace. Blending in with the visitors as much as possible, Steven led Amanda down the walkway. The wolf exhibit was at one end of a wide corridor. It was the only exhibit that had open space, pine trees, and rolling mounds of brush. Granite boulders stretched for a hundred feet behind the front bars.

Strolling toward the wolves, they passed the coyotes, the foxes, the beavers, the muskrats, and porcupines. Steven didn't stop when they reached the wolves. Instead he kept on walking and secretly studied the visitors. Nothing seemed unusual.

"Suppose it's not the wolf," Amanda said slowly.

"It's the wolf," Steven repeated stubbornly. "It has to be."

By now they had passed the den. Out of the corner of his eye, Steven had checked the animals. The big male was sunning himself on a tall slab of granite; three females lolled underneath his sight. He couldn't see the rest of the pack but he was satisfied that they were safe by the unconcern of the male.

"We can't just keep walking back and forth," Amanda said. "My uniform doesn't exactly fit in with the crowd."

About thirty feet from the exhibit, Steven paused and looked around. There was a planted hedge, a small circle of succulents, and a few rest benches. At the other end of the open ground was a corral—the bare wooden beams of the children's zoo.

"You're finally going to get your chance," Steven said. "Come on."

He led her past the tiny gate and into the throng of children.

The ground was bare dirt, packed hard by shoes. A dozen goats were ambling through, variously nuzzling pant legs and chewing on shoelaces. Three unshorn sheep, covered with straw and twigs, stood in the center like overstuffed pillows. They moved their lower jaws in unison, surveying the screaming, shouting children with contemptuous eyes.

Steven shooed an alpaca away with an arm and led Amanda to the side of the corral. From where they stood, they had a perfect vantage point. The wolf den was just across a low hedge and a bench. There were a few trees to the left which hid part of the corral, but from the children's zoo the view was unimpeded.

"Here's where I want you to stay," Steven said. "The only way he can get to the wolves is through the front of the exhibit by the bars and you can see everything, all the way up the corridor."

"I don't have my camera."

"You don't need it. No camera this time. Take this." Steven gave her one of the transceivers she had used before. "Call me."

"I'm supposed to stand here and watch?"

"That's right," Steven said. He turned and started to leave.

"Hey!" Amanda protested. "You can't leave me here."

"I'm coming back," Steven said over his shoulder. "I've just got to get something."

■ ■ ■

Steven took the shortest path back to his office. Luckily the wolf den was only a hundred yards away, although the path twisted through rows of primate exhibits and a line of pheasant cages. Instead of going through the main door, where he would have to encounter Harriet, Steven silently opened the side door and slipped inside. He made his way across the office floor with quick steps. Stopping in front of a large wooden cabinet, he grasped the handle and pulled. The long drawer creaked on seldom used rollers. As the light exposed the interior, something metallic gleamed inside.

Steven pulled the drawer out as far as it would come. He stood over the opening and looked down at the rifle. A Holland & Holland .375 elephant gun. It was Charlie's old rifle, thinly oiled and resting on a bed of soft velvet. The oil had attracted a layer of fine dust that barely dulled the smooth gleam of the blued barrel. The stock was heavy Southern hardwood, worked walnut, and polished smooth by years of rubbing against his uncle's hunting jacket. The rifle had killed just about everything under the sun that weighed more than fifty kilos and would make a good picture lying stiff on the ground, head propped up, and Charlie spreading the jaws to show off the teeth. In the heydays of the twenties and thirties, when the great cats were being slaughtered on safari, when the rhinos were laid low heaving on the plains, when the water buffaloes were slain by the thousands, when the twelve-foot crocs and fifteen-foot Kodiaks were laid thrashing by smashing hollowpoints thudding into thick skulls, Charlie's rifle was kept warm and polished.

Animal trapping was an ambiguous business then; the boundaries between collecting alive for zoos and collecting heads for sportsmen often shifted according to the prevailing market prices. When the fifties came and the economics favored the living animal, the rifle became a useless tool. For the same price it was stupid to wrestle down a mature beast when a young baby suckling was far easier to steal—providing of course that the parent wasn't left alive to protest. In the sixties, if you tried to walk through airport customs in any of the emerging African states with a rifle, no matter how much money you pressed into palms, it was "not done anymore." That was the decade Charlie retired.

Steven fingered the box of shells stacked in the corner. Magnums. He had never seen the rifle taken out of the cabinet. As far as he knew it had been used only once—ten, maybe fifteen years ago. He had heard the story from Gordon. A visitor had been teasing a lion. The cages were the older type then, indoors and with little separation from the public. The visitor was shaking a piece of hot dog with his left hand and holding a camera over his eyes with his right, hoping for the lion to open his jaws. With each movement of the piece of meat, the cat twitched his paws. The visitor leaned further over the railing, hoping for one last good shot, when the lion fully extended his arm and sank his claws into the man's shoulder. The camera dropped to the floor as the man was yanked against the bars of the cage. The huge mouth opened finally and the enraged growl shook the building. His snout banged against the bars; the rods whined in the concrete. He treaded his paws in the man's flesh for a better hold, trying to chew the man's head off. It was a stalemate. The lion couldn't get a good bite because of the bars and the man, fully conscious, couldn't tear himself away when the lion shifted his hold.

The keepers tried everything, from throwing hunks of horse meat in the opposite corner to buckets of boiling water in the lion's face. Gordon was sent for and while hundreds of people watched, he loaded the rifle and bolted it. He lifted the barrel to the lion's ear and waited for it to settle down. What he wanted to do was shoot the man.

The lion was old and half-blind. A white filmy layer covered his left eye; both had cataracts. His gums were thick and black; most of his teeth had fallen out. Given another hour, it would have been possible to tear the man away from the lion's grasp but Gordon knew what would happen then. The lion would be branded a killer, a bloodthirsty danger to society, and his menacing presence would not be tolerated by an enraged public. Gordon held the rifle steady. And how much longer would the ancient lion live anyway? Already he had problems chewing meat; the keepers had to scrape the flesh from the bones and mince it. What kind of a life? Gordon pulled the trigger. The lion slumped. The keepers pulled the visitor free from suddenly limp paws. There had not even been a roar.

Steven slid open the box of Remington cartridges. He wondered how old they were. Had Gordon kept the ammunition fresh? He was about to check the date on the box when the transceiver squawked.

Steven fumbled in his coat. *"Yes?"*

"I see him."

That was it. The three words jumped out of the little transceiver and then there was nothing. *"Amanda?"* Steven called her name again but there was no answer. Static. "Amanda?" He pressed the transmit button again. Nothing.

Steven looked at the rifle, the box of ammunition, the cloth lining the drawer. His right hand reached for the stock while his left dug into the box for a dozen rounds. The brass cartridges were cold; the steel-jacketed heads were colder.

Just as suddenly, he opened his left hand and spilled the heavy slugs into the bottom of the cabinet. He lowered the rifle and slammed the drawer shut. He shivered as he realized how close he had come to loading the rifle. That might be Charlie's solution; it wasn't his. He walked quickly out of his office without what he had come for.

It took less than a minute to reach the corral. He vaulted over the fence and ran across the packed dirt to the corner where he had left Amanda. He could see her by the time he was halfway through a scurrying flock of sheep. She was pressed against a fence, half hidden by an overhanging limb of a Monterey pine.

"Where is he?"

Amanda didn't turn around. She stared at the wolves. "There," she said, not bothering to point.

The man stood next to the guard rails, reading the information sign with an air of intense concentration. His hands were resting in the pockets of a short brown coat. His head moved slightly, as if checking the animal with its identifying portrait on the sign, and his sunglasses gave off a momentary flash of reflected light.

Steven didn't bother to ask if she was sure. There was no need. The way he was standing and the awkward way he thrust his hands in his pockets marked him as no idle visitor. This man was paying too much attention to the wolves.

"He hasn't taken his hands out of his pockets," Amanda reported. "I was petting a goat and just looked that way and there he was. Standing in front of the den. I know it's him. He's the man that got on the tram."

Steven didn't answer. He climbed to the top of the fence and dropped to the other side.

"What are you doing?" Amanda cried, following him in the climb. "Wait for me."

"Hurry up," Steven said over his shoulder.

"Why?"

"He just took his hands out of his pockets."

Amanda stared at the wolf den. The man had finished his examination of the sign and was now moving slowly to the center of the bars. His left hand swung freely; the right held something that looked round and pink. A little larger than a tennis ball. He started to wave the pink mass.

The dominant male wolf was sunning himself on the rock and only incidentally glancing at the man in the brown coat. The three females below were asleep. When the pink ball began to bob just outside the bars, the timber wolf raised his nose and tested the air. For several seconds he sniffed. Then he gave a short gruff snort and stood on the granite, stretching his legs. Immediately the females awoke and pressed their heads toward the ledge to see what caused his actions. By now the male had located the pink ball as the source of a smell that had wafted through the air. With a short spring, he landed on the sloping ground and began to trot toward the front of the enclosure. The females followed.

Steven began to run.

"Hey!" Amanda cried, putting on a burst of speed to match his.

Steven ran faster. His legs pumped furiously. His eyes locked on the man's arm. The pink ball rose higher in the air.

The man hoped that the ball of hamburger meat was large enough. The wolves were much bigger than he expected. But as the pack ambled toward him, his concern mounted as he tried to choose which of the wolves to throw the meatball toward. The big leader? But he was too dumb looking. The grey one on the left with the quivering snout? Or the one behind the rest, slavering for an opening to dash in? He had prepared the treat carefully—mixing the hamburger in a large bowl with chunks of stew meat and chicken livers and a dash of MSG. It was more of a meatloaf, really. For the final spice he had put on a pair of kitchen gloves and opened the can of caustic lye. Carefully measuring a large portion, he spooned the crystals into the center and meticulously shaped the meat around it.

He decided on the skinny wolf at the edge of the pack. It had intelligent eyes. More drool was coming from its lips than the others. He couldn't wait any longer; he must not attract too much attention. Already the wolves were whining against the bars, straining their snouts for the meat. His hand gently began its lob.

And stopped.

His wrist was caught. An arm had reached over his shoulder and grabbed his wrist.

"Drop it," Steven ordered.

The man froze, facing the snarling wolves. His eyes began to dart left and right. "Who are you?"

"The person you've been writing letters to."

The man whirled around, kicking his feet. His wrist squirmed loose and he crammed the meatball in Steven's face. He pushed hard, into Steven's mouth, and the juice dripped.

Steven choked.

The man searched frantically for a way to escape. His back was pressed against the guard rail. He saw a woman in a zoo uniform coming at him. People were staring.

Steven's hands clawed at his mouth. The quickness of the thrust had surprised him and he couldn't shut his teeth in time. Some of the meat forced its way into his mouth and it tasted salty at first. Then it began to burn. He gagged, stumbling backward. His hands flew up and flung the meatball away. Then he began to vomit.

The meatball landed a few feet away, a scant yard from the bars of the cage. The wolves lunged toward it, scrambling for position. The big male forced his way closest to the meat and he stretched his paws through the bars. His nails scratched the ground trying to roll the ball closer. The females yelped. Their slavering heads growled in frenzy.

Steven clawed at his face. One of his fingers had smeared a gritty piece of meat near his eye and it suddenly erupted into flaming pain. The tears came then, trying to flood the stabbing burn. He brought up his shirt sleeve and rubbed as hard as he could.

The man was genuinely worried. How had the message been decoded? He looked around him. People were walking quickly toward them. He had to get out of there.

Steven forced his eyes open. Through the flood of tears he saw a movement—the man was slipping away. He reached out a hand to grab his shoulder and then he saw the blow coming. Steven ducked. He lowered his head and rammed his body forward into the man's belly.

The charge forced both of them against the railing. Steven heard a gasp of air from the man's chest and the clatter of sunglasses flying across the ground. Then a knee came up and slammed into his chin. The thud of bone against his chin made him forget his burning tongue. He clenched his fist and threw it as hard as he could into the man's windpipe. Then he wrapped his arms around him as both fell to the ground.

Amanda didn't know what to do. The only thing she could think of was to start kicking but the two men were rolling over so fast there was no chance to land a shoe. She looked around for something to grab.

Steven found the man's throat and squeezed. He rolled on top, slamming his knee into his groin. His mouth was filling with burning saliva but he didn't bother to turn his head to spit. He spat the grey froth into the man's face. Through his tears, Steven saw the man's eyes flare, like a cornered animal. Then he remembered.

"*The meatball!*" Steven yelled to Amanda. "Get the meatball away." Steven raised a hand and pointed toward the wolves. The man twisted underneath and Steven slugged him on the chin.

Amanda looked where Steven had pointed. The pink hamburger ball, squashed and flattened on one side, leaned against a large pebble. Only the stone kept the meat from rolling down a drainage slope into the cage. The male wolf had just about succeeded in hooking his nails into the meat. His jaws snapped, there was an audible clicking of teeth. Behind him the females shoved against his flank; the pack was worked up in a yelping frenzy.

Amanda ducked under the guard rail and stood as close as she dared to the cage. Slowly she stretched out her leg, pointing the tip of her shoe toward the meat and the scrambling flurry of paws. Her toes started to shake.

The male wolf snarled and Amanda jerked her shoe back. The wolf was eying her leg now, venting his frustration at anything near the meat.

Amanda put all her weight on both feet, trying to keep her knees from shaking. Behind her she could hear the sounds of the two men grappling. The wolves in front were straining their forelegs, clawing at the air.

Taking a deep breath, she bent down and slipped off her shoe. Aiming slightly above the snout, she flung the shoe at the biggest wolf. With a roar of rage, the wolf's jaws sprang open. And open. The shoe disappeared into his maw. He snapped his jaws shut and only the thin black shoelaces dangled outside his mouth.

As soon as she threw her shoe, Amanda bent down and reached for the meatball. Her fingers inched over the dirt and felt their way closer. She touched it. One more inch and she could grab it. Her hands curled over the pink ball; she could feel the air move over her fingers from the snapping jaws. The meat was finally in her grasp.

Her knees buckled. The two struggling men rolled under her, pushing her toward the cage.

She didn't have time to think. She put all her weight on the foot with her remaining shoe and jumped. At the same time she arched her back and sprang backward. She was in the air for only a second, an eternity. She felt the scrape of nails sliding across her sole.

She landed hard on her back, knocking her breath out. Steven and the poisoner had their hands on each other's throat and lay thrashing within inches of the frenzied wolves. One of the females had succeeded in hooking a nail in the poisoner's coat. With a flick, she slashed open the material. Drawing the tattered piece to the bars, she ripped the shred into long strands. The pack set up a howl even louder than before.

Stunned, Amanda groaned and started to feel her spine. Looking down, she saw the flattened meatball clenched in her hand. It burned. Flinging it behind, she scrambled to her knees and crawled down the ditch toward Steven.

The two men were squirming in the dust. Steven was on top but the other man had both his hands around Steven's back and squeezed tightly. Steven slammed his elbow against his neck and pressed. The man began to choke and loosen his hold.

Amanda grabbed Steven's feet and pulled. She braced herself against the railing and tugged as hard as she could. Slowly, the two men stopped rolling.

Steven wrenched his right hand free and landed it against the man's chin. Blood began oozing from his mouth and his arms went limp.

"Get away," Amanda yelled. "The wolves—"

Steven dug his heels into the dirt and dragged the poisoner away from the paws. He pulled him under the guard rail and slammed the man's head against the asphalt.

"The police," Steven gasped. "Get the police."

The man was lying still, his mouth bloodied and covered with dirt. Steven had twisted his arm behind his back, just before the breaking point, and the pain screamed from his eyes.

"Go!" Steven yelled. "Get out of here."

Amanda stumbled backward. She looked around her, at the dozens of people standing with horrified looks. Turning toward the main gate, she started to run for help.

"You sonofabitch!" Steven screamed. He twisted the man's arm harder. He spat blood. Steven lifted his head and slammed it down again on the asphalt.

"What did you put in that meat?" Steven yelled.

"I can't—breathe," he choked.

Steven loosened his hold. He kept an arm bent in a vise grip, applying pressure. The man's eyes were white, filled with terror. A gurgling of blood sounded in his throat. He tried to talk.

Steven swiped the blood from the man's mouth. "Why did you try to kill them?" he demanded.

The man shook his head. "Didn't."

"You were going to poison the wolves."

"Free them. I was going to free them."

The man's face contorted in fear. The words spilled from his mouth without sense, like the blood dripping from his glistening wet lips. His body shook uncontrollably. Like a half-alive mouse clamped in a trap, the shaking spread outward from the points of pressure. He gasped as his eyes widened in recognition. "It's *you*," he gurgled. His eyes rolled as he focused on the man hovering above him. He had never seen the director before, but he hated him more intimately than he had ever thought possible. The air was heavy with the vapors of hate, of putrid agony, of unremitting disgust. This man knew! He *feels* the animals, too. But he's so twisted by evil he has completely warped himself.

"I'm going to get you!" the man screamed. "I'm going to punish you."

"Shut up."

"You're the Devil," the man hissed. He whistled the truth to the firmaments. "The Devil of the cages of Hell. May God burn down your concentration camps."

"You're not going to do a damn thing now."

"All my life I've been freeing the slaves. I was liberating the oppressed. But I was wrong. All the time I've been stopped. I've failed. And it was *you*, you all the time, wasn't it? You in all your hideous disguises. Now I recognize you, the Devil himself. You've been hiding everywhere, watching me."

The man's eyes bulged like fat grapes as his words growled and tore loose from the bottom of his stomach. "You've always tried to silence your enemies. But I won't be quiet. *I'm going to get you!* If it's in my power I'm going to destroy you because you are the root of all evil. And when you die the shackles shall be broken and the beasts will be free."

Steven raised his head, trying to spot help. The man was completely mad. Of course he had to be, Steven knew that all along.

To knife an antelope? To feed razor blades to a hippo? To poison sea lions and wolves? But there was crazy and there was this crazy. This was *real* crazy and it scared Steven like nothing had in his life. This man was insane.

Steven thought he could understand perversion; he could rationalize why a teenager would shoot BB's at a deer. It disgusted him, but he could *understand.* He could understand someone hating a hyena and throwing a rock at it. Or pulling a tail feather off a peacock or stepping on a snake. These were things people did without thinking. If you caught them after the act, they became quiet and sullen. They *knew* they had done something wrong. But this bleeding sick man underneath him was on a psychotic crusade. Even that, Steven thought, he could eventually come to grips with. All except *I'm going to get you.*

Steven saw the police coming. Far across the plaza Amanda was running ahead leading them to the wolf den.

The man growled. The blood was drying on his face. As it coagulated, it felt as if someone had smeared his lips with thick paint. He was feverish. He felt his breath coming in flashes, shallow pants, like the time he was in the dentist's chair and the drill started to scream and disappear into his mouth. I can't move, he screamed to himself. He swallowed and felt the salty-sweet taste of his caked blood. Above him, he saw the Devil. He leered down with a fat hiss. The wicked smile of the serpent. A jeering face, laughing at failure.

"I'm going to get you," the man choked.

Yes, he vowed. I will. I'm going to punish you. I'm going to free all the fallen angels you've stolen and held within your power. Francis was right. You have no right to capture them like . . . like common children. You shut them up in cages when they really want to fly up to Heaven. Soaring up there with their souls shooting through space.

He felt himself being pulled to his feet. Two more blue devils grabbed his arms to prevent his escape. He felt himself being dragged across the ground, past the pits of Hell. Shoved in the back seat of a purple devil car. He heard the sound of a lock.

Caged! Windows barred. No escape. Trapped! He felt himself urinating out of control. He clawed at the window.

"I'm going to get you!" he screamed at the Devil.

■ ■ ■

"Well," concluded Lieutenant Tadich, "you got him."

Out of the corner of his eye Tadich studied the heads on the director's office wall, the hides covering the chairs, the horns, and the furs. He caught himself mentally comparing his own office with its cheaply framed photographs, yellowing commendations, dented Formica furniture, and tarnished bowling trophies. What would the wall behind his desk look like, for instance, with a stuffed moose head? Or one of those antelope things with the long curved horns? Tadich frowned and let the idle thought pass. It was no good unless you shot them yourself and how was he going to afford a hunting trip like that? A chief of police could afford a trip like that. A mayor could afford it. But he had enough troubles paying off his Buick. Goddamn loan.

"Did you find out who he is?" Steven asked.

Tadich continued his briefing without moving a muscle in his face. He was good at briefings. "Of course," he said, shrugging. "We were going to pick him up where he worked. Toll collector. He's a toll collector on the Bay bridge. His landlady tipped us off; we got his prints and were just going to pick him up. Bernard Quintavalle. Odd name, isn't it?"

"Why do you think he did it?"

"Who knows?" Tadich said. "I don't. We talked with his boss at the bridge. Quintavalle worked there for years. Quiet, no trouble. Came on time and never took sick leave. Ordinary kind of guy."

"Killing animals isn't ordinary."

Tadich shrugged. "Better animals than—" He stopped.

"No," Steven said. "Go on. What were you going to say? *Better animals than people?*"

"I didn't mean it like that. Skip it, okay?"

"I can't skip it. It's my job to understand why it happened and make sure it doesn't happen again. But at least now I'll know in the future how much help I'll get from the police department."

"Let me tell you something," Tadich said. "I've got plenty of work to do. Always have. Always will. I'm going to be drawing that paycheck because there are always people screwing other people and giving me work. That's how I see it. You, you got off lucky. You caught the bastard. You have enough on him for a case. Half the *homicides* in this city don't have a case like you have. And you're worrying about understanding? I don't get it. How the hell do I know why he hates animals? Maybe he loves them. You always hurt the one you love, right? Maybe he thinks he's brave; maybe he hates himself. Maybe his girl's cutting him off. I don't know."

"Thank you, Lieutenant."

Tadich started to leave but paused at the door. "Let me give you some advice. You have a nice job. Nice office. Happy people running around. Keep it that way, huh? The Mayor was on my ass about this case. He was pushing me hard. But it worked out okay; nobody made any mistakes, nobody got hurt. You came out smelling like a rose. You put one over on the Mayor. He's sweating like a pig now."

"Pigs don't sweat."

Tadich allowed a rare smile. "This one is. When you caught Quintavalle you stuck a hot poker up him. He can't blame you, he can't blame me, he can't blame anybody. And when a mayor can't blame somebody, he's in trouble. Nothing to work with. He walked out on a limb and you sawed it off. I read what the *Chronicle* is doing to you. You're a hero. You're grabbing a lot of space now."

"Space you think the police department should have?"

Tadich shook his head. "You still don't understand me, Cooper. I didn't want any part of this mess. You dragged me into it and I did the best I could. I had you on my back and I had the Mayor. Who do you think weighs more? I don't like getting caught in the middle. But I don't play politics because I want to stay around long enough to pay off my Buick and take my kids to Disneyland once a year. . . . Like I said, you came out on top. Keep it that way."

"What's going to happen to Quintavalle?"

"We're holding him on four counts of animal cruelty. He's already been arraigned. With the *Chronicle* on the judge's back, he's moving the case to the top of the calendar. Don't worry anymore about him, he's on ice."

∎ ∎ ∎

"Good morning, ladies and gentlemen. Welcome to the San Francisco Zoo. This is *your* zoo if you live in the Bay Area but if you're from out of town, I'd like to extend a warm welcome to you also. As our tram continues, I'd like to remind you that arms and legs should be kept inside."

Amanda looked at the tramload and continued after a slight pause. "As we move along, I'd like to give you some statistics on the zoo, some facts and figures."

"I thought we were going to see the animals," a fat man in a Stetson hat objected. He grinned at the others in the tram.

"You can see the animals much better on foot, sir," Amanda said coolly, eying his paunch squarely. "And it's excellent exercise."

The smile on the man's face faded. He stared back with narrowed eyes. Amanda continued brightly. "As I said, I'd like to give you some facts and figures. I've always felt that most people zoom right past the animals and don't really learn much about them."

"What is this, teacher? A school?" The fat man needled Amanda, squinting his piglike eyes and chortling.

"This is a zoo," Amanda said, keeping her eyes from the fat man and speaking to the tram. "We have all kinds of animals here, most of them are in cages. As I was saying, about my facts and figures—"

"Hey, teach," the fat man joked. "You got a nice figure but you'd better skip the facts. Show us the animals quick before they're all poisoned."

Amanda swallowed hard. She gripped the microphone so tightly her fingernails turned pale. "I happen to *like* lectures," she said tensely. She gulped inside as she heard herself speak the words. "I like lectures," she repeated lamely. Why did she feel this way? Hadn't she always run the tour like this? *"We're going to hear a lecture,"* she growled threateningly. The fat man in the Stetson fell back, momentarily stunned by the ferocity of her attack.

Amanda was about to continue the facts and figures when an old lady waved a handkerchief for attention. The lady sat at the rear of the tram, clutching a worn carpetbag purse.

"Yes?" Amanda said.

The woman gingerly piped, "I don't know about the other people here, but I would certainly like to hear about the animals." She nodded primly at the rest of the tramload and seemed to want to add something more. "My name is Mrs. Fleisher," she stated. "And I've been coming to the zoo for many years. I think we all should respect a moment of silence for the hippopotamus. His name . . . was Harold."

The fat man snickered. "A moment of silence isn't enough for a hippopotamus. How about an hour?" His jowls shook as he laughed at the people, urging them to join him. The tramload stared grimly back.

"Perhaps," Mrs. Fleisher continued, "we could all write a note to the Mayor. To tell him how much we miss Harold. Perhaps he could—"

"I think that's an excellent idea," Amanda interjected quickly. "We all should do that. Maybe you, sir—" she aimed her eyes at the fat man—"would like to write also."

The man smirked again. "For a hippopotamus?" He stared incredulously at the crowd. "Don't you people *know?*"

"Know what?" Mrs. Fleisher demanded, cocking her head.

"There's not going to *be* a zoo much longer." The man nodded, as if confirming a fact. "The Mayor's going to—"

"The Mayor is a good man," Mrs. Fleisher stated firmly. "I've read magazine articles about him. He's a good family man. Perhaps if we all wrote—"

"Hah," the fat man chortled. "You're—"

"See here," a new voice spoke up. Amanda saw a man in a glare-blue suit suddenly clear his throat. "*I'll* sign my name."

"Name to what?"

"Why, the petition of course," the man in the suit said, puzzled. "Isn't that what we're talking about?"

Mrs. Fleisher waved a piece of paper in the air as fifty-nine hands grabbed for it. Suddenly the tram was awash with a sea of pens. Bags of peanuts were hurled at the man with the Stetson; he ducked under the barrage and scowled with darting eyes. The children began shouting to join the confusion and Mrs. Fleisher beamed. The tram rocked dangerously from side to side as people jumped out of their seats to add their name to the circulating list.

Amanda grabbed a post to steady herself. Her eyes blinked at the sudden revolt.

"*Bears!*" she shouted. "On our right is Yogi the bear."

▬ ▬ ▬

After walking in unannounced, Amanda closed the door and leaned back against it, her arms folded around a sheaf of papers. "You ought to get an agent with all the publicity you're getting in the *Chronicle.*"

"No, thanks," Steven said. "One more week and that's it."

"A week?"

Steven nodded. "The hospital called and said Gordon will be released a week from today. The minute he steps through the gate I'm leaving."

"Back to school?"

"Yes," he said. "The zoo is Gordon's problem. My leave of absence runs out in seven days and I've got dumb kids to teach the mysteries of life and dumber articles to write. But I want to get back. I have a lot of work piling up."

"Work left to do?" Amanda butted in. She quietly fumed. "Look at this dump," she said, scowling. She crossed to the window and viciously yanked the curtains open. The late afternoon sun streamed in, setting the room ablaze. Steven blinked his eyes and for the first time, Amanda could see the lines of worry creasing his temple. "What's with the face?" she demanded.

"When I took this job I made a promise. I said I'd keep the zoo for Gordon."

"You did."

"No," Steven said, shaking his head. "I screwed it up. It was my fault the animals died. I bungled it. Trying to keep quiet about it, hoping it would go away. And all I was doing was waving a red flag in front of the bastard. And the Mayor—he's been waiting years for a chance like this. Licking his chops for the zoo to fall on its butt."

"He won't do anything now," Amanda said. Her voice took on a strange self-assurance.

"Who's going to stop him?"

"You still don't know, do you?"

Steven didn't hear her. "Seven sea lions. You know we could have caught him there? All we had to do was think."

"Will you stop it?" Amanda shouted.

"What?"

"I've had enough."

"Of what?"

"Of you and your goddamn self-pity. Can't you see out your own office? Can't you look out there?" Amanda pointed out the window. "Are you blind?"

Steven looked where she pointed. From his window he could see most of the main plaza, the entrance gates, and the tall eucalyptus trees bordering the highway. It was crowded. Steven frowned. *Too* crowded.

He rose from his desk and walked to the window. The plaza was packed. The visitors were jostling past each other shoulder to shoulder. More were streaming through the main gate. Steven checked his watch. Two hours before closing. There was even a line snaking down the street outside waiting to get in. They were three abreast. Steven had never in his life seen so many people in the plaza. It had been crowded after the first article in the *Chronicle*—they had over four thousand that day. But there must be that many in the plaza right now. And the rest of the grounds?

"Why didn't someone tell me?" Steven said. His eyes blinked at the sunlight.

"Because we've been working all day handling that crowd. All you had to do was look out your window."

"Harriet." Steven flipped the intercom switch again. "Harriet?"

"She's not there," Amanda said.

"I heard her come in after lunch."

"I asked her to help me outside."

"Help you?" Steven asked, puzzled. "What for?"

"For these," Amanda said. She flung the papers in her hands at Steven. About thirty sheets fluttered in the air and swirled past his face. Steven grabbed at one. It was regular typewriter paper; someone had drawn lines across the page with a ruler and numbered them. In ink, pencil, and crayon, each line was filled with a scrawled signature.

"What are these?" Steven asked. He bent down and grabbed another piece of paper. It too was covered with signatures.

"Petitions," Amanda said. "Those are just the ones I collected on the tram. Harriet's catching them when they come in the gate."

"Petitions? What for?"

"To save the zoo. What else?"

"You can't—"

"We are," Amanda broke him off.

"Whose idea was this?" Steven demanded. "Yours?"

"No," Amanda said, shaking her head. "It was some old lady's. She said she gets on the tram free because she's a member of the Society or something. She stood up at the first tour ride and said wouldn't it be a good idea to write a letter to the Mayor about the zoo. Tell him to ask the City Council for money to buy another hippopotamus. Then someone said that would be a waste of tax-payers' money because there wasn't going to *be* a zoo very much longer. And then everybody was quiet. For two seconds. Then they started yelling. I never saw anything like it. They were standing on the tram, yelling and screaming, throwing popcorn and candy wrappers at the guy and then the petition got started. The old lady waved the paper in the air and it went around."

Steven half listened to her. He bent down and picked up the papers, scanning the rows and rows of names.

"That was the first tram," Amanda continued. "I told the tour manager and he let me take a few minutes off to see Harriet for more paper. She liked the idea and went around the grounds herself to give paper to the keepers. Everyone's handing them out now."

"But—"

"You'll believe it when we start stacking them up. The visitors are even taking blank sheets home for their neighbors to sign. We're going to have ten thousand names by tomorrow."

"Ten thousand?"

"Don't tell me you couldn't see it coming?" Amanda stared at him in disbelief. "I tried to tell you yesterday when you pushed me off the tram. Everybody was talking about the zoo. *Talking.* They weren't sitting there staring at the animals with dumb looks on their faces like they usually do. They weren't looking for something to get rid of their boredom. They were *talking.* Asking me questions about what's going to happen to the zoo and I couldn't answer. I didn't know."

"I don't know either."

"But all these names know," Amanda said. She rattled the pile of papers in Steven's hands. "They know enough to want to do something about it. When's the last time you took a ride on the tram? When's the last time you walked around outside?"

Steven closed his eyes and began to rub the back of his neck. Then he stood still, staring at the petitions. "These . . . these aren't enough."

"Of course they're not. But it's the start you need. Now you can—"

"Now Gordon can," Steven corrected her. "My leave of absence is over in seven days, remember?"

"You're impossible. Doesn't any of this mean something to you?"

"It means a lot. When my father comes back, he'll finally be getting the support he needs."

"Steven!" Amanda screamed.

"What?"

But he never found out what she was going to say because Amanda stormed out of the office, slamming the door with a resounding crash.

■ ■ ■

The zoo maintained the crowds for the entire week. The turnstiles clicked incessantly and the grounds were packed more thickly than at any time Steven could remember. And everyone who worked there, from the concession workers to the keepers, strutted with new smiles on their faces. Their feet lifted higher with enthusiasm. And Steven couldn't be happier. He *wanted* the zoo to wake up, that's what he had tried to explain to Amanda. What he objected to was that it had taken a disaster to do it. Silver linings were fine, but it wouldn't return the sea lions or the hippo.

As he watched the crowds, Steven wondered how long their enthusiasm would last. It had already affected the Members' Society. They were having talks with Gordon daily at the hospital. Suggestions were buzzing and plans were being made.

But plans had always been made, Steven thought. What changes had ever taken place? What they didn't realize was that you had to follow through with them, to keep on plugging when that first burst of enthusiasm sagged. He had learned that lesson early in his life when he had the burden of responsibility for the animal business. Could Gordon do it? He had to, Steven decided, in every sense of the word.

The killer had been caught. But Steven knew that Quintavalle wasn't the real killer of the zoo. What really stalked the zoo, and had for years, was public apathy. He realized that fact as the petitions piled up. The fact that they *were* piling up only underscored the previous depths to which the zoo's irrelevance had sunk. And when will this false spurt end? A question for Gordon to answer, Steven shrugged to himself.

But the petitions didn't stop.

■ ■ ■

Steven woke early every morning refreshed and well rested. In the quiet hours, he made his walk. He passed the bombastic edifices of the WPA architecture, so grandly disastrous for animal comfort. So much eloquence had gone into the design of the exterior that the dark, tomblike cubicles inside—the "homes" of the animals—were satisfactory only for storing square bales of hay or uncomplaining moles.

Steven took the same route through the grounds, the same turns and twists he had memorized from years of following Gordon. He studied the zoo carefully. Some things changed, most didn't. It was still impossible to keep sea gulls out of the duck pond. Goats still climbed on the picnic tables and bantam roosters still defended their tiny patches of dirt along the paths. The prize for the messiest, most disgusting enclosure still was not to be found among the animals but in the public rest rooms.

And Steven strolled through the quiet grounds in the early hours. He greeted the keepers as they arrived for work and he chatted with them about their animals. Steven valued their dedication the most; without them and the kind of people they were, animals would never have survived as long as they had. Keepers were animal people. To be a keeper was to experience the most extraordinary bond between animal and man that existed. The keeper alone was responsible for his particular animal's food, water, shelter, and absolute well-being. The keeper in hour-to-hour contact provided all of their reinforcements and he alone experienced the feeling of total dependence from his animals.

When the zoo opened its gates and the visitors streamed in, Steven instantly felt the change in the animals. They knew the second the zoo opened; their behavior altered. They braced themselves and endured.

It was on Tuesday that Steven found himself standing in front of an outdoor bird cage. Inside the exhibit was a grey desert roadrunner. And staring with wide eyes and absorbing interest at the bird was a girl of about seven. She had separated from her school group and stood as if slightly unsure of herself. Her neat little dress danced in the breeze but she stood still, staring.

"Excuse me," she said to Steven.

"Yes?" he said, bending down.

"Can you tell me something?"

"What do you want to know?"

With a chocolate-stained finger, she pointed at the roadrunner. "Why doesn't he go beep-beep?"

"Because roadrunners don't go beep-beep. They only do that in cartoons."

"He doesn't go beep-beep?"

"Cartoons aren't *real*," Steven explained. "In real life, roadrunners don't go beep-beep."

"Do they run?"

"Yes. They run very fast."

"I never saw one before."

Her teacher blew a whistle and the girl dashed toward her group. Steven watched as she joined the giggling, shouting cluster of children. The girl pointed back toward the roadrunner and her classmates became silent as she lectured. All of them turned their heads toward the cage and tried to see inside.

Steven continued his walk. It was a stupid incident; ten years ago he would have laughed at the kid if she had asked him the same question. It would have made a great story, like one of Charlie's. But on Tuesday of that week, Steven thought about the girl's question and why she had asked it. It bothered him. It was an irritation somehow—funny at first, but annoying the more he pondered. If he hadn't told her about the bird, who would have? And it wasn't just the roadrunner, but what about every other exhibit in the zoo? What other stupid misconceptions were being left unchallenged?

But Steven forgot about the roadrunner, the ritual morning walk, and the quiet talks with the keepers that marked the beginning of his last week at the zoo. They fled from his mind because on Wednesday, on Wednesday afternoon, the animals began to die.

▄▄ ▄▄ ▄▄

Steven got the call from the joey's keeper near closing time. The keeper led the way to the back of the field.

It was a kangaroo, a tawny yearling. The keeper pointed at the brushy spot and Steven bent down. The roo was lying near the exhibit fence, his left hind leg snared by a piece of piano wire. The blood that collected from his severed foot had coagulated.

"I was making the afternoon count," the keeper choked, "and came up short. I found him here, in the back."

Steven unlooped the wire from the joey's leg. Loose slices of apple were lying around the fence, as if someone had lured the roo to the brushy back of the exhibit and left the snare to finish the deed. The roo, trapped and struggling, had died from shock.

"I don't want you to breathe a word about this to anyone," Steven said. "That's a direct order. Do you understand?" The keeper nodded grimly.

Steven piled mounds of grass over the corpse and then jogged to his office. He burst through the doors and yanked the telephone off its cradle. Punching the numbers angrily, he waited for the connection.

"Lieutenant Tadich," the voice acknowledged wearily. "Who is this?"

"Steven Cooper," he snapped. "One of my kangaroos was murdered. Isn't Quintavalle in jail?"

"I was going to call you," Tadich tried to explain. His voice echoed remotely over the wire, flat and hollow.

"Is Quintavalle in jail?"

"No."

"What do you mean? Didn't he go to trial?"

"The judge sentenced him—"

"Is Quintavalle in prison?"

A pause, a longer pause, and then "No." Steven held the phone like a cube of ice, his ears hearing the lieutenant's words from a far distance.

"Your assault didn't stick and all the judge had was four counts of animal cruelty. One of those was dismissed for lack of evidence. Quintavalle pleaded guilty and the judge gave him the maximum. Two hundred and fifty dollars on each count."

"A *fine?*"

"He was fined seven hundred and fifty dollars and released. The judge ordered him to go six months to a mental health clinic for private treatment under outpatient status."

"What?"

Tadich grunted. "That's what is on the books. I don't have anything to do with it."

"Feeding razor blades to hippos, poisoning sea lions and wolves—a seven-hundred-and-fifty-dollar fine and that's *all?*"

"Like I said, I don't have anything to do with that. These cases hardly ever go to court. Usually it's some fruit peddler beating his horse—that's the only time anyone around here remembers booking this rap."

"I don't believe it. You've got to be wrong."

"Sorry," Tadich said. "I like animals as much as you do. Hell, I bring my kids to the zoo. But laws are for people and their money; Sacramento doesn't stay up nights worrying about monkeys."

The lieutenant coughed and the shrug of ineffectualness carried over the wires. Steven fell back in his chair, stunned. No prison sentence? A two-hundred-and-fifty-dollar fine for each count? If it wasn't so horrible it would be ludicrous. Steven had blithely assumed that once the killer was caught he'd be put in prison and that would be the end of it. He had taken it for granted that a just punishment would be exacted.

He had fought the *Chronicle*. He had fought the Mayor, the police, and even Charlie. But Steven had *won*, the killer had been arrested. Damn it, that means something. The zoo should be safe now. It should return to the way it was before he took over.

"Someone's killing my animals!" Steven screamed into the telephone. He yelled at Tadich as if the lieutenant had never believed him.

"I doubt if it's Quintavalle this time," the lieutenant began, his calm voice allowing no trace of a reaction to Steven's scream. "Did you get a note?"

"No," Steven said icily. "There was no note."

"I saw Quintavalle's face at the trial. White. Bloodless. He was shaking like a sinner, getting it over with. I've seen his type before. Once the shakers get caught they never do it again."

"Someone is—"

"It's not Quintavalle!" Tadich snapped. "Will you believe me?"

"How do you know?"

"Because I put a man on him. We're watching him every second. There's nothing he can do."

"Where was he yesterday?"

"In Fisherman's Wharf. He's there all the time he's away from the clinic."

"What does he do there?"

"He stands around, watching some statue. Maybe he's trying to get a tan."

"What statue?"

"I don't know, but he stares at it for hours . . ."

After Steven hung up he realized who was responsible for the kangaroo's death and the knowing made him sick, too sick to tell the lieutenant. Nobody believed me, Steven thought as the sweat collected on his neck. The reporter didn't. The reporter didn't believe the *Chronicle* story would set off every animal nut in the Bay Area against the zoo. Now it was coming true.

Steven asked Dr. Lewis to stay on the grounds after the keepers left and when night fell, they went to the meadow to collect the body.

"Do you want an autopsy?" Dr. Lewis asked as they carried the roo back to the hospital.

"No," Steven said. "I know how he died."

On Thursday Steven spent the entire morning walking the grounds and talking with every keeper, maintenance worker, and concession operator. Without revealing the kangaroo death, he ordered them to study every visitor, every person who looked as if . . . "As if what?" they asked, puzzled. And Steven couldn't say. As if they might kill animals? As if they might run amok? Quintavalle wasn't caught that way. Quintavalle was the most ordinary looking person Steven had ever seen. "Just look around," Steven said. "Keep watching."

And Steven waited, paralyzed. He walked the grounds in a stupor, poring over every step of the disaster that had started only weeks ago as an easy baby-sitting job. He was halfway across the main plaza when he saw him.

It *was* him, Steven gulped, twisting his head. Wasn't it? The man far across the rose bed, standing in front of the crocodiles? The brown coat. The same brown coat. Steven rose on the tips of his shoes as a crowd of high school kids blocked his view. The sun glared at a bad angle.

The crowd was huge; it moved in an endless herd. Steven rose higher and shielded his eyes from the sun. He stared at the corner of the alligator pit. A service truck drove slowly past, pulling a trailer of hay. Steven twisted his head, trying to see through the space in between. He couldn't move. The kids blocked him completely.

There! A flash of brown. And for an instant, a quick line of profile. It was him . . . wasn't it? No sunglasses, but it was the face. Wasn't it? *Wasn't it?* Steven's mind screamed.

He saw a break in the crowd and elbowed his way through. Vaulting over the rose hedge, he landed with his legs kicking for more speed. He reached the alligator pit. Nobody. Steven leaped on a bench and scanned the area. For a long minute he studied the crowds. There! The flash of brown. He was standing a hundred feet away in front of a grounds map, now wearing sunglasses.

Steven pushed himself through the crowds once more, elbowing toward the map stand. Then he was beside him. The man lifted his hand. He raised it to his head and took off the sunglasses. Excuse me, he said in a thick German accent, but could you tell me how to get to the koala bear exhibit? Steven's breath slowed and he smiled weakly. He pointed the way and asked the man if he had liked the crocodiles. Can't stand crocodiles, the man objected vehemently, you'll never find me anywhere near the ugly beasts. But I saw you standing next to the pit, Steven said. No, no, the man denied, I haven't been near the crocodiles in years, ever since an ill-advised African tour. Steven nodded numbly.

Exactly twenty-four hours after the kangaroo was found, Steven was led by a pale and shaking keeper to the peccary pen. The small piglike creature was hidden by a rock formation next to the exhibit's rear fence. The blood from the cut neck coated the rocks like glistening enamel paint.

■ ■ ■

Gordon grinned. The chuckle spread across his belly until the entire hospital bed shook. He laughed at the joke and the girl laughed with him. He couldn't remember anyone laughing around the zoo in years and how long did she say she had been there?

"More carrot juice?" she asked, holding up the bottle. "I know you can't stand roughage."

"No," Gordon said, staring at the graduated medicine bottle. His smile only slightly faded. "Thank you but not right now."

He eased his head back onto the pillow and made himself comfortable. Her joke had made him scatter papers all over and he put on his eyeglasses to see better. As he straightened the pile, he sneaked quick glances at the woman sitting by the bed. He remembered the first time he noticed her, really noticed her. Was it three or four nights ago? The zoo people had started to leave; Harriet was scolding and nudging them from the room like a clucking hen. They came every night, Harriet and the keepers. Staying for a few hours, they noisily exchanged gossip, delivered children's letters, and offered small presents of nuts or fruit. Zoo food, Gordon fumed to himself; he begged for a box of greasy fried chicken or a taco, but they shrank back in horror and shook their heads sternly.

Gordon devoured the gossip, firing off rounds of questions at the keepers on their animal charges. He compared his mental orders with the ones Steven was giving but found no great gulf. Steven was doing a good job. Through some unspoken pact, nothing was ever mentioned in the hospital room of the deaths. Often there were uncomfortable pauses, lowered eyes and tensing of voices, but they were always broken by Harriet bursting in with a fresh tidbit of news. The keepers clustered around his bed, filling up the bare room with a cheerful presence. And one night they ambled away at the end of visiting hours and Gordon saw her standing by the door.

"Hello," Gordon said. "Who are you?"

"I work in the children's zoo," she said. "You don't know me."

"Children's zoo?" Gordon said, puzzled. "I thought Bob Christo—"

"He was promoted to reptile keeper. Steven put me in the children's zoo yesterday. I used to work on the tram."

"Oh," Gordon said. "How do you like the petting zoo?"

"Great," she said, smiling.

"I'm glad. It's good training, you know. The goats get a little boring but you won't have to stay there long before—"

Amanda nodded slowly, smiling weakly. "No, I won't be there long."

Gordon bobbed his head vigorously but the woman remained at the door. She raised her head and looked at him.

"You wouldn't mind, would you—"

"Mind what?"

"If I came back again tomorrow?"

It was the next night that he realized that she was the girl who had started the petitions. Harriet had told him a tour guide had done it but didn't mention her name. He beamed at her, his smile only slightly fading when he opened her present and found the carrot juice. She came the third night, and the fourth.

"Tell me more," she said.

Gordon grunted. "Charlie. Charlie tells them better than I do."

But Gordon watched the woman's face when he told the stories everyone else had heard a dozen times. Her eyes hung on every word. And when there was a lapse between the tales, they gossiped about the zoo. Gordon was surprised to hear how well she knew Steven.

"He's a sonofabitch," she said.

Gordon nodded enthusiastically. Again the curtain lifted between them and words flew in a gush. By God, this girl *knew*. She jumped from her chair and it was all Gordon could do to keep from hopping out of his bed and joining her. He listened to her gripe about his pigheadedness, his black moods, and his fanatical devotion to lectures.

"Yes!" Gordon rasped, agreeing with every word of her denunciation. "You have him pegged exactly. I don't know where he picked that stuff up. It wasn't inherited. But you know what would settle him down, don't you?" Gordon's finger rose to make a point.

"No, what?"

Gordon was about to say it when his face reddened. He was staring at Amanda, looking into her wide eyes, and another curtain disappeared. His searching stare bore more deeply than he ever thought possible. What he saw made him cringe with embarrassment. His jaws wagged silently and he eased back into his pillow.

"Carrot juice," he croaked.

■ ■ ■

The crowds streamed past, marching like vast herds of bleating range stock toward the vats of steaming crabs, loaves of fresh-baked bread, and tacky stands of tinsel jewelry and cheap art. The cries of the vendors shrilled like a bazaar, the jangling of the cable cars beat out frenzied tunes, and all around the common people rushed toward their earthly pleasures totally oblivious of a man in agony pacing in a corner of a parking lot in Fisherman's Wharf. He was an ordinary-looking man; from his perplexed exterior it would have been guessed that he either forgot where his car was parked or in which pocket his missing wallet had been, but in truth Quintavalle was a man engaged in an intimate conversation with nobody. His talk was quite spirited at times and his arms flung out in animated gestures to seemingly empty space. But whomever he pursued his argument with was evidently quite a passionate antagonist, for as time wore on it was apparent that Quintavalle was losing.

Although the crowds streaming past were oblivious to Quintavalle, there was a man on the opposite side of the parking lot who did indeed pay attention. The observer was a thin bored man sitting in a late model sedan with what appeared to be an inordinate number of headlights inconspicuously mounted on the dashboard. Pear-shaped from years of sitting, he sat trimming his already immaculately groomed fingernails with a key-chain clipper while eying Quintavalle. When he finished his hourly ritual of trimming his nails and making a notation in a notebook, he occupied himself with a cheap novel and occasionally lifted his eyes between chapters to yawn and blink at the mesmerizing figure pacing incessantly. He yawned particularly enthusiastically at one point and noted that now, on the fourth day, even the pigeons ignored Quintavalle's shoes and refused to scatter. When the yawn showed signs of promise, he rolled up the car windows and turned on his air conditioner. A pleasant humming emanated from the machinery and the cool air powerfully soothed him. He rested his head against a support, still eying Quintavalle, and yawned again. The more things changed, the more they stayed the same, he thought. The originality of the thought inspired him and he settled even more comfortably in his seat. As one eye drooped lazily, the other idled on Quintavalle's pacing.

The crowds hurried by, unaware of the private communion. There was a time when Quintavalle would have been embarrassed at talking aloud in public but he did not want to miss the signal. The longer he waited among the jostling crowds the more his friend was likely to speak. Quintavalle wanted to know what he must do next and the more he waited in limbo the more his agony increased. Sunlight swooped down with a favored grace; the light was reflected like a perfect mirror as Quintavalle shielded his eyes from the glare and blinked.

"I can't look at you for long," he confessed. "You're too bright."

He blinked harder; the light of the mirrored stone hurt his eyes and tears began to stream down his cheeks. For days he had waited, for afternoons in sunshine and in rain, for the words. Now, after nearly a week of patient waiting, they were coming.

It took only an instant, between the blinking of an eye, for the sign to be revealed. Stone lips moved, mica in the marble glinted, and the statue in the parking lot of Fisherman's Wharf became again a conduit of passion. The statue's eyes rose above the parking lot, above the crowds of tourists, and pointed as it did before toward the foggy reaches of the Great Highway and the zoo.

In his excitement at receiving the message, Quintavalle had to forcibly order his limbs to stop shaking. Control, he muttered to himself, control. He nodded at the statue, to let him know the orders had been received, and he caught himself swooning. "Francis," he whispered, "you were so sure of yourself they *had* to make you a saint."

The statue became cold and silent, lapsing into a mute timelessness as if the effort of speaking had wearied it beyond recovery. Only the rock remained and it stood, dignified and composed, the sun reflecting brightly from the specks of fire embedded in the dazzling stone.

The pear-shaped man was napping in his car as Quintavalle melted into the crowd. His steps were measured and quick, as if he were late for an appointment. He looked back once, smiling at the statue with reverence.

"Francis," he whispered.

■ ■ ■

Gordon removed his glasses and coughed. Papers scattered over the bed sheets and fell to the floor. He sat upright in the bed, pencils and fountain pens crammed in the pockets of his hospital gown. He coughed again and stared at his son.

"You haven't been listening," he croaked. He lifted an accusatory finger and brought it smartly down on a stack of papers. "We're going to do it this time, Steven."

"Sure," Steven said.

"Sure, sure, sure. Is that all you can say? We're going to do it this time, Steven. The Members' Society has come up with some good ideas. We're going to try the referendum again, break the zoo from politics and run it independently. A private society with no interference."

"That takes money."

"Of course it does," Gordon snapped. "And we'll get it. You

sound like a goddamn accountant. No, Steven. You do these things first, then you find the money. It's the only way. Don't you remember how Harry started the San Diego Zoo?"

"Yes," Steven sighed. His father began to sound like Charlie spouting off another story.

"He got a lion," Gordon said. "He stuck the beast in a plywood crate and said he was starting a zoo. Then he went to the city and said he couldn't be held responsible for what happens if the lion escapes. They hand over the money and tell him to build a stronger cage but get out somewhere in the hills. Harry builds the cage, the biggest and best-looking cage in Southern California, and goes back to the Council. He says now he's got the best cage in the world but nothing to put in it except a toothless, fleabitten lion. San Diego looks cheap. We'll have to buy more animals. And look what happened. He got away with those things, Harry did."

"I've heard that story a million times, Gordon. I was raised on it, remember?"

"Then I did a hell of a lousy job raising you," Gordon croaked. "You know, she said you wouldn't listen."

Steven raised his head. "What? Who did?"

"The girl."

"Which girl?"

"If you haven't noticed her you're sicker than I am. The girl who shoved these petitions in my lap. She's been coming to see me every night."

"What for?"

"She says she's been working in the children's zoo forever and now she wants to be a keeper."

Steven's jaw dropped. "She's lying. I just transferred her."

"I told her to ask you how to become a keeper. She said you wouldn't listen and you'd be gone tomorrow. She said you only listen to lectures and you get mad when you miss them."

"Gordon, she's—"

"She's *animal people!*" Gordon rasped. His face colored and the words strained from his throat. In his nervous agitation, his glasses slipped from the bed and clattered to the floor.

Steven bent down and picked the glasses up. They were old-fashioned bifocals, with tarnished wire rims and scratched lenses. Rubber bands had been wrapped around the side of the frame to keep it from slipping off Gordon's ears. And all Steven could think of was why his father couldn't buy new glasses. These were old, falling apart, and the rotten rubber bands left a sticky residue on his finger. When was the last time Gordon had his prescription checked?

Steven stood and tried not to look at his father. He could hear Gordon's wheezing, the cough and rattle that signaled the arguments that had always ended this way. But not this time, Steven swore to himself. He wasn't going to do it this time. No poison. *No more poison.*

"Okay," Steven said. He controlled his words carefully, trying to calm his father. "I'll help you weekends. I'll try to arrange my class schedule. We'll see what happens, okay? What do you want me to do?"

"First you can get me out of this damn hospital tonight for the members' banquet."

"No." Steven said, shaking his head. "The doctor said the last tests won't be finished until tomorrow."

"Then I'll walk out of here myself if you won't help me. I'm through with this hospital. I've got work to do."

Steven started for the door. "Goodbye, Gordon. I'm not going to argue with you. Argue with the Parcheesi lady. I've got to go back to the zoo."

"You'll be there tomorrow? Ten o'clock?"

Steven smiled weakly. "I'll be there. The whole goddamn zoo will be there. They want you back."

"We're going to do it this time, Steven."

"Of course we are. Didn't I say I'd help?"

Gordon waved him out of the room but Steven paused. There was something else. Something he had to say now, before his father returned to the zoo.

"Gordon," he began slowly. Steven found that it was easier to look at the floor as he spoke. "I'm never going to argue with you again. I want to help you. There are still . . . things left unfinished. Problems. I'll tell you tomorrow. Problems. You don't know."

"How can I understand if you don't tell me?"

"No more poison," Steven blurted. "I'm never going to argue with you again. I read your letter. Charlie didn't want to show it to me."

Gordon put his glasses on. "Letter? What letter?"

"The letter you typed to Charlie. He was forced to show it to me. It was an emergency."

Gordon blinked through his bifocals with a blank look on his face. "What are you talking about? I didn't type Charlie any letter."

Steven raised his head from the floor and stared at Gordon. His father wasn't lying. He really didn't know what Steven was talking about.

"*Shit!*" Steven yelled.

"Steven!" Gordon croaked. "What the hell is going on with you? Come back here."

Steven slammed the door and stalked down the hall with stomping feet. It was beginning to fall into place. The call at his lecture hall, the drive to City Hall, the big speech. The letter. Charlie had faked it. He had typed it because he couldn't forge Gordon's handwriting. Charlie had no intention from the beginning of taking over the zoo. Everything had been plotted and Steven fell into the trap like a fish. It explained why Charlie avoided the zoo except when "he smelled trouble." It explained everything—except why.

■ ■ ■

The Japanese lanterns made the plaza look festive. It was nearly midnight but the party was over. The waiters cleared the long tables covered with rented linen, punch bowls, serving trays, and

· 200 ·

flowers. Groups of people in evening clothes and shawls stood quietly talking.

The alpacas and sheep from the children's zoo wandered through the thinning crowd, nibbling somewhat less feverishly. The annual zoo Members' Night was their only chance to mingle with adults and they made the most of their elevation into society—variously sipping from champagne glasses, devouring cheese spreads, and taking an occasional hopeful sniff at genuine silk. Earlier one of the goats had eaten a lantern and was only narrowly rescued from electrocution by a quick-thinking Society member in a tailored safari jacket. The goat protested, sending the man sprawling into a patch of succulents. There he rested, slightly drunk and vaguely bewildered at the lowered horns trapping him in the bed of ice plants.

Steven skillfully nudged Amanda out of a group of tuxedoed stockbrokers and led her to a quiet place near the turnstiles. She was wearing her new children's zoo uniform with a stripe on the shoulder for "Animal Service, second class."

"I'm drunk," she said. "How about you?"

"Still standing," Steven answered.

They paused under the dark eaves of the ticket seller's booth.

"I haven't had a chance to talk with you," Steven began.

"What did you want to talk about?"

Steven looked sharply at her eyes but couldn't fathom the tone of her question. He waited a long minute. "How's the movie business?" he asked cryptically.

"I guess I'll find out tomorrow, won't I."

Steven nodded. He waited again. "Gordon's coming back at ten in the morning. Is there any chance you—"

"I have a flight at eleven. I think I can just make it."

"Good. He . . . asked for you. You never told me you were seeing him."

"And you?"

"What about me?"

"Are you going to be here?"

Steven nodded slowly. "I have a lecture in Berkeley at noon. Another quarter's starting and lots of—"

"Steven—"

"Yes?"

"You don't have to say anything."

Steven lit a cigarette. The flame flared and he dragged deeply. "Are you a good actress?" he asked. The ashy tip of the cigarette glowed red at his words.

"If they ask, then you can't be very good."

"I'm sorry. I didn't mean—"

"Skip it, I don't know what I was saying. Do you want another drink? I'm beginning to see clearly again and I think I need another one." She made a move toward the plaza.

"Wait," Steven said. He touched her arm. "When will I see you again?"

"After the party?"

"And after that?"

"We never did talk about that, did we?"

"You never wanted to. You always stopped me."

"Steven—" Amanda said.

"I want to talk about it now, before tomorrow."

"You're not ready to talk about it," Amanda said. "And I'm not drunk enough to listen. Steven—"

"Do you want that drink?" Steven interrupted her. For some reason he didn't want her to finish that sentence. "Let's go."

"Have you seen Charlie?" he asked as they headed back for the tables. As he spoke, his eyes continuously scanned the thinning crowd.

"No. I looked for him like you told me to but I haven't seen him."

"He said he was going to come," Steven said.

"It's not like him to miss free drinks," Amanda agreed. "But you know Charlie, he only shows up when there's trouble."

Steven looked at her sharply. "Why did you say that?"

Amanda shrugged. "I didn't mean anything. I was just thinking of his stories, that's all. I could listen to them for hours. Why do you want to see him? Won't he be here tomorrow when Gordon takes over?"

"There's something we have to settle before that. Something important."

Steven saw the headwaiter giving him a dark look signaling that overtime started in ten minutes for his crew. "Keep your eyes open for Charlie," he muttered to Amanda, and returned to the banquet area.

About fifty people remained in the plaza, clumped in groups and talking in low murmurs. The excursion tram was shut down and the special lights for the zoo grounds were already dismantled and packed. The busboys scurried around, folding chairs and unwiring the lanterns. Steven circulated slowly, gently guiding the groups toward the gates. His wrist ached from shaking hands all night and his mouth seemed frozen in an optimistic smile. Gordon needed the Members' Society. They were the strongest supporters of the zoo and they were flushed with the coming victory. Most of them had joined long ago, as a way of helping beyond just visiting. Now they found themselves pleasantly in the position of community leadership. Their opinions were eagerly sought and they willingly thrust themselves into active promotion.

It was after midnight when he said goodbye to the last person, a weaving matron with a drooping felt hat. Steven locked up the gates and joined Amanda in walking along the darkened path. Both of them were drunk and the chilly air made them hold each other closer.

Inside the cottage, Amanda pulled him to her. She kissed him without a word and they walked into the bedroom. He undressed and joined her under the covers. He was hungry for her. Her breasts were warm and he drank in her body, tasting her everywhere. She was just as hungry, running her hands over his legs and guiding him closer.

The wine wore off as they made love. The sweat rose on their bodies as Steven forced her mouth open with his tongue.

When they became still, when the beating in his chest slowed and he rolled aside to drift into sleep, his hand slipped between her thighs and rested on her damp hair. Amanda stirred, falling into his breathing rhythm, and she pulled the covers higher.

But the sweating didn't stop. It had started earlier that evening when he looked around the zoo party and realized that nobody knew what was going on. They were laughing and enthusiastic about Gordon's plans and they eagerly awaited his arrival in the morning. For them the chapter with Quintavalle was finished; the threat had been extinguished. Nobody knew about the kangaroo and the peccary. And Steven couldn't tell them.

The sweat didn't stop. What could he do? Time was running out. And as he lay on the bed next to Amanda, the dream came on waves of sticky sweat. Steven heard the roar of the hippo spraying blood, the sucking of the drainpipe as the inert sea lions, their bodies like stiff leather punching bags, twisted slowly in the current. The buzzing of flies collected around the antelope's throat. The wolves. He felt himself rolling down the drainage ditch with Quintavalle, rolling toward the bars and the hellish howling of tendon-straining throats. His hands were around Quintavalle's neck, choking. The spittle was spurting from Quintavalle's mouth like pulses of semen, Quintavalle shuddering in an orgasmic tremor of locked limbs and moaning ecstasy. The saliva drooled from his lips in the consummation of a holy and totally carnal desire. The kangaroo. The thick red paint that was blood. And then it came again.

The nightmare. The same one. He was burning. A ring of faces surrounded him. Hyenas. Their grinning sharply pointed teeth laughed at him. They were burning, too. Fur slid off their skin in flaming patches. The ground cracked open in pits and snakes squirmed out to escape the steam and heat. He tried to run but his feet had melted. He looked down and saw a turtle moving away. It crawled but it moved faster than he could. Then it stopped. Steven bent down and touched it. The shell crumbled into a flaky ash, singeing his fingers.

The cages were burning. All the animals were screaming. A gorilla! A magnificent mountain gorilla grasped the red-hot bars and strained to pull them apart. But they were too hot and he roared with pain and confusion. He beat his massive chest and bellowed. Ashes singed his hair. White. He was old. He was Boss-Man.

Steven groaned. The sweat ran down his face and he couldn't breathe. He yelled and jerked upright. The telephone jangled on the nightstand.

Amanda's hands were over him, wiping the sweat off with a cloth. She stared at him with horrified eyes.

"Steven! Are you all right?"

Steven gasped for air and looked around him as if he didn't know where he was. The telephone screeched.

"Should I answer it?" Amanda asked worriedly.

"Don't touch it," Steven shouted. Amanda drew back and stared at him in shock. The telephone. Steven looked at it. His hand slowly reached out and touched the receiver. Hot. It burned his fingers as he lifted it like a glowing coal near his ears.

"Yes?" Steven said.

"Steven Cooper? Is this Mr. Cooper?"

"Yes."

"I'm Dr. Mason, from UC Medical Center."

"Yes."

"I don't know how to tell you . . . it's very hard to say. Your father . . . Gordon . . . just passed away. Less than half an hour ago, peacefully, in his sleep. His nurse found him on her nightly rounds. I'm . . . very sorry to—"

"I understand," Steven said dully.

"The last tests I ran on him came in. They were . . . bad. I'm afraid he didn't have much—"

"You don't have to explain."

"I just want you to know that it was peaceful. He suffered no pain. He was a very brave man. I—"

Steven dropped the telephone on the cradle and stared at it. His body started to shake.

"Steven! What's wrong? What happened?"

"Gordon died," Steven said slowly. He shuddered. Boss-Man was dead.

"Oh, my God," Amanda cried, covering her mouth with her hand.

"Just a few minutes ago."

Amanda tried to touch him. "Steven, I'm sorry. I know how you—"

The scream stopped her cold.

Both of them jerked their heads toward the window. Steven

leaped out of the bed and ran toward the glass. The scream came again, this time louder. It started off on a high pitch, warbled, and then the tones separated as if ripped apart. It was piercing. The shriek held its strength, surging into the bedroom as if it were on some electronic feedback circuit. It whined. It cried like a broken bagpipe. Amanda's skin began to crawl. She covered her ears with shaking hands.

"What is it?"

"I don't know," Steven whispered.

"What do you mean? It has to be right outside the window."

"It's farther away."

A pause. "Is it a person?"

"No," Steven said. "It's an animal."

Amanda shivered. The high-pitched howl began again. The scream shuddered, fell in a throaty gurgle, and rose again. It was out of control this time; the notes blared without sense. It fell to a choking moan, then leaped again in a sirenlike blast.

"What kind of animal could scream like that?"

"I'm going to find out," Steven said, putting on his clothes.

"Wait. I'm going with you."

"You'd better stay here."

"Not on your life," she said. Amanda's hands grabbed her zoo uniform. "Nothing can keep me here alone with that noise."

Steven finished dressing and waited for her to catch up. He stood near the window, trying to stare through the darkness. The scream started again. And stopped.

Exactly in the middle of its wail it choked off. It had risen in pitch, gathered intensity, and then erased itself abruptly. There was a silence then, louder and emptier because of the howl that preceded it. Steven didn't know what animal it was. The sound was like nothing he had heard before—the gurgling, the shriek, the wavering trumpetlike screech. It had burrowed into his ears and burned inside. He was sure of only one thing—the animal was dying. He grabbed a flashlight and hurried down the hall. Noiselessly, he crept outside, motioning for Amanda to follow. Keeping to the side of the cottage, they headed for the bedroom window.

The moon was full. A dim mist had crept in from the ocean and lay like a blanket over the zoo. The moonlight filtered down in pale patches. Steven felt his way by memory; he didn't want to expose himself by turning on the flashlight. Their feet made no noise on the grass. Like the light, noises buffeted through in soft waves. The low din of the honky-tonk carnival rides rose and fell. Traffic noises from the highway seeped in. The mist itself could be heard settling on the leaves of trees.

Objects took on curious shapes, looming larger and more ominous. A rosebush stood a few feet away. A cluster of thin pine seedlings. He could see less than a dozen yards in the gloom. A small marble birdbath. Another bush. He strained his ears. Nothing. Signaling for Amanda to keep behind, he headed away from the cottage into the misty eucalyptus grove.

Step by step the huge trunks loomed into view. Steven stopped at the edge of the grove and waited. Nothing. He started to move inside. Like a door closing off a room, the sounds stopped. The trees baffled all noise. Strangely enough, there was more light inside the grove. The smooth eucalyptus bark reflected the moon glow. The ground was littered with rubble—seed pods, bark strips, and dried leaves. Then he heard it.

Far off, at the end of the grove, a crunch. A dead branch cracked. Footsteps hit the asphalt of the path beyond. Steven ran. He kept the flashlight dark, leaping across the rubble in high jumps. Like a deer flushed into flight, he ran toward the asphalt. He could hear Amanda crashing behind him, her shoes snapping on the seed pods.

At the end of the silvery grove Steven plunged into the suddenly darkened mist beyond. He felt the path under his feet but he had to stop at a fork. Turning his head, he listened for the footsteps. There! Left. Steven lifted his legs to run. He took two steps and sank into a shadow. But it wasn't a shadow. It was soft and giving and he fell. He rolled his shoulder to take the sprawl but the flashlight smashed into pieces.

Amanda finally caught up and he could hear her panting above him in the dark. Steven reached his hand toward the dark shape and touched it. It was warm. His fingers tried to smooth the ruffled feathers but most of the quills had been snapped. Automatically he felt for the bird's head and his hands passed up the neck. There was no head. A flap of skin slipped and a hard point of a neck vertebra jabbed his thumb. The bone jutted out; more blood oozed from loose spaghetti veins.

"Is it dead?" Amanda asked.

"It couldn't be deader," Steven said bitterly.

"What is it?"

"A peacock."

"Did it make the noise?"

Steven scrambled to his feet and pulled her away from the bird. They started running toward the footsteps. The moan still whined in Steven's memory, a sharp wail that rose ever higher. It cried in a blaring, trumpetlike call of terror. Higher, ever higher, the peacock whined. And stopped. Cut off from its scream, stopped midway, its blood surged through a suddenly severed throat.

Steven ran. The mist rolled through the zoo in great ground clouds, like wagons. Between the patches the moon exposed the dark shapes of cages. The animals were quiet. Most of them were asleep but the nocturnal beasts moved silently within their confinement, seeing everything but reserving comment.

They saw the light at the same time—from the open door of the elephant house, a momentary burst of flame. It vanished quickly and darkness again shrouded the area.

Steven nudged Amanda off the asphalt into the grass border as they approached the building from the cover of brush.

Mist hid the huge doors in a slowly churning cloud. Soon the fog rolled by and in the clear moonlight a figure could be seen just inside the elephant house. He was on his knees, fumbling at some sort of bucket. Another burst of light flashed; a long kitchen match trembled in a shaking tremor.

Steven gasped. Piles of straw from the elephants' bedding were heaped around the bucket. The dry tinder was smoking. A five-gallon can of gasoline lay on its side. The match sputtered out and the figure lit another one, lowering it to the rag-stuffed bucket.

Amanda cried softly, "Fire." It was all she could manage before Steven grabbed her arm.

"Get back to the cottage," he ordered. "Call the fire department."

"I can't leave you," she protested.

"Get away. Tell them to get here fast. Damn fast."

"But—"

Steven pushed her away, shoving her toward the cottage. Amanda started to object again but the look on Steven's face scared her. She turned. Her legs started to pump and she flew down the path into a cloud of mist.

Steven stared into the elephant house, trying to see the person's shape. When he recognized him, he also began to run.

Quintavalle prayed to the elephant as he had prayed to the hippopotamus, the great behemoth of Bible writ alone of God's creatures capable of sweating blood. He genuflected and knelt, begging forgiveness but yet prepared to justify a higher sanction. He prostrated himself before the elephant's stall and felt the ground tremble at the nervous stamping of the beast. His own heart fluttered. Never had he been so intimately close to such a mighty and intelligent creature and the experience catalyzed the familiar intoxication. He felt a tingle cross his skin as if he were in the presence of an unseen force concentrated and focused lenslike through the two immense all-seeing eyes of the land whale. Quintavalle's prostrate body scraped the dung-littered stall and he raised his head in awe of the chained beast enclosed in its boarded pyre. A current of highly polarized powerfully charged particles pulsed in a surging flux down his arms and through his wrists, forcing his stiffened fingers to repel one another. The elephant coughed, a massive throaty rumble of discontent, and Quintavalle received his commandments. The instructions were so clear, emblazoned upon the creature's forehead with a scarlet crystal script. The celestial vision hummed from laser eyes.

You know me, the elephant roared, *and the knowing will set me free.*

"Yes!" cried Quintavalle. "I know you." Quintavalle rolled in the elephant's dung, his coat and pants acquiring a scarecrow littering of soil and straw. "I know you as no man does," he called. He fumbled for his matches and when he grasped the wooden sticks Quintavalle could feel the cleansing power concealed in their heads. He was about to begin his rite of purification when he saw him. He thought his mind was playing tricks.

"Ack," Quintavalle grunted, and scowled. He blinked hopefully but it was no use. The Devil was approaching, running out of the mist. From deep within, Quintavalle had always prepared himself with the inevitability that the more ardently he consummated his devotions the more vigorous his opposition would grow. It was the way of the world, he sadly concluded; with the knowledge of the planet's workings came only a confirmation of his already bleak suspicions. He accepted the conflict as an eternal dilemma relegated to perpetuity and almost wearily rose to do battle for his colors. "Ack," Quintavalle groaned. He studied the Devil now flying through the barn door toward him and wondered why the manifestation still bothered to disguise his hooves with shoes, his tail with pants. Quintavalle finished striking the match and lowered it to the rag-stuffed bucket.

The flame instantly exploded and Quintavalle cowered before the fiery bucket, mesmerized by the chain of events he had initiated. He mumbled a few hurried incantations and blinked again in faint hope of projecting the charging Devil to another less immediate astral plane. As the fire spread to the stall, the hay litter absorbed the flames hungrily and the stamping of the elephants was shattered by the piercing trumpet blasts of terror. And still the Devil came!

He was ten feet away and springing for his final leap when Quintavalle spied the pitchfork. He grabbed the handle, jerked the tines toward the Devil, and stood.

The impact was extraordinary as the Devil in one moment saw the pitchfork, tried to stop, couldn't, and dropped his jaw as his belly ran into the tines.

Quintavalle saw the Devil's arms rise in a useless slow-motion flap and he felt the Devil impaled and connected through the trident like a speared sea fish wiggling in terror. Quintavalle clucked triumphantly, drooling in exultation, and in his excitement let loose the pitchfork.

"Ah-*eee*," he cried. "I've caught you now."

The flames, now a dozen feet tall and lapping up the beams, were reflected like ruby veins in Quintavalle's quartz eyes. He cackled and began to dance in a mad waltz around the crumpled Devil, still clutching the pitchfork embedded in his belly.

"I've caught you now," Quintavalle cried. "You're trapped by your own iron. Can you speak, Devil? Look at the iron. Your iron. The blasphemy of your trade."

"Stop . . . must put out the fire," the Devil gasped.

"It is the last fire," Quintavalle howled. "The holiest fire."

"More?" the Devil choked, clutching the pitchfork tines with bloody fingers. "You set more?"

The booms of the terrified elephants drowned Quintavalle's answer. His cheeks danced in agitation and he shivered in the heat of the burning barn now intense with crackling flames. "I've set the fires all over the temple," he cried. "The flames of freedom are alive."

With eyes that refused to blink Quintavalle stared at the disguised Devil. When his shaking hands grabbed a bull hook he prodded the writhing archangel below him with short anxious probes. "Where are your hooves?" Quintavalle demanded. He tapped the Devil's shoes and the hook shook with exasperation. "Your tail," he demanded. "Show me your tail. Produce your horns, I tell you." But the choking Devil refused to do anything more than clutch his belly and spit and utter feeble curses. "*I want to see your hooves!*" Quintavalle screamed. An answering bellow thundered from the elephant behind him and the barn now echoed with the furies of many enraged beasts. Quintavalle began to dance. "All I want," he cried, "is the sign. Can't you see what I want? The last sign."

Just as quickly as the mad waltz ebbed from his electric feet, the vast aloneness clutched Quintavalle's lungs. The bull hook dropped from his hands as he crept from the burning barn into the hotter mist.

Now he could return with honor to his pets—his kittens, his guppies, and his birds. He would sit on the outside of the cages and look at himself looking out. He would go to work at the tollbooth, in his box on the bridge, and collect tolls from other moving cages belching sulfurous fumes. Maybe Francis's voice wouldn't bother him anymore. The final steam was collecting around his body and he shivered.

It was surprise at first. Steven knew exactly how he felt. Surprise that the tines broke his skin so easily. Surprise that the metal rods punctured his flesh so casually. They slipped in so easily, so deep.

And the pain—that was a surprise, too. There was none. Steven looked down and saw the tines in his belly. He saw the handle wobble and the movement carry deep in his guts. He staggered backward. All he could think of was to hold the pitchfork so it wouldn't tear his organs.

Steven collapsed. His leg muscles vanished and he crumpled to the ground. His mind screamed. *Don't fall on it!* He landed on his back. His hands fumbled at his belly, feeling for his wet intestines. The flames marched higher on the walls of the elephant house but he couldn't see. Everything was moving in freeze frames, trapped in a strobe light's explosions. The pitchfork was shiny. Then it became dark with blood.

Bamma trumpeted. The elephant stamped her legs furiously and rattled her chains. She tugged at the links, straining to escape her bondage with the flames leaping at her flank. A siren's wail drifted into the barn, shrilling between the crackles of fire and the elephant's screams. Steven heard the fire engines in the distance, the squealing of the service gate being rammed, the rumble of trucks scrambling on gravel. The din grew closer as his mind grew quieter.

Steven saw someone leaning above him, a face twisted with

fear. The pitchfork was pulled out of his belly and Steven's hands clutched the bleeding wound. Sirens. The barn was full of smoke and people. Hissing. The CO_2 extinguishers exploded like steam into the hay. The choking air burned with fumes and raw heat. He felt himself lifted and he protested. Someone slapped him across the cheeks and he found he could become angry. Outside someone laid him on the grass. Gritting his teeth, he screamed at his belly.

The clearing in front of the elephant house was packed with fire trucks. Dozens of dark-coated firemen leaped off running boards with axes in hand as they attacked the barn. A nurse truck rumbled and geysers of water sprayed the night. People were shouting, running, yelling orders. And as Steven held his stomach in, he realized why.

Flames crackled across the entire zoo. Far to his left he could see yellow fire licking the trees of Asian Hill. Several hundred yards to the right a generator plant erupted in spark-showers. The eucalyptus grove was completely engulfed in flame. The oils in the strips of bark sputtered in colors and lifted the fire higher into the crowns where a gusty wind threatened to spread the flames to the cat house. Then Steven heard the sounds.

The monkeys shrilled. They clumped together on the summit of Monkey Island's mountain and shrieked. The cats roared, the deep-throated roar against a fire they smelled but could not see. The zoo reverberated with the coughs, the panting, choking exhalations of hundreds of small animals. They had never known fire in their lives but they reacted instinctively to the fumes, the clouds of smoke, and the screams of their neighbors. The bears began to clatter their claws against the bars. The rodents clicked their teeth against the cage wire and the owls hooted. An elephant trumpeted. The tremendous blast was joined by another, then another. Bamma!

Steven screamed at his legs and as if in terror, his toes began to answer. They moved, Steven could feel them, and then they began to follow orders. Steven felt for broken bones but could find none. Only one of the pitchfork tines had embedded deeply and when it was pulled out no more damage was done. Blood still poured from the puncture wound but Steven felt it diminish. He staggered to his feet and panted. The pain was blinding but he could move!

He pushed himself away from the barn and lurched to the control car with the heaviest collection of flashing red lights. Searching for the fire chief, he hobbled into a group of men.

"The elephants," Steven choked. "You've got to unchain them."

The group parted and the fire marshal looked at Steven. "Who are you?"

"I'm the director," Steven shouted. "You've got to get the elephants out of the barn."

As he spoke, Steven realized that the order was unnecessary. The firemen had already chopped the chains with their axes and the ground shook as the elephants charged from the barn. Their trunks boomed in the raised call of danger against the only enemy they feared. Their broken chains dragged along the asphalt as their heavy feet stampeded toward open ground. They blasted the air—thundering like a succession of giant cathedral organ pipes, a terrified fugue.

"The animals," Steven shouted. "You've got to let them out of the cages."

The fire marshal's transmitter sputtered with reports from his units. His cool eyes studied Steven with a professional glance. Passing his hands over Steven's wound, he ordered softly, "You're going to be all right. You're in shock, do you hear? You'll be okay if you don't move. There's a lot of blood gone but you're okay." The marshal brought up the transmitter to his lips and barked loudly, "Bring the ambulance to the elephant barn. We have an injury." Then he turned back to Steven. "Lie down. Don't move." He motioned a fireman to lead Steven away to a bed of pine needles.

"I can't," Steven protested. "I have to get the animals out."

"You're not doing anything," the marshal snapped.

"The animals!"

"Right now I'm in control."

"But—"

"Listen, if I don't stop it, you won't *have* any animals left. Get out of here. You can't do anything in your condition."

"It's my zoo."

"It's *my* fire," the marshal yelled. "Get the hell out of our way."

The fireman pulled Steven away and dragged him to a clearing where he collapsed. He lay on his back and saw the marshal ordering more equipment and directing the ladder trucks toward the Mammal House.

The sweat came, pouring over his face in waves of salty wetness. He gagged and his stomach twisted in pain. He began to choke from the smoke pouring from the elephant house and he felt his vision fading. Steven realized that he was going blind. The circle was closing; it was dark all around.

No! he said. *I can't.* He had to keep awake. Now all he could see were two circles, ends of binoculars. He was growing cold. He wanted to sleep. Cold and dark. The noises faded.

No!

Steven bit his tongue. He stuck it between his teeth and bit hard. He tasted blood. Harder he bit, the pain searing his brain. Pain. He needed the pain to keep awake.

He rose in a crouch, staggered, and leaned against a tree. Slowly, incredibly slowly, he raised his body straight and tested his legs. He bit his tongue again to feel the pain that was his only life. He had to call the keepers. He had to get help. Why didn't Amanda come back?

Steven found a stick and hobbled away from the elephant house toward the cottage. The phones. He had to get help. Where was Amanda? He had to tell her.

The carnival was on his left. The lights sprayed the path with fiery colors. Why didn't she come back? Where was Amanda?

———

Amanda slammed the telephone down. She had called the fire department and Harriet and now she thought furiously. Who else? There's no time, she decided. Steven would know what to do. She had to get back to Steven.

Amanda fled from the cottage and ran toward the elephant house. She was just passing the carnival when it happened.

To her right was a small grove of pine trees between the zoo and the carnival grounds. A trash can was set in the middle and as Amanda passed, it exploded into flames. A five-gallon gasoline can was hurled like a mortar shell and landed in dry pine brush. The carpet of needles flared up and in seconds the saplings caught fire. Dry as tinder, they burned intensely. The sap vaporized and then only the main outline of the stems could be seen in the cone of flames. As Amanda stared in horror, the bed of fire spread laterally, eating into the bigger trees. The grove was only yards away from the carnival fence, where the canvas tents and pennants beckoned like a fuse.

Amanda gasped. A tall pine tree had sucked a fireball up its trunk; it whirled up like a burning tumbleweed. A breath of wind fanned the ball and flaming pinecones shot out like hand grenades over the fence.

She had to warn them. They didn't know. Amanda turned away from the elephant house and ran toward a safe part of the fence. She scrambled up the chain links and dropped into the carnival's back lot. Just beyond the row of tents came noisy sounds of laughter and cries. She burst through a side tent and the lights blinded her. Above the carnival a steel tower jutted above a midway—its support legs emblazoned with flashing trails of incandescent displays. A calliope shrilled. A pounding organ moaned from a neon-sprayed carousel. Thudding target pistols exploded. The loudspeakers in front of the sideshows blared scratchy snippets of music; barkers exhorted the streaming throngs of giggling, shouting merrymakers. The carnival stayed open late on Saturday night; the crowd boiled in their lurching, weaving search for noise, light, smells, and packed movement.

Amanda literally pushed herself into the stream. She felt herself caught up at once in the current of sweating, wild-eyed bodies rushing everywhere. Her legs hurt. Her uniform had been torn by the fence and the scratches began to bleed. She had to warn them.

"Fire!" she screamed. She held her hands around her mouth and shouted as loud as she could. *"Fire!"*

Someone jostled her. A man in a Coast Guard uniform. He grinned at her before she was swept away. Amanda felt herself spinning around. She was being pushed backward. The jangling of the carousel started and the strains of tremendous organ music screamed in her ears.

"Fire!" she yelled. "You've got to get out of here."

She pounded on the backs of two men with fringed leather jackets and cowboy hats. They scowled at her and moved away.

"Fire!" she shouted. "Can't you hear me?"

A woman turned around and laughed at her. She giggled and tossed her electric yo-yo into the air. It sprayed blue sparks across the dazzling sky before it snapped back on its return spring. The woman laughed louder and flung the yo-yo again into the air. The string broke, sending the spark-flashing piece of plastic in a soaring arc.

Amanda spied a barker in front of a tent. He was standing on a bally and exhorting the crowd to enter, join the fun inside, get close together and laugh as you've never laughed before for the price of a thin half dollar that will prove to your lady you're not cheap and is that a bargain, men, or is it not a bargain? He swung a bullhorn in front of his mouth and boomed into the ocean of faces streaming past. The bullhorn. She must get him to warn the people.

Amanda shoved her way through the crowd and made the bally. Reaching to pull herself up, she saw the barker eying her suspiciously. Still spouting his patter, he moved over, put his foot on her toes, and pressed. "Cool it, sister. Lay off the sauce, eh?" Then he continued his spiel and exhorted the crowd to step right in.

Amanda screamed as the man stepped on her toes. She beat his ankle and punched him in the shins. "Fire," she yelled. "You've got to clear the carnival."

The barker looked down at her with another sneer, then he heard the sirens. He glanced where Amanda pointed. From his height on the bally he saw the flames attacking the first row of tents. The sneer faded from his lips and he dropped the bullhorn. Taking a running leap from the bally, he jumped into an open space and fled toward the highway.

Amanda scrambled up on the stand and grabbed the loud-speaker. The people whirled in front of her in spinning confusion; their heads twisted, and all Amanda could see were mouths thrust back in howls of laughter, shiny eyes, and faces flushed with fever. "You've got to leave the carnival," she yelled. Her voice boomed into the crowd. "Do not panic. There is a fire in the zoo and it's coming into the carnival. There's plenty of time if you leave quickly."

The screams started then. The first wave of flames engulfed the cotton-candy stand and poured into the lot. People were shouting. They ran in terrified madness away from the fence.

Hundreds fled past the bally—shoving, pushing, and dropping food. Coke bottles clattered on the ground, spinning against stuffed animals and bronze horses. Cheap porcelain prizes crunched under the onslaught of stamping feet and cotton candy stuck like pink burrs to pant cuffs.

The entire carnival plunged into darkness. The screams erupted louder. A fireworks display of sparks shot from a power shed. The smell of burning insulation added its stink to the smoke. Then the lights burst on again and the carousel organ went wild. The shrill protests of its bearings screeched as the giant wooden platform sped faster. The whirling carousel flung people off; they shot out like stones and landed in heaps on the ground, where they picked themselves up and joined the mad flight.

The lights flickered and Amanda smelled the smoke and the sweat of fear. The people thinned in front of her. Gradually the ground came into view with its littered carpet of trash. Nearly everyone had run for the safety of the highway and only a few stragglers remained. Jumping off the bally, she made sure nobody was left in the penny arcade or the shooting gallery. Then she started to run past the carousel away from the fire toward safety.

She stopped. There was someone left in front of her. Like a beach wave slipping back to sea and leaving a chunk of driftwood stuck in the sand, the man crouched. He was thirty feet away, hiding under a lurid trailer poster advertising fat freaks and lizard people. His back hunched under the poster, as if clinging for security. His eyes jerked left and right, his tongue flickered out like a nearsighted snake testing for danger. Then Quintavalle saw Amanda.

Amanda screamed. But the sound wouldn't come out. She opened her mouth but nothing could come out. She screamed because Quintavalle was coming toward her.

He was taking short jerky steps. His head rolled from side to side and his eyes were white. His body jerked in a quivering St. Vitus's dance. Waving his hands in front of him, his fingers twisted in spastic passes as if he were warding off a spell. A strange chant screeched from his lips. But Amanda wasn't watching his mouth; she stared in horror at the carving knife that had appeared like a flash from inside his coat.

She stumbled backward. She was trapped. The fire was only fifty feet behind her and coming faster. Her stomach began to fall. The knife, it couldn't be real. He won it in a penny toss game. Amanda cried in relief. *Plastic.* It was a plastic imitation.

Then Quintavalle swung the knife at an awning and the thick canvas parted like cheese.

Smoke poured into the lot, great rolling clouds of ashy particles. She moved to the side, almost tripping on a bottle. Her hands wavered for balance and she felt the side of the shed that controlled the carousel. The organ music thundered above the lot, into the air, into her ears. Deserted! There was nobody left. Everyone had fled. Quintavalle stalked closer. He waved the knife, passing it back and forth with contorted hand signals. He bent his knees, twisted his body, and straightened again. Each time the knife rose higher in the air.

Is this what it feels like to die? Amanda cried to herself. Why can't I stop thinking? Why can't I shut off my mind? Is this how the animals felt? I can't move. My legs won't move. Even my toes. Is this how the animals felt? *I can't move.* Why can't I stop thinking? It's not hypnotism, I know who I am. I'm in control— but that's a lie. I can't control anything. Is this how it feels to die? Why can't you move when you're going to die? Why can't you think? *The carousel!*

The knife was slashing toward her neck when Amanda turned and jumped. The carousel thundered past; she flung out a hand and grabbed a pole. Swept off her feet. The merry-go-round yanked her arms from her shoulder sockets and the organ screamed in her ears. She saw colors spin past—blue light, pink glows, red sparks. Her feet scrambled to find a perch on the moving platform. Her ankle caught a leg of a carved wooden horse and she clung to its hooves with straining hands.

■■■

Quintavalle was seeing things again. He was a broken man. Failed, he thought, the Devil has finally won. He has sent his army after me. She is wearing the uniform of the Devil's army. I will never be safe. He found my apartment house because my righteousness was growing too strong for him. He was only teasing me. He's playing with my mind, to make me see things that aren't there. Sulfur! I smell sulfur burning and the Devil is here. What kind of magic,

O dear God, what kind of magic can protect me? I am not prepared, I don't know anything. Please help me.

Quintavalle passed his knife in the air, then swirled it like a hashish-crazed Kurd, like a ganja-mad Rastafarian. He grunted in cabalistic mutters. I see you, he screamed at the Devil's angel. I see you but I know you're not real. I know that if I cut your neck, if I slice you in pieces, you'll still haunt me. Each piece of you will grow like a starfish leg and follow me like a heathen voodoo Baron Samedi. You are not real. If I stab you your flesh will part like soft butter. *But the Reaper must reap.* Quintavalle swung his carving knife down, slashing at her throat.

Gone! Vanished. The angel took flight with invisible wings and Quintavalle cowered with fear. O dear God, he moaned, help me. My mind is infected and I cannot see the clear path. Something is rotting inside me. I smell my own putrid stink. The fires. The fires are scalding my brain and I cannot lead anymore. Help me.

Quintavalle opened his eyes. The angel was flying toward him. She was riding a horse, a magnificent black stallion with eyes of burning rubies and snorting clouds of steam. Such a powerful steed he had never seen! His heart beat faster. Quintavalle cried in awe and slashed at her again, thrusting with all his might.

Missed! His knife found only air. The angel taunted him. Quintavalle cried. Tears streamed down his cheeks and he sobbed. His eyes flooded with tears and when he took in a breath, he saw it. God sent him the miracle!

He heard it first. The bells. The silvery bells and then the horns of Gabriel. Quintavalle cried but they were tears of joy. Had the sounds been there all along? Hadn't he seen it? The miracle was before him, the sign was a spinning whirlwind. THE ANIMALS ARE COMING! The words of joy dribbled from his mouth. The animals! Oh, they were so wonderful. Oh, glory, oh, sweet glory. He licked his lips and tasted.

Following the Devil angel marched a legion of stallions, each saddled and bridled for the chase. Quintavalle gasped. A rabbit, a giant smiling rabbit. A bird! A hawk? An eagle? A gyrfalcon? Such a fine bird it was, with beak of silver and talons of steel. It clawed at the heels of the stallions, forcing them *on, on, on.* A dragon! A flame-breathing Chinese glory in sparkling scarlet and gold. He was saddled, too, with blankets of silk, stirrups of gold. A camel! A two-humped desert camel dripping with the blinding finery of the Orient. A stag! A leaping, bounding Irish stag with mighty antlers that jabbed the camel *on, on, on.* A panda! A herculean black-and-white panda with glory upon his face. A blazing flamingo, dagger neck, flying *on, on, on.*

Quintavalle rocked on his heels, flushed with dizziness. He was astonished at his miracle. He wanted to drop on his knees, kiss the ground, and utter a thousand thanks for his astonishing vision. But something was wrong. Wrong. And then he frowned, the same painful frown that had twisted his cheeks so many times when he had tried to see clearly. Quintavalle shook his head. Spoiled. An irritating anomaly threatened to spoil everything. Devils did not belong in miracles, nor did their hirelings. Quintavalle took a running jump and leaped at the hated angel, his knife flashing.

He landed in a heap under the hooves of the leaping stallions. He shielded his face but the blows never came. The stallions were frozen. Quintavalle felt the world rumble and shake under him. He studied his miracle as a conscientious and awed explorer finding himself suddenly on unmapped territory where every leaf and pebble was a novelty. Wood. Wooden floorboards, creaking and jerking. He tried to stand and felt the wind whistling past his ears. He was flying! A great force threatened him, forcing him away from the center. He crouched, hanging on with his weaponless left hand to poles that pierced every animal. If the angel had stabbed his animals and frozen them, then the same punishment must be given to her.

There! The angel was in front of him. She clung underneath a coal-black stallion in the lead. Quintavalle lurched toward her. From one horse to the next, he dragged himself forward. Lights flickered. Darkness. The horns of Gabriel melted. And blew again! Faster! He was flying faster. The wind slapped his face; great streams of tears poured down his cheeks. Quintavalle cried and pulled himself forward. The angel was below him now; she, like his animals, was frozen in fear.

Quintavalle prayed and with his prayers sought guidance and strength for his final oath of fealty. Dear God, we've won. She's lying there with fear in her eyes. Dear God, help me guide my weapon true to her heart. Dear God, help me lead the animals to Heaven.

Quintavalle raised his carving knife high. The wind whipped his hair and whistled past his shrieking teeth. He plunged it toward her lungs.

■ ■ ■

Steven heard her screams. He heard her voice above the carousel organ and above the crackling flames of the pine grove. But the heat pushed him back. The hot wind punched him in the stomach and he held his belly tightly. He had stumbled up a mound of chaparral, reached the unburned section of fence, and now looked down upon the carnival a hundred yards away.

He saw the empty lot and Amanda in the center. Someone was walking toward her, hopping erratically. She was crying and Steven saw a knife glint. Quintavalle! He saw her jump on the carousel and Quintavalle's knife narrowly miss her throat. Then Quintavalle jumped on the carousel and crawled toward her.

Steven's fingers grabbed the chain links and he tried to pull himself up. But as soon as his arms rose, the pain in his belly screamed and he started to drip blood. He pressed his face against the fence, staring at Amanda. He couldn't move. Her uniform flashed every time the carousel revolved but Steven could only watch helplessly. She spun in a circle; Quintavalle crawled closer.

Steven began to slip to the ground, his fingertips clutching and releasing each link as he dropped in a faint.

The wind. From the south?

The wind, fanned by the zoo's fires, rose in strength and charged over the grounds. The hot air burned Steven's belly. The wind, Steven thought, the fires of hell.

Damn it. From the south?

The wind is from hell, Steven swore to himself, and it's blowing over the pits of steam. He was going blind again. The tunnels of his vision narrowed into cones, into smaller circles, and finally into pinpoints. I don't care about the wind, he silently screamed. Leave me alone.

If you're not going to tell me, then get the hell out of my way.

Go away, Steven swore, leave me alone. Quit yelling at me. I can't see. I'm falling.

"Get the damn hell away from the fence. You're shaking it, Steven."

Steven released his hands. He fell in the dirt and watched the fence stop its shaking.

"Stand up. Help me, goddammit."

Steven bit his tongue again. The pain came. He twisted his head back. The greyness left. He could see!

Charlie sprawled on the ground less than a dozen feet away. He lay on his belly, his legs spread out wide for balance. His left elbow rested solidly in the dirt, his right arm cradling the Holland & Holland's butt against his leather shooting patch. He was swearing at Steven.

"The wind! Which way is it coming from?"

Steven swallowed his blood. He coughed and tried to rise into a crouch, clutching his leg. He stared at Charlie. "What?"

"The wind? Is it from the south? I can't see."

Steven looked around him, at the ground and the fire.

"Not here, damn it. At the carousel."

Steven pulled his head back and stared through the fence and the hundred yards beyond. Wind? What did Charlie want? The wind! Steven saw the pennants of the penny arcade next to the carousel. They flapped in the strong breeze. The east!

"East!" Steven yelled. "It's from the east."

Charlie swore and shifted the barrel of the rifle a millimeter to his left. He strained his eyes through his bifocals and clenched his teeth. "The sights," he shouted at Steven. "Did you change them? Did you touch them?"

"No," Steven yelled.

Charlie grunted and muttered another curse at the rifle. "They were set for fifty yards. How far is the carousel?"

Steven raised his head. "A hundred. A hundred yards."

"Bullshit," Charlie thundered. "You're blind. It's a hundred-fifty. You were always blind, Steven." Charlie raised the tip a millimeter. He had corrected for wind drift and now he was locked in on distance through the critical sights.

"It's a hundred," Steven cried.

"Bullshit."

"Charlie!"

"My glasses, damn it." Charlie coughed. He could handle the rifle, he could cradle it like a baby because he had learned from the best. And Percival, the limey Percival, had taught him the spots forty years ago, the pressure not to shoot until the one perfect spot presented itself. The Holland & Holland .375 was the smallest elephant gun made. It was too small—outlawed because nobody could bring down a bull with it for sure. Unless you knew the spot. The lions had their spot—just above the shoulder blade, between the two large ribs. The rhino had its spot, and the Cape buffalo. He had learned the spots from Percival and he learned to wait for the one good shot that always came and you took it if you were good and you jumped it if you were bad. Charlie was good. He had been the best. But he didn't wear glasses then. He never saw the spot waver in fog and then completely disappear as the mist and sweat condensed on the lenses, blinding him. He couldn't see.

"A hundred," Steven yelled. "It's a football field away."

"A hundred-fifty," Charlie yelled.

"Charlie!"

Charlie squeezed.

■ ■ ■

Amanda groaned. She was lying fifteen feet from the carousel which was now slowly grinding to a stop. She didn't remember letting go, sliding across the boards and shooting off the carousel like a centrifugal missile. She didn't remember the hiss of the wind and the shriek.

She groaned again. With her eyes closed she ordered her muscles to respond. Was anything broken? She moved her legs, her feet. Okay. But her arm. Something was pressing her left arm.

Her eyes fluttered open and it was then that she saw Quintavalle's body lying on her left arm. He was on his side and Amanda saw a small spot in his breast pocket. It was dark, like a tiny dimple, right above his heart. She tried to pull her arm away and then she saw Quintavalle's back. His coat was gone; handfuls of flesh from the bullet's exit wound hung loosely by strands of tissue. Shattered pieces of his spine and ribcage poked out. The soft lead slug had flattened upon impact and tore, twisting, into his heart. Exploding out, it left a hole—a trench—a foot across.

Amanda pulled her arm free and she rested, panting. Close my eyes, she ordered, close my eyes. She couldn't move. Her breath came in great lungfuls and she lay exhausted and sick.

Finally she pulled her body away and Quintavalle's frame convulsed in spastic tremors. His tongue jerked and slowly, sickeningly slowly, he tightened into a fetal position. Then he was still.

She heard the siren of the ambulance coming closer. It raised great clouds of dust as it sped across the lot and slammed its brakes in front of the carousel. The back door flew open and Charlie jumped out with two medics.

"Quick," Charlie yelled. "Get in. He wants you to go with him to the hospital."

Amanda stared in confusion. The medics had picked up the corpse of Quintavalle and shoved it inside the ambulance under another stretcher. There was another body in the ambulance and Amanda, numb and shaking, walked closer.

"Steven!" she cried.

Steven raised his head at her cry. He blinked his eyes and tried to raise a hand. He couldn't. "The fire," he gasped, "get away before it gets you, too."

Amanda jerked her head to stare behind her. The carnival was in flames but behind, in the zoo, the grounds blazed even fiercer. "Steven—"

"Get in," Steven said. "Come away with me."

"Steven, I can't—"

"Get away from the fire."

"Steven. The *animals.*"

"Burning," mumbled Steven feverishly. "Come with me."

"Who's going to save the animals?"

Steven blinked his eyes again and he stared with delirious eyes. "Come with me," he choked.

"Who's going to take care of the animals?"

Charlie roared. "Make up your mind, damn it. The fire's coming."

Amanda cried. She took a step for the ambulance and stopped. Then she reached out her hand and grabbed the door. Slamming it shut instead, she screamed at the terrified driver. "Get away," she yelled. "Get him away."

The driver accelerated in a scramble of stones and roared out of the smoking lot. The siren began its howl and then the flashing red lights were lost in smoke. Amanda turned to Charlie.

"How do we get back? Is there time?"

"Follow me," Charlie ordered. "This way."

Steven stared at the medics hovering over his legs. They were attaching plasma bottles to a stand and the plastic tubing started to drip its fluid into his veins. They attacked his blood-soaked pants with scissors and packed the wound with sterile gauze. A pillow was stuffed under his head and he could see the zoo flash by through the tiny back window. The ambulance passed the park grounds and Steven saw the fires burning. The nightmare had happened. He was one of the few who saw their dreams come true.

But were the screams he heard real? Could he really hear the lions' howls above the screaming tires? Was that the elephant's trumpet above the siren? The ambulance had a tiny vent near the floor. Steven stared at the hole and saw the lane markers of the Great Highway flash past at sixty miles an hour. And then he saw the ticket.

The medics had cut away his pants and the admission stub protruded like a bit of lint in his right pocket. How long ago had he bought it? Two weeks? Three weeks? Why did he buy it?

The bit of paper dropped toward the floor of the ambulance. The stub spun in the air and was sucked out the hole. His job was finished. He had kept the zoo for Gordon.

Who's going to take care—

Amanda's face hovered over his eyes. Why didn't she come? He needed her.

—of the animals?

Charlie bent over him, yelling in his ear.

There's nobody else.

One of the medics cursed as he stumbled over Quintavalle's corpse. He shoved the body away and then wiped his foot off. Steven's head flopped over and he stared at Quintavalle. So it was true what Amanda had said when she ran away from Steven after their first meeting. Amanda was right when she said Quintavalle looked like Steven. They were the same height. The same color of eyes. The same build. He had never really looked at Quintavalle before. In death, the body of Quintavalle looked even more ordinary. But it's not true, Steven thought, how much different Quintavalle's life would have been. A pet. If only he had had a pet when he was young. If Quintavalle had been allowed to take care of an animal, to love it, to respect it—none of this would have happened. It would have been so easy for someone to have given him a pet when he was young and just left him alone with it. The love for animals would have naturally progressed, the respect would have instinctively matured. Why hadn't someone given Quintavalle a pet?

The medic hovered over Steven's face. "Quiet," he ordered, laying a wet cloth over Steven's temple. "You're in shock. You don't know what you're saying."

But Steven stared at the ceiling of the van hurtling down the road. He stirred. The poison was breaking. He felt the fresh plasma surge into his veins, displacing the venom. And it was Charlie who had killed Quintavalle, Charlie and his stories.

"Don't talk," the medic ordered.

■ ■ ■

The gibbons howled. They clustered and shrieked and much to their surprise, the sun rose upon command just as it always had. The pink glow spread over the acres next to the ocean and as always, the gibbons hooted. But they had seen the light before, the red brilliance that had flooded the zoo in great shafts of fiery radiance. The gibbons' arithmetic was poor; three suns in two days added in only slight confusion. Their subtraction was poorer; they could not understand why the old male was missing. The young male instead led the pack's first whoop-whooping. He filled his air sac almost until it burst; he expelled his whoops with a freedom that was only equaled by the delight he felt in being out of his cage. The troupe gathered upon the highest crown of a pine tree. Below them, the black bark smoldered.

The gibbons interspersed their whoops with a few snarling hisses directed toward the ground where three men with nets yelled back. They thrust long poles at the gibbons and hollered. The gibbons hooted enthusiastically; they welcomed all the help they could get in raising the sun.

From their perch high in the pine trees, the gibbons saw the smoke rising in wispy plumes across the zoo. The charred stumps and lumber puffed last gasping trails. Small jets of water spraying from garden hoses spurted here and there as keepers doused the last stubborn glows. A flock of Barbary sheep streaked across South American Hill in complete disregard of geographical distribution; an alpaca chewed disdainfully at tufts of burned grass among the African plains. A snarling warthog backed into the women's rest room and curled his lips to expose fierce tusks at two men who hopefully pushed an open crate toward the beast. And as the sun climbed the sky and flooded the zoo, the air resounded with hooves clattering on asphalt, horns scraping against hastily thrown lassos, and carpenters' hammers attacking plywood.

Charlie gulped his coffee, the first nourishment he had taken in ten hours. He swore silently at the taste. Harriet was passing out candy bars and coffee from the urn set out in the main plaza. She handed the steaming cups to the long line of smudge-faced workers. Charlie had established "temporary camp headquarters" on the lawn in front of the main gate and he listened to the keepers' reports as they staggered in. He didn't know what to do. Everything was getting too complicated. He couldn't think.

The sweat poured from his face, leaving streaks in the layer of soot that caked his skin. His clothes reeked of smoke; the lack of sleep made his eyes redder than the scarlet macaw still uncaptured on top of the tram garage. He looked past the army of exhausted faces but for the first time that morning he didn't see any remaining smoke.

The fire had destroyed a quarter of the grounds before the firemen brought it under control. Amanda had sounded an alarm to Harriet and the emergency calls went out to keepers at home. They poured into the zoo in pajamas, raincoats, and bare feet— unlocking the cages of threatened exhibits and chasing the animals to fend for themselves. The fire marshal contained the blazes and dispatched trucks to drench the most important areas. He left the forests to burn themselves out and instead concentrated on saving the evacuated animal buildings. In spite of his efforts, half of the cat house was destroyed and two jaguars perished from smoke inhalation, but the cat house was the only building besides the elephant barn to sustain permanent damage.

Charlie gulped another cup of coffee as he listened to Dr. Lewis.

"—supplies in bulk. We need them now and I don't know who Gordon orders them from. Do you?"

Charlie shook his head wearily. "It's somewhere in his office, I don't know either."

The vet's voice droned on and Charlie watched the faces of the keepers wearily taking the first rest from the night's work. The elephants had taken hours to track down and lead back. Their barn was destroyed but Charlie tethered them to ground stakes and piled up feed in front of them to keep them happy. The elephants munched the hay hungrily and were oblivious to the smoldering remains of their cramped quarters.

Charlie had taken charge of the trapping; it was the one thing he knew well. He was amazed that so few animals were hurt. Except for the jaguars and a slow-moving pangolin and a gibbon, all of the animals had escaped serious injury. The minor bruises, scratches, and mental strain had taken full toll, however, and now taxed Dr. Lewis to his limits. Charlie could trap the animals but where was he going to put them? He had no idea what to do now. Everyone was giving him conflicting advice. The keepers shouted opposing orders and began to argue heatedly.

Harriet came over to him then. She refilled his cup and they looked into one another's eyes. No words were spoken. Both of them knew the frustration, the defeat. Both of them knew the legacy Gordon had left.

"I'm glad he never saw this," Harriet said slowly.

Charlie nodded. "Gordon never could have taken it."

"It was all going so well," Harriet said. Her eyelids were trembling and Charlie tried to turn away so he wouldn't see her tears. "He would have come back this morning and—"

Charlie swore. The public was packed against the entrance gates and staring inside. They had lined up since the fire started last night and it was all the guard could do to keep them out of the way. They stared inside with gaping mouths and clicked their cameras at the weary keepers leading the animals back into the enclosures. Now a fight had broken out in the parking lot and Charlie cursed them. Probably some argument over who had the best spot.

"He would have been sixty years old today," Harriet said. Her eyes were completely wet now.

Charlie gave a start. It *was* his brother's birthday today. He had completely forgotten. Some birthday present, he thought. The noise from the fight grew louder. Someone was shouting.

"The zoo was all he had," Harriet said. She gently rocked back and forth. Her hair was falling in grey curls over her ears but she didn't bother to pin it up.

"God*dammm*it," Charlie muttered under his breath. He gave a dark glance at the noise across the gates. He had half a mind to go over to the troublemaker and punch him in the nose.

"It was his life," Harriet continued. Then she stopped because she heard the argument too.

A single voice rose from among the crowd and the tone was unmistakably angry. Charlie froze. He turned his head to Harriet whose jaw had almost fallen to the ground.

Both of them gasped at the same time. *"Gordon—"*

Dr. Lewis paled. "It can't be."

He heard the voice and he trembled. The old keepers raised their heads and perked their ears. But Charlie was the first to start running.

"Goddammit, you blockheads," the voice shouted. "Out of my way."

It was him, it *was* his voice. Charlie's feet pumped and his lungs screamed. The same pitch, the same cursing obstinacy. My brother's voice, Charlie swore.

The old keepers put down their coffee cups. They looked at one another, their eyes wide open in astonishment; then without a second glance, they took off in hot pursuit of Charlie. Dr. Lewis jerked his pipe from his teeth and hobbled forward.

"What's the matter?" he yelled at Harriet. "What's going on?"

Harriet cried, "It's Gordon. Over there."

Dr. Lewis looked at the running men and heard the voice again.

"Will you let me into my own damn zoo? Out of the way!"

Dr. Lewis threw his half-eaten doughnut on the table and waddled toward the main gates. The entire zoo force was now rushing toward the voice and as they hit the turnstiles they vaulted over and dove into the crowd.

"Back off, you bastards," the voice yelled hoarsely.

Charlie threw himself into the crowd, pushing and shoving as he scrambled toward the voice. Then he saw it—the ambulance parked in front of the main gates. It had stopped because of the crowd and the driver angrily honked his horn. But the back door had already been flung open and two medics were carrying the stretcher.

"Not that way, you idiots. Over there."

The voice! Charlie pushed away a camera-snapping reporter and lunged for the stretcher. He grabbed the rim and thrust his face over the sheets to stare at the voice.

"Well, you're one dirty sonofabitch," Steven growled at his uncle. "Did you keep it for me?"

"*Steven!*" Charlie yelled.

"Will you tell these idiots the way to get inside?" Steven croaked. "They don't know their asses from first base about zoos."

"Steven!" Charlie gasped. "What are you—" He turned to the medics with a bewildered look on his face. He didn't know what was going on. "Through the main entrance," he told the medics. "That way."

"Like *hell,*" Steven choked. He spat the words out and raised his hand. The bandages wrapped mummylike around his body tightened his voice. "I'm not going in that way."

"What?"

"*That* way," Steven said, lifting his arm and pointing. "The employees' gate. Will you tell the bastards to make room? I'm going in the employees' gate or you can let me rot out here. Take your choice."

Charlie stood on the tips of his shoes and swelled into his six foot three inches. He glared at the people and they shrank back, terrified.

"Make way, you bastards!" Charlie roared.

The procession charged through the employees' gate. As the stretcher cleared the entrance and was carried across the plaza, Steven lifted his head and looked at the grounds. He studied the blackened trees, the wet glistening puddles, and the smoldering ruins of the far-off cat house. He raised his head higher but the swarm of keepers and maintenance men crowded around the stretcher blocked his vision. Steven's eyes passed over the faces around him, searching intently. He closed his eyes.

The keepers shoved the medics aside and grabbed the stretcher. Three abreast, they swiftly ran Steven down the plaza until they reached the operations table, where they gently deposited him.

"How many did we lose?" Steven questioned Charlie.

"Two jaguars, a gibbon, and a pangolin," Charlie said grimly.

"Thank God jaguars breed like flies," Steven muttered. He turned his head to Dr. Lewis. "Injuries?"

"A lot," the vet began. "Bruises, minor burns. But we need to get—"

"I know what we need," Steven interrupted. "We need everything."

"The cat house is half-burned down," the lion keeper blurted almost hysterically. "It'll take weeks to repair. We don't have enough cages for the tigers."

"Half-burned down?" Steven slowly raised his upper chest and stared across the zoo toward the blackened ruins. Then his head slumped down and he spoke quickly. "Take the cats out. Move them to the vet's compound holding pens. Then I want the cat house *all* burned down. The whole goddamn building."

"What?" the lion keeper gasped. His face was aghast.

Steven looked hard at him. "We're not going to repair a goddamn thing; do you understand? We're going to get a *new* cat house. We'll keep the lions chained to parking meters outside until we get it." He stopped, looked at their faces, and tried to shout. "Don't you people know how Harry started the San Diego Zoo?"

"Steven," Charlie broke in. "What—"

"Well, Harry knew a good opportunity when he saw it. Haven't you heard that story, Charlie?"

"Steven. You can't—"

Steven turned his head and lifted his arm to someone across the plaza. "Will somebody tell those guards to let them in?" he asked.

But the guards had already checked the passes and the small group of young graduate students exchanged nervous glances as they approached Steven's stretcher.

Steven waved Dr. Lewis to come nearer. "I brought you some help," he said. "Degrees. Every last one of them have degrees but they don't know what to do with them. I'm sorry I couldn't do better. They want to study animals, Dr. Lewis. But I don't have the heart to tell them there aren't any anymore. They're about twenty years too late. The only place you can find them anymore is zoos."

"What do you want me to do with them?" Dr. Lewis asked. He puffed on his pipe furiously and bent down to the stretcher as Steven motioned him closer.

"Make them shovel shit," Steven hissed. "Make them shovel shit out of cages until they start rolling in it. If they're going to take care of animals, they're going to learn which end is for what. Most of them will quit when they have enough shit experience. But we might get one or two that stays. After that, you know what to do with them."

Dr. Lewis sucked his pipe. "I'll see what I can do."

Charlie beamed. He wiped his forehead and laughed. "Steven, you look great. You look just like the time—"

Steven choked. He coughed and a racking spasm shuddered his chest. Immediately the crowd surged closer and stared in horror. Steven shook his head, clearing it from his tremor and he barely gasped, "Harriet—"

"What?" Harriet had been at the outskirts of the crowd but as she heard Steven mutter her name, she moved closer.

"Here," Steven gasped. "In my pocket. A letter."

"What?"

"A letter I want you to read it aloud. Take it."

Harriet bent over Steven and felt in his pocket. She found the folded piece of paper and looked at it strangely.

"Gordon wrote it," Steven whispered hoarsely. "Just before he died. I want all of you—the whole zoo—to hear what he said. Read it, Harriet. Read it aloud."

" 'Dear Steven,' " Harriet said loudly and slowly. " 'I don't know how long I'll be around but I need you to do something for me. Keep the zoo, Steven, keep it for me. Do the best you can. Everyone who works there are the best people I've ever known. They're animal people, you know what that means. Make it the best, Steven. I want the best zoo this side of the Mississippi. I want San Francisco to beat the pants off Harry's dump in San Diego. San Francisco is the city that knows how. Let them know and they'll find the how.' " Harriet read further and stopped. She tried to fold the letter.

"Don't stop," Steven whispered. "There's more. Go on," he ordered.

" 'P.S.,' " Harriet continued. " 'I don't need to tell you about Charlie. He's a good man, Steven, he means well. It's just that he makes other people do his own work unless he's forced to. But he means well. I want you to promise me one thing. Instruct every keeper that he will be docked one day's pay for every minute he listens to one of Charlie's sea stories while on duty.' " Harriet folded the paper and reached over to tuck it back in Steven's pocket.

"Wait a minute," Charlie growled. He grabbed the paper and read it himself. "It's typed," he said, puzzled. "It's not his—"

"I'm sorry," Steven croaked to Charlie. "I don't think Gordon wanted you to read that. But that's Gordon for you, isn't it?"

Charlie stared hard at his nephew. Steven coughed and stared back with sorrow in his eyes.

"Yeah," Charlie snapped. "That's Gordon for you."

Steven looked at the silent sea of faces staring at him. "Well?" he croaked loudly. "What are you looking at? Haven't you ever seen a sick man before? Get me into my office. I've got work to do. Do you think you're getting paid to stand around in pajamas and drink coffee? San Diego's got a hell of a start, a hell of a start."

Charlie ordered the keepers to lift Steven's stretcher. As he was raised. Steven again craned his neck to stare at the workers around him. A flash of brown hair. Steven opened his mouth but he stopped when he saw her turn. It was only a concession worker.

"Charlie," Steven said slowly.

"Yes?" Charlie answered, bending down toward the stretcher.

"What time is it?" Steven tried to keep his voice steady.

Charlie looked puzzled. "Noon," he said. "Why do you want to know?"

Steven shook his head and fell back. "I just wanted to know. I'm an hour late."

Inside the office, Steven had Charlie lay his stretcher by the window. Bright sunlight streamed through the pane, intensified by the absence of shade from the denuded eucalyptus trees. Steven watched the crowd of workers break up around the coffee table.

"How bad are you hurt?"

"What?" Steven jerked his head back. He was shaken by his uncle's question.

"The guts," Charlie said.

"It's okay," Steven said, shrugging. "I'll be wrapped up for a couple of months."

Charlie nodded. "As long as it missed the groin. That's the devil's business there, when you get it in the groin. . . . I remember once in Anchorage—"

Steven listened to the story with a weak smile. When Charlie finished, Steven nodded with a satisfied grunt. He looked at the two keepers who had been listening with gaping mouths at Charlie's description of the Eskimo woman and where she had put the tattoos. "That's a good one," Steven chuckled to the keepers. "It was worth a day's pay, wasn't it?" His face suddenly hardened.

The keepers paled. They exchanged terrified glances and fled from the room.

Steven stared out the window at Dr. Lewis, who was carrying his bag to attend a raccoon with a limp. "That woman," he began. He tried very hard to keep his voice level. "The tour guide I transferred to the children's zoo—"

"Amanda?" Charlie asked. "She left about an hour ago. Said she couldn't wait."

Steven nodded. "Did she say anything else?"

Charlie thought for a moment, then shook his head. "She said she had work to do."

"Yeah," Steven said. He nodded his head and turned to his uncle. "We all have a lot of work to do, don't we?"

Steven listened to Charlie's description of the fire and the condition of the exhibits. His uncle's voice rapidly and concisely reported the situation as Steven bit his lips. The rebuilding would take a monumental effort. But there was no question now that it would be rebuilt. If ever he was sure of one thing, that was it. Shacker's carnival was totally destroyed; his land would be perfect for a grazing North American exhibit. All that was necessary would be to keep up the momentum. But for the first time, Steven felt no worry about the momentum. It *was* going to happen. San Francisco *was* going to have a better zoo than San Diego. He had the people to do it, didn't he?

And the more his mind wandered, the faster it returned to her. He could have called the airport, damn it. He shook his head. His hands felt sweaty. Charlie's voice droned on in the thick air. But he came back as soon as he could, didn't he? No, he could have called. But what would he have said?

"I think we can get some lumber donations from a warehouse up the street," Charlie continued.

Steven nodded dully, not hearing a word that was said. Why was he sweating? He could have called, damn it.

"Charlie," Steven said.

"Yes?"

"Dial this number, will you?" Steven fumbled in his pocket for his address book.

Charlie looked at the number with a shrug. He walked over to the phone and lifted the receiver.

"Person to person," Steven said softly. "When you get the connection, I'd like to be left alone."

"Sure," Charlie said, nodding. "Who are you calling?"

"Person to person for Amanda Newman. If she's not there, get a number where she can be reached. It's important."

Charlie stared back. The puzzlement on his face was growing greater. "Amanda?" he asked. "Why are you calling?"

"Because she left," Steven said. "And because I want her back."

Charlie's face turned red. "I said she left," he said slowly. "But she left for the children's zoo. She said she had work to do in the corral."

"Goddamn you, Charlie!" Steven screamed. His fist rose in the air and he shook it wildly. "Moving. Get me moving, damn it," Steven roared.

"Sure, Steven, sure. Whatever you say. Don't get the pressure up. I'm just trying to help."

■ ■ ■

Amanda heard the shouts from the direction of the main gates but she figured it was another animal escape. She reached in her back pocket for a pair of wire snips and bent down to the hay bales. A herd of goats eyed her hungrily and charged her pockets. Scowling, she brushed them away.

After the hay was loosened, she piled it in a corner for the sheep and goats to browse. As she straightened up, she stared at the menacing layer of manure that had collected in only a few hours' time. She groaned and picked up the shovel. The dung was fresh and it stunk like only goats could stink. The wind died and the air grew warm, very warm.

As she shoveled the dung into a corner pile for the tractor pickup, she glanced at her shoulder. The patch on her uniform was smudged with ashy particles. She stopped for a moment and rubbed hard. Gradually, the scarlet "Animal Service, second class" shone through the soot.

"Second class," she muttered, piling up the manure. She looked across the asphalt track at the rows of bear pits and the men keepers. As a matter of fact, she considered, *all* the keepers were men. As a matter of fact, she considered once more, *all* the keepers were men. The only women in the zoo were either tram guides as she had been, or girls who worked the concessions.

Then she began to decide which animal she wanted. Bears? Maybe. But the cats were interesting, too. And the elephants. The giraffes? It's about time for first class to get a little more class.

Should she wait until this afternoon or tomorrow morning? She didn't exactly know Charlie's condition. Certainly he couldn't handle a general strike at this moment. But maybe that's the best time to organize it, she considered. She shoveled the dung and thought some more. The flies hovered around her boots. Hell, she thought, the shit a woman has to put up with these days.

A cough interrupted her deliberations and Amanda turned. Two men stood at the edge of the burned corral. Both were dressed in immaculate three-piece suits and both carried tanned leather attaché cases. Gold amulets dangled from open neck shirts; their chests glowed with a rich tan. One of them was flicking a particle of soiled sawdust from his Gucci loafers.

"Amanda!" the other called out in forced heartiness. "I want you to meet someone."

As Amanda ambled toward them, they exchanged a flurry of heated whispers that immediately turned into wide grins when Amanda stopped.

"Hello, Frank. How'd you get in here?" Amanda asked. "I thought the Reptile House was still intact."

Frank's grin widened and he jostled the shoulder of the man next to him. Then Frank's smile faded and was replaced by a brisk coolness. "A good agent looks after his client, especially when they're a little confused."

"Who's confused, Frank?" Amanda asked.

Frank's smile vanished. "You missed your flight, I checked the airport. Like I was telling Mr. Evans here, the producer, you probably got tied up with this . . . research you're doing for another role and missed your connection. Well, no matter. Mr. Evans happens to be flying down to LA in his own plane and—"

"Yes," Mr. Evans broke in with a smile. "Glad to have you on board. We'll have to rush. I think we're going to make a great team, Amanda. We'll be down there in time for dinner. I thought we could discuss a few things about the picture."

"Sorry," Amanda said. "Can't make it."

Frank's voice had long since lost any pretense at politeness. "I'm afraid you don't understand, Amanda. Your contract starts tomorrow for three weeks. You *have* to be on the set tomorrow. Mr. Evans will overlook this little eccentricity but he expects a certain level of professionalism from the people he hires."

Amanda stared mutely at Frank, meeting his gaze with just as much stubbornness. The warm air grew warmer.

"Perhaps," Mr. Evans broke in, "there's been a mistake made."

"Mistake?" Frank asked.

"Yes," Evans continued. He spoke in a particularly slippery tone of voice. "The role I had in mind might not be exactly the right type for Amanda after all."

"Just a minute," Frank sputtered. "We have a contract. You can't—"

Evans waved his hand. "I'll make good your fee. But the woman I need has to have a certain . . . sophistication. From her photographs I thought Miss Newman would be perfect." He looked at Amanda with a frown. "Perhaps I was misled. No offense, I'm sure you understand, dear. But I was looking for a more, well, attractive type."

Amanda leaned against her shovel. Sweat had collected on her temples from the noon sun and it poured down her cheeks and throat, carrying with it soot and dirt. Her hair was tied roughly with a torn strip of rag and bits of bark and hay nestled in it like the wool of the sheep flocking about her. Her eyelids drooped from lack of sleep; her stomach growled from the doughnut and hurried cup of coffee that had been her breakfast. With an exhausted arm, she wiped her face. As she stared at her sleeve, she found it black with collected grime. Her lips trembled as she stared at the two men standing before her who controlled her fate. She had fought for the role against three hundred other women; she had done commercials, showcase theater, and haunted every casting director for months.

"No offense, dear," Mr. Evans repeated with a sweet smile.

Amanda lifted the shovel and dumped a yard of goat shit on his gleaming Gucci loafers.

She went back to the hay bales. The sun rose higher and the air was now shimmering in waves of heat. She never turned back at the two men. They evaporated like the water in the goat trough.

"You're doing it wrong."

Amanda pushed a greedy goat away from the middle of the hay to let the others have a chance to feed. She ignored the jeer.

"You're supposed to spread it around."

Amanda grunted but refused to acknowledge the keeper taunting behind her back.

"*Goddammit, do I have to give you a lecture?*"

She dropped the shovel. The handle slammed onto the ground and raised a tiny cloud of dust. Whirling around, she sucked in her breath.

Steven ordered Charlie to lean the stretcher against the remainder of the fence, then he waved him away. Raising himself up as high as he could, he blinked his eyes at the slowly approaching figure emerging like a blackened chimney sweep from a packed herd of braying sheep. She swatted their flanks to move

· 242 ·

them away and they broke for the water trough. A great cloud of dust and ashes rose in the air, swirling like a choking sandstorm.

And Steven stared at her—at her torn uniform, the scratches on her arms, and the nest of straw in her hair.

"I thought you had to go back to school," Amanda said.

"So did I," Steven said. "But you know Charlie. He can't run a zoo."

Amanda nodded, staring at his bandages. "Are you all right? You shouldn't be—"

"Don't tell me what—"

"I'll tell you what I damn well—"

"Stop!" Steven barked. "Will you just listen for once?"

Amanda grinned. "The lecture? The lecture's finally coming?"

"You better believe it."

The dust had settled. The flock of sheep returned and noisily crowded the stretcher, sniffing at Steven's pockets. Steven swatted them away. "You're hired," he said grudgingly.

Amanda's jaw dropped. "Hired for what?" she demanded.

"The children's zoo. You've got the job for good. Providing, of course, that you plan on staying here awhile. Are you?"

Amanda blinked. Her breath began to come in short, gasping chokes as her cheeks flushed crimson. "Why, you—" she stuttered, pointing an accusing finger at his startled face. "I—" she stammered.

"You what?"

"I want a transfer," she gasped. "Do you think I'm going to spend the rest of my life in this dung heap? Hell no, buster, I want to be a keeper. I want to work with animals, not sheep."

"These things take—"

"They take as much as I'm going to grab. It's easy for you to say that, lying in a cot and—and what are you doing for dinner?"

"Huh?" Steven cocked his head, puzzled at her sudden shift in tone.

Amanda eased into a casual slouch. She ran her eyes appraisingly over Steven's body. "Maybe we can talk over dinner. If you're not busy," she added offhandedly.

Steven stared at her suspiciously. There was some vague uneasiness lurking in the back of his mind, a distant feeling of—of
what? The scent of the master woodsman, the subconscious tingling of approaching a path that was too neat? Hogwash, Steven
thought, and brushed the idiotic idea from his mind. For a moment he had almost sensed the particular phrasing of Charlie in
her words.

"Dinner?" Steven said, smiling. "Why, that would be great."

"I'll bring a bottle of wine," she said.

"You don't have to," Steven said, grinning.

"Oh, I'd like to," Amanda urged.

"No," Steven said. "Don't bother."

"I'm going to," Amanda stated.

Their voices rose. Steven stirred on his stretcher and his lips
clenched tightly as their argument stampeded the flock of sheep.
Amanda's voice grew louder and Steven's grew firmer. The
sounds of their quarrel carried up to the crown of a pine tree
where six long-legged gibbons began to hoot in unison. As they
whooped and shrieked on their perch, the leader began ripping
pinecones and flinging them down like baseballs at the scattering
sheep.